AUBURN RIDE

DAVID STEVER

Cinder Path Press, LLC

AUBURN RIDE

Cinder Path Press, LLC
5319 Tarkington Pl.
Columbia, MD 21044

www.davidstever.com

Cover Design: Brandi McCann/ebook-coverdesigns.com

Cover Photograph: Marina Svetlova/Shutterstock

Interior layout and design by romantic suspense and young adult author P. J. O'Dwyer http://indieauthorsbrew.com

ISBN: 978-09983371-0-4 (paperback)
ISBN: 978-09983371-1-1 (ebook)

Printed in the United States of America

To Helene, with love

AUBURN RIDE

1

SHE WAS TWENTY-FOUR, FIVE FOOT EIGHT, HAD blonde hair that fell to the middle of her back, was being held for ransom, and it was my job to find her and bring her home.

The Blair Trucking Warehouse and Distribution Center was in the industrial section of the city with train tracks on the south side and truck loading docks on the north side. Located on Mechanic Boulevard, I drove by twice before I backed into a driveway of an adjacent construction company that provided a good vantage point for observation. A large structure about the size of a football field, it had truck loading bays every forty feet and security cameras mounted at the corners, but I couldn't do much about that.

It was midnight, the night warm and quiet, and after an hour of no activity and no security patrol, I drove to the warehouse and parked my car between two large trash bins in the rear of the building. I made my way to the side door on the narrow west side. It was unlocked, just as the note instructed. I slowly turned the handle and the heavy steel door opened without a sound. I slipped inside.

The warehouse was dark; the only light came from night safety lights mounted over each loading door that cast a dim light around the doors but left plenty of dark areas throughout the building. I waited a few moments to allow my eyes to adjust. I had worn my black jeans and black leather jacket and stayed in the shadows along the wall. A check of my watch: 1:10 a.m. Doctor Richard Pitts was expected at two o'clock with the ransom money. The wrinkle here was the kidnappers were expecting Pitts and a bag of cash, not me an hour early.

Doctor Pitts hired me two days ago, right after he received the ransom instructions. Five hundred thousand in cash in exchange for his daughter, Katie. Do not call the police. From what we figured, Katie had finished playing tennis at Greenwood Country Club where the doctor and his wife are members. She never showed at home that evening; her car was still parked at the club.

Pitts found me the next morning through a doctor friend, an Irish urologist named Sullivan, who I helped out of a mistress mess last year. Sullivan thought I walked on water and told Pitts that if I could cover up his affair and save him a cool million in a divorce settlement, then I could get Pitts' daughter back. Pitts agreed to my five thousand dollar retainer without hesitation.

The ransom was to be delivered to the warehouse and Pitts was to come alone. The whole deal smelled amateurish. Pitts said when he received the ransom call, he heard trucks in the background. Did they make the call from the same location as the ransom drop? Not the smartest pigs in the pen.

The plan was to take them by surprise, pull Katie out of there, and then call the cops. The cops would have my ass for not calling them first, but that's the nature of my business. I wanted a peek at Katie, too. The Pitts showed me pictures of their only child but all I saw were the long legs and blonde hair.

Rows and rows of large wooden pallets, loaded with household items, toasters, blenders, and coffee makers filled the warehouse. Each pallet was eight feet high and six feet square and wrapped in a heavy-duty plastic wrap. The aisles intersecting the rows could fit two forklift trucks side-by-side. I crept along the perimeter wall, my Beretta in hand, praying I wouldn't have to use it.

A man spoke in Spanish. I froze in place. The voice had a tinny sound to it and after a few seconds I realized it came from a Spanish radio station. I followed the sound and crept another ten yards or so along the wall when Katie Pitts came into view. Illuminated by a small propane camping lantern, she sat in the center aisle on a metal folding-chair with her hands tied behind her. Duct tape secured each of her legs to the legs of the chair and tape covered her mouth. Her long, blonde hair hung in a tangled mess and her cheeks were streaked with mascara tears. And the kicker: she only had on a white bra and lacy, white panties. I guess our kidnapper figured she wouldn't run away without her clothes. Or he wanted to humiliate a rich, white girl.

He sat in a chair opposite her. A short, pudgy, south-of-the-border greaser. His black hair was slicked back; he wore dirty blue jeans and a dingy wife-beater T-shirt and had a plastic straw hanging out of his mouth. He slouched in his metal chair while he tapped his foot to the music. The portable radio sat on the floor beside him, surrounded by empty beer cans and candy wrappers.

I moved around two of the pallets and made my way to the center aisle, behind him and facing her. She saw me and her eyes went wide. I put a finger to my lips, hoping she was smart enough to not react. As I got closer, I could see her chest heave and her breathing increase. I motioned for her to stay calm. I tapped him on the shoulder and he shot from the chair as if I hit an eject button. He turned toward me and my fist crashed into his mouth, landing him hard on his back. I thought he was out cold but he rolled over and scrambled to all fours. I grabbed the chair, swung and caught him on the side of the head and dropped him back to the floor. Now he was out cold, at least for the time being. I checked his pockets for weapons and found a decent switchblade, which I pocketed. I went to Katie and gently pulled the tape from her mouth and then untied her hands.

"Thank God. Are you the cops?" Tears spilled down and she wiped them with the back of her hands, which only smeared the mascara across her cheeks like war paint.

"Not quite. Is he the only one?"

"No. There's two. The other guy is around here somewhere."

“They have weapons?”

“I didn’t see any.”

“Are you hurt?”

“No.”

"Your clothes?"

"They took them."

I got the last bit of tape off her legs and she jumped up. I took off my jacket and she slipped it on. Something about her wearing my leather jacket with the lacy panties almost made me lose my focus. "Stay beside me. I'll get you out of here."

"Wait." She picked up the chair and lifted it to smash it down on his head but I grabbed it from her.

"I don't blame you but we got to go. Too much noise. Come on." I reached out my hand and she took it, squeezing as if she would never let go. We hurried back into the shadows along the wall, heading to the door where I came in.

We were a few yards from the exit when the second kidnapper came in, carrying a bag from a taco joint. What self-respecting kidnappers would go for take-out tacos an hour before the ransom drop? I guess these guys. The safety lights above the door provided enough light for him to recognize the money end of my Beretta as I stuck it in his face.

"Drop the bag." He did. "Hands up." He did. He shook so bad his keys rattled. I frisked him; he had a pistol tucked into the back of his jeans, which became mine. A long spool of plastic wrap was nearby. It was five feet wide—the self-sticking stuff they wrap around the pallets to secure the products. I had Katie pull off a long stretch of the plastic and lay it in the middle of the aisle.

"Seńor?" His eyes went wide. He knew what was coming.

"Shut up. Lay down on the plastic."

"Seńor, please."

"Make him take off his clothes," said Katie.

"What?" I said.

"What?" he said.

She took a step closer to him. "Take off your clothes, you bastard."

Again, I couldn't blame her. She deserved some vengeance. "You heard her. Strip."

"Seńor, please. I can't," he pleaded.

"Take off your clothes, you spic son of a bitch," Katie screamed. It scared me and I know it scared him. He stripped off his clothes in seconds. "Yeah, now who's the big man? What is that, two-inches?"

And I was into Katie Pitts. Leather jacket, blonde hair, black streaks across her face, and bra and panties—a cross between an underwear model and an Amazon warrior.

"Lay down on the plastic," I said. He did but still had his hands outstretched. "Put your hands to your sides. You're about to be a human burrito." I rolled him in the plastic while he cursed me in Spanish. The naked man wrapped in plastic floundering around on the warehouse floor put a smile on Katie's face. "Can we go?"

She went to our plastic-wrapped kidnapper and smashed her heel into his ribs a few times. A muffled scream came from the plastic roll. "Now we can go."

We got outside and made our way to my BMW. I opened the trunk and pulled out a sweatshirt. "Put this on. Give me my jacket." Even though she was sexy in my leather jacket and her underwear, it was still my leather jacket. She complied. I had bottled water in a cooler and handed her one. She gulped it down. "Sure you're not hurt?"

"No. I'm okay," she said.

I handed her my phone. "Call your parents and let's get you

home."

"Wait. What's your name?"

"Delarosa. Get in."

It took twenty minutes to drive to her parents' large colonial in the affluent Wood Grove section of town. Katie filled in the details of the past two days with her abductors. She recognized one guy as a maintenance worker from the club, and said the other must work at Blair Trucking because he had keys to the place. They held her in their apartment, didn't mistreat her; only sat and stared at her for a day and a half. I used one of my throw-away phones to call the police emergency line and anonymously reported a break-in at the warehouse. I doubt the morons would cop to a kidnapping. The police would check their immigration status, and with any luck, they'd be deported.

The reunion at the Pitts house was tearful. Their tears, not mine. I stood next to my car in their driveway and thought Mrs. Pitts would never let go of her daughter. Doctor Pitts walked over and handed me a check for twenty grand and couldn't stop thanking me. I slipped the check into my jacket pocket and he threw his arms around me in a giant bear hug. I gave him one more chance to report this as a kidnapping but he wanted it quiet. He explained if the word got out about this kidnapping, then others like him—wealthy folks—would become targets. He didn't want to give anyone any ideas. Sounded pretentious and paranoid, but didn't matter to me. Pitts was a cardiologist and offered me free cardiology checkups for life. I'll need it if my cholesterol keeps going north instead of south.

Katie broke free of her mother, ran over and threw her arms around me. This hug I didn't mind. "Thank you. Thank you so much."

"I'm glad you're okay."

She let go and I shook the doctor's hand again. Mrs. Pitts came over and hugged me. I got into my car as the three of them headed into the house, arm in arm. As they got to the front door, Katie turned back and gave me a wave. A wave I felt in my gut. I waved back. It even pulled at my heartstrings a little. I'm glad for the happy ending, even happier for the nice payday. I put the Z4 in gear and headed home.

It was three in the morning when I got back to my condo but I was too keyed-up to sleep, so I put a Miles Davis CD into the player and stripped off my clothes. With the shower as hot as I could stand it, I allowed the water to sting my skin for a good five minutes, and then stepped out and wrapped a towel around me.

I pulled a seven-year-old Chianti from my wine rack and opened it, grabbed a glass and went to my balcony to stretch out on the lounge. The music and the wine were just what I needed to come down from the night's job. My condo was on the fourth and top floor of the building and provides me a panoramic view of Port City. Straight out from the balcony looking north are the lights of downtown and the suburban sprawl beyond. To the right and east is a view of the harbor. From my high vantage point sometimes I feel like an overseer or a protector. Especially when jobs go well—like tonight.

The eastern sky was turning a light gray as I filled my glass for a second time. The red wine felt good going down and I got a nice burn from the alcohol. I kept going back to Katie Pitts. The little wave she gave me as I left her house stayed with me. I had this feeling, and after twenty years in the department and six out on my own, I always trusted my gut, my instinct, my sixth sense. I had not seen the last of Katie Pitts.

2

THE NEXT MORNING I GOT TO MY OFFICE AT ELEVEN. Mike had called to tell me I had a potential client waiting. Mike is Mike McNally and my office is the back corner booth of McNally's Irish Pub. The bar is on the ground floor of my apartment building so I don't have a long commute. Mike—a large, barrel-chested, red-haired Irishman—was my partner for twelve years in the department. If ever two guys were soul mates, Mike and I were. We saved each other's ass more times than I can count.

He retired after twenty-five years and bought himself the joint. It became a cop bar in no time and grew in popularity. The locals in the neighborhood liked it because a lot of cops hung around and crime went down in the area. Located in a working-class, blue-collar neighborhood, with decent food and fair prices, the folks enjoyed having a safe place to talk and drink.

After a couple of years, business was good and Mike decided to bring on another bartender. Shelly Colamanti filled the bill—and the uniform. Being half-Irish and half-Italian meant she was either mad or holding a grudge all the time. The regulars loved her, though. With her low-cut tops that revealed just enough cleavage to keep the guys hanging around buying drinks, she had the perfect mix of sass and class and complemented Mike's gregarious personality. They played off each other and made for a fun team. That lasted a good year and everything was working smooth until Mike's wife Janice showed up one night after closing time. She found Mike and Shelly, both naked, with Shelly on a table with her legs pointed toward the ceiling and Mike banging away like she was the last lover he'd ever have.

That's how I became half-owner of McNally's. I bought half of the business so Mike could pay off Janice in the divorce. We never saw Shelly again, either.

Two of our regulars were on their usual stools, working on an early liquid lunch. Mike had poured two fingers of bourbon and had it waiting for me. "Be careful." He nodded toward the back.

"Thanks." I took the drink and got a fix on at the last booth in the back. All I could see were long, slender legs. "I see what you mean."

The woman sat at an angle, with her back toward the front of the bar. Her legs extended out into the aisle, with a white skirt riding halfway up her long, tan thighs. Auburn hair cascaded down her back against the sharp contrast of her white suit jacket. I got to the booth and moved around to face her. She was movie actress gorgeous with vivid green eyes.

"I'm Delarosa. Looking for me?"

"I am. I'm sorry I didn't call ahead."

"No problem." I slid in opposite her. "How do you know me? I don't exactly advertise."

"Referral," she said with half a smile.

I'm sure her beauty carried her a long way but she knows who I am and now I need to know who she is. "Not good enough," I said. She ignored my comment.

"Mr. Delarosa, I need you to find something for me."

"That is...?"

"Money. Money owed to my family. My mother."

"Okay?"

"I'm afraid there's not much to go on."

"Why don't you start by telling me your name?"

She hesitated. "Claire Dixon. From Philadelphia." She pulled a slip of paper from her purse and slid it to me. Two names and a phone number were written on the paper.

"This is it? This is your information?" I took a swallow of my bourbon and leaned back. I couldn't stop looking at her green eyes, reddish-brown hair, and perfect, oval face. I figured her to be around thirty. She had an air of confidence and sophistication about her which was unusual. Most of my clients come to me out of desperation, panic, or looking to settle a score.

She reached into her purse, pulled out an envelope and

set it in front of me. "Twenty thousand dollars. Your retainer. If you complete the job, you'll receive another one hundred and eighty thousand."

Or walking in with twenty grand gives you all the confidence you need.

Now, she had my attention. She was either smart and fearless, or naive and way out of her league. Flashing that kind of cash made me nervous. Every red flag in my brain waved. Every cautious nerve ending and stood on end. My work comes via word of mouth. I built a reputation of doing a good job, maintaining discretion, and always putting my client first no matter the legalities involved. I never take a job without knowing who I'm working for, where I'm going, and what I'm up against.

"Pretty impressive start. I like money just as much as the next guy, but I need details. When did this happen? How much was stolen?"

"Two million dollars."

"Two million?" I took another sip of my drink, without taking my eyes off hers. "I'm going to need a lot of details. Who is your mother for starters?"

"I don't mean to be secretive or evasive...but, it's complicated. My mother died two months ago and there are people who will have an interest in the money—and let's say they're not the most upstanding of citizens." She tapped the piece of paper. "Start here." She got up from the booth. "I hear you're the best. Now, should I take back my money?"

I peeked in the envelope. *Loaded with cash all right.*

Against my better judgment, I put the paper in my pocket.

"My phone number is on the paper. Be careful." She turned and walked toward the door.

"Wait—" She didn't stop.

The sunlight streaming in through the glass door made her white skirt translucent and every guy in the place knew it. We stared until she went through the door and turned up the street. The guys all turned toward me. Mike went to the front window. I grabbed the envelope and went to the bar. Mike came back, writing on an order slip.

"New Audi. I got the plate."

"Ask Junior to run it." I handed Mike the envelope full of cash.

"Whoa—she's serious." Mike grabbed my arm. "What have we learned over the years, partner? Gorgeous broad with that much cash is dangerous. Got to be a woman scorned, mad, or out for revenge. Been there before, buddy. Bad for your health."

I went to the window but she was long gone. I turned back to Mike. "I have that feeling—

the gut thing—and I don't like it when I get the gut thing. This could be the one where we get rich—or we get dead."

3

TONY THE SCAR WAS THE FIRST NAME ON THE paper Claire gave me and he was no stranger to law enforcement. Tony Scarazzini and his brother Sammy own City Salvage. They handle used auto parts and about anything else you might want to buy. Law enforcement was well aware the junk yard was a front business, but if you wanted anything of a questionable nature, including information, you went to Tony and Sammy.

They also ran the biggest bookie operation in town, owned a strip club, Stiletto's, and a massage parlor. But with all their interests, legal and illegal, the Scarazzini brothers' greatest talent was staying out of jail. Neither one had ever been arrested. They stayed in business by giving the boys in blue good insider information from time to time. Not exactly confidential informants, more like part-time informants. They had an ear to the street at all times.

Genius at working both sides of the law.

Their salvage yard was on Lincoln Road between a recycled tire business and a gas station-convenience store. I pulled into the dusty parking lot a little after noon. The office at City Salvage was an old mobile field office they had poached from a construction job site in their younger days. I stepped inside and was smacked by a wall of cigar smoke. The brothers were in their usual spots: perched behind the counter, each with a sports page spread out in front of them. They dressed the same every day: khaki shorts, a dingy, faded white T-shirt, and beat-up sneakers with no socks. Both fat, bald, with three-day old beards, and Churchill cigars lodged between yellow teeth. Tony was the oldest, over sixty now, with Sammy a few years younger and many IQ points slower.

Tony glanced up from his paper. "Well I'll be God-damned."

"I told you we should keep the door locked," chimed Sammy.

"You son of a bitch, Delarosa."

"Been a while."

"Damn right it's been a while."

"What, three or four years?" added Sammy.

"I'd like to say I missed you guys, but..."

"You only grace our presence when you need something," Tony said.

"That hurts my feelings. I'm just checking to make sure you guys are staying on the right side of the law."

"I would believe that if you were still Detective

Delarosa. But now that you're private dick Delarosa, something tells me different," chided Tony.

"Mean, Tony, mean. Sammy, we're still buddies, right? C'mon."

"Yeah, you're still okay," said Sammy with a half- smile.

"Good, cause I need to ask a question."

"I knew it. You're a son of a bitch, Delarosa."

"Hey, you guys owe me."

"Really? What do we owe you, Mister Private Dick?"

"Well, remember the time your strippers were turning tricks in the back of the club and the city threatened to shut you down? Then the threat went away. And what about the time we had a district attorney who had a bug up his ass about illegal sports book operations in town? Anybody get charged?" Tony shot a sideways glance at Sammy. I leaned on the counter. "Get the bottle and let's toast the old days."

"I always said you're a stand-up guy." Tony grabbed the bourbon and three small juice glasses from under the counter.

He poured a shot-worth in each glass. We toasted and threw it back. I put my glass on the counter. "Good. We're all friends again. I do have a question."

A customer opened the door and came in. Sammy moved over to help him. "Ask away," said Tony.

"My client, a woman, is looking for some money she claims was stolen from her. The problem is she doesn't have much to go on. Just some old family rumors."

Tony shrugged. "I don't hear a question yet."

"Go back a few years. Does someone running around

with two-million dollars ring a bell?"

Tony took the cigar out of his mouth and put it on the filthy counter. "Why would you ask me that?"

Interesting.

"You know all and see all when it comes to back alleys and the scumbags in this town."

"Who's the woman?"

"Tony."

He slid the glasses around a bit. Nervous like. "Want another?"

"Sure." He poured two more and we downed those.

Did the two-million strike a nerve?

"Sounds like a real interesting case you have there. Wish I could help you."

"You're sure two million doesn't jog your memory?"

"When did this happen?"

"I'm not sure. Hoping you can shed some light."

He stuck the cigar back in his mouth. "I would remember two million."

"Let me ask Sammy."

"Nah, he won't remember anything. He can't remember what happened yesterday."

Tony's body language backed up his words. He looked me in the eye. He held my gaze. "Here's the problem, Tony. My client gave me two pieces of information. Two names."

"So?"

"Yours is the first name on the list."

"Yeah?"

"Yeah. Why?"

He shrugged. I laid my card on the counter. "In case you think of something."

He picked up the card and flipped it around in his fingers. "Johnny, how old is she? Your client?"

Now we're getting somewhere. "Thirty or so."

"Any chance she has red hair?"

"Dark red. Sort of auburn-like. Why?"

"I'll call you."

"When?"

"Real soon."

"Tony?"

"I promise. Tomorrow."

"Okay." I tapped the counter. "Thanks for the drink, old friend."

4

I LEFT CITY SALVAGE CONVINCED I OPENED AN OLD wound on Tony the Scar. His reaction and his promise to call me—which wouldn't happen—only fueled my curiosity.

My phone rang as I got to my car. Dave Richards, Jr., is now a lieutenant in the department. He was one of our running buddies back when the cops were still in charge. He runs tags and pulls criminal records for us in exchange for food and beer at Mike's.

"Junior."

"Hey boss. Got yourself a real interesting client."

"How so?" I said.

"The car registration address is a private mailbox place downtown. Mike asked if we could sit on it for a while. Willie wasn't doing anything so he hung around and got lucky."

Willie was Willie Stewart, an African-American cop who works a lot of undercover vice and narcotics. He's friends with Junior and helps us out. "Really?"

"Said the red hair is hard to miss."

"No doubt," I said.

"He tailed her from the mail box place to the Marriott on Washington."

"Okay."

"He followed her in to try to get a room number, but no sooner did he go in she came back out and walked right past him. Said she's better-looking close-up, too."

"Junior."

"Here's the cute part. From the Marriott, he follows her to the Harbor Court Motel over on Harbor Boulevard. Registered there, too."

"She's checked into two hotels?"

"Well, yeah, if you can call the Harbor Court a hotel."

"She was by herself?"

"Yep."

"Now why would someone check into two hotels? With one in the sleaziest part of town."

"Well, either hiding or wanting to throw somebody off track. Like I said, boss. Got yourself a hot one. Anytime you need us to watch that red hair, give a shout."

"Will do, buddy, will do. Thanks—good work."

"Yep."

So my client drops a twenty grand retainer on me, says she's looking for two million owed to her, only has two names to go on, and she's booked into two hotels.

Junior is right; we got ourselves a hot one.

5

IF CLAIR DIXON WAS GOING TO RENT A HOTEL ROOM, the four-star Marriott—among the finer hotels in the city—would be an obvious choice. But, if she's going to rent two hotel rooms, one in a four-star and one in a sub-zero-star motel ready for the wrecking ball, then my expert investigative skills told me to start with the dump.

It was 1:00 p.m. when I parked my car in a McDonald's parking lot across the street from the Harbor Court Motel, a one-story motel built in the sixties where you park your car in front of your room. Between a dive and a flea-bag, I'm sure the front desk had no problem renting rooms by the hour. The area consisted of project apartments, boarded-up storefronts, and homeless sleeping on the sidewalks. I'm sure the motel has its share of vagrants, hookers, and junkies hanging around. The cost of a room for a week was less than what I'm sure she pays for a day at the hair salon.

Her black Audi was parked in front of room 112. Driving an Audi A6 in this part of town begged for attention—and for it to disappear. Things weren't adding up. Too many years of police work told me Claire was less than forthcoming. My concern was I would uncover some secrets that were better off buried. The Scarazzini brothers aren't your church-going, family-men, Rotary Club types. Raised on the streets, they never left. They were street smart and street tough and Claire was in over her head and way out of her league. Although, maybe that's why she hired me. Making her the smartest one of all. Nevertheless, something smelled fishy in this seaside city.

Twenty minutes went by before the door to room 112 opened and Claire came out. The unmistakable red hair, tied back into a pony tail, bounced as she walked to her car. She wore tight jeans, boots, and a red blazer. She drove out of the lot and turned east on Harbor Boulevard which runs toward the harbor and the docks. I waited a few seconds and then pulled out behind her putting a city block between us. To my knowledge, she didn't know my car and I hung back far enough that she wouldn't notice me. She stayed on Harbor for a mile and then turned south on Ocean Avenue. Ocean runs parallel to the beach and after three miles or so, the real estate is more expensive and the people are better-looking. High-rise condo buildings line both sides of the avenue, along with some of the more upscale restaurants and shops. This part of Ocean Avenue is known as the Silver Strip—a mile-long section that contains the most pricey real estate in the city. The large hotel chains all have oceanfront properties here, mixed in with some independent hotels that had not yet sold out to the big operators.

Claire turned left into the parking lot of the Marquis Seaside Resort Hotel. A newer, four-star property, it gobbled up three smaller hotels and a mini-golf a few years ago. I pulled to the side of the road and watched as she parked her car and walked into the lobby. I turned into the lot and parked on the far side, opposite her car.

I keep an assortment of coats, jackets, sweatshirts, and hats in the trunk of my car for an occasional disguise. I put on an old, tan jacket and a floppy fisherman's hat. With my sunglasses on, I tried to look as touristy as possible as I entered the lobby. I've been in the Marquis a few times and made my way to the bar. The bar overlooks a restaurant; the restaurant has a deck that overlooks the beach. Unless Claire was headed up to a room, she'd be in the restaurant. I took a chance and found a seat at the end of the bar that had a view of the restaurant.

The bartender came over and slid a cocktail napkin in front of me.

"Gin and tonic," I said.

"Sure."

He went for the booze and I turned to the restaurant. As sure as the sun was shining down on the white sand outside, there was the red hair and red blazer being led to a table. An attractive brunette, maybe mid-sixties, stood at the table and extended a hand to Claire. She wore a smart blue suit and heels; her hair framed her face and fell to her shoulders. The waitress took an order and went off. They both sat upright in the chairs, nodding and smiling. Their body language suggested this was more of a business meeting instead of two old friends getting together for lunch. The bartender brought my drink.

"Start a tab?"

"No. Who's head of security here?"

"Security?"

"Yes, head of security. Somebody broke into my room and I want the head of security."

"Umm, yeah, hold tight. I'll make a call."

I sipped at the gin and tonic while I watched Claire and her lunch companion. Nothing more than two attractive women having a lunch on a pleasant spring afternoon. After a few minutes, a mountain of a man lumbered up to me. I'm six one, one eighty-five and he had at least two inches on me and was twice as wide. "Can I help you? I'm with hotel security." He wore baggie khaki pants and a blue sport jacket at least a size too large. His white shirt was open at the collar, necktie loosened, and his gut hung over his belt so far that I knew he hadn't seen anything below his waist for years.

I extended my hand. "Name's Delarosa. PCPD retired. Private work now." He stood there with his hands on his hips. He didn't bother to shake my hand.

"You a guest? The call said you had a break-in."

"Not exactly. Need some info. Name's Delarosa, retired PCPD."

"Yeah, you said that. How about some ID?"

"Sure." I showed him my police retiree card and my PI license.

"How long were you on the job?"

"Twenty years. Vice and Homicide. Got tired of the bullshit. You?"

"Fourth Precinct. Down on the docks. Got tired of the corruption. We were ineffective. Only there to make it look good. I took this job to get fat and rich. Only part of it's working. Name's Worthington."

This time hc extended his hand and I shook it.

"I'm hoping you can help me."

"Okay, but why the ruse? You could've just asked for me," he said.

"Sorry about that but I didn't want to leave my spot here and wasn't sure how much time I had. The table in the middle of the room with the two women, one with the red blazer and red hair?"

"Yeah."

"You know either one of them?"

He sat down on the stool next to me. "Don't know the redhead, although I wish I did. The older one is Elena Garver. She's in here a couple of times a week. Loaded with cash. Lives in a condo a few blocks from here. Socialite. Does some charity work. Sponsors a fund-raising dinner once a year here in the hotel for Children's Hospital. Bit of a do-gooder and they say she's high maintenance. On husband number three."

"Is that where the money comes from? The husband?"

"I think so. Or she inherited it. Someone said her father was the old mobster, Aletto."

"Oh yeah?"

"Yep. Is she cheating on him or is he cheating on her?" He winked.

"Neither. I'm keeping an eye on the redhead."

"Well, with any luck you'll catch her cheating and she'll want to work out a deal with you." He chuckled and elbowed me. "She's a looker."

"She is at that. But this one is all about money."

"Aren't they all?" He got up from his stool. "Need anything else from me?"

"Nope, thanks," I said. "And sorry about the ruse."

"Hey, no problem." He dug a business card from his pocket. "Ever need another set of eyes and ears, give me a call. I can use a change of scenery."

He gave me a slap on the back and walked off. I turned back to Claire and her companion in time to see Elena stand, throw her napkin on the table and storm off. The friendly lunch just went sour. Claire sat there for a few minutes and then put some money on the table and left. I threw a twenty on the bar and headed for the parking lot, only to get there in time to see her hop in her car and drive off.

On my way back to the office, I drove past the Harbor Court to see whether she went back to the motel. I parked in the McDonald's lot again. The Audi was in its spot, but her room door was open. After a minute or so, Claire stepped out of the room, waited for a few seconds, turned and went back inside. She left the door open. A moment or two later, she appeared back in the doorway. She kept looking toward the motel office, leaning against the door frame with her hands folded across her chest.

A minute or two went by before a tall, skinny guy, older—around sixty, I'd say—came out of the office and went to Claire's room. *The front desk clerk?* He wore a white T-shirt, blue jeans, and had long gray hair pulled back into a ponytail. He reminded me of one of those guys who played in rock bands for the last thirty years, only to wake up one morning realizing his time on the road was over, the big recording contract never came, and he never opened that 401K like he always intended. So he takes a job in a flea bag motel to live on minimum wage and the memories of his sex, drug, and rock-and-roll days.

Claire turned in to the room; he followed and closed the door.

Fifteen minutes went by before the door opened again. The guy came out and went back to the office.

So my mysterious client was registered in two hotels, met a wealthy broad for lunch, and had a fifteen-minute visit with the front desk clerk of a seedy motel. Never a good sign when I have to start my investigation by investigating the person who hired me. My client needed to provide more answers instead of creating more questions.

6

THIRTY MINUTES LATER, I PULLED UP TO THE second name my mystery client—Claire—gave to me. Carlo Bocci, CPA. His office was on the second floor above a small strip of stores in a commercial area on the outskirts of the city. The strip contained a Chinese restaurant, a liquor store, a tattoo and piercing parlor, and a check cashing place. A door next to the restaurant had his name on it.

Before going into the building, I took a quick look around, in case something or someone looked out of place. Claire dropped twenty thousand on me and that kind of money could attract slimy characters of all shapes and sizes. Plus, I didn't know enough about this job to even form an investigative strategy. The money had me curious, but my guard was up.

I climbed a set of creaky, wooden steps to Bocci's office

on the second floor. Most of the walls were bare plaster. What remained of the faded pale-green paint was peeling and lying in chips on the stairs. I knocked on the door and stepped inside. An old metal receptionist's desk sat in an outer office along with two large wooden file cabinets, but judging from the layer of dust no one had sat at that desk for years. It was as though time passed this place by. "Anyone here?"

"Back here." A soft, high-pitched voice came from a back office.

I opened the door, expecting to see a woman. Behind another large metal desk sat a small, pasty-white slender man, in his sixties, with a terrible comb-over and small, gold wire-framed glasses. If this was Carlo Bocci, he sure didn't fit his tough-guy name. He wore a paper-thin white dress shirt, a skinny black tie, and brown pants. He had a pocket protector in his shirt pocket that held two pens and two mechanical pencils. He was such the stereotypical, nerdy accountant that I thought I'd been pranked. Central Casting couldn't have done a better job.

"How can I help you, sir?"

He kept his head down, concentrating on a large accounting ledger on his desk.

"Well, I'm not quite sure. My name is Delarosa."

"Cop?"

"No. Doing some private work."

He peeked up from the ledger and gave me a once over. "You from Twenty-Second Street?"

I knew what he meant. Twenty-second is in the heart of

the Italian section of the city.

"A couple streets over. Twenty fourth." He nodded, as if he approved.

"I'm here on behalf of a client," I said. "Looking for some money."

"All the clients are looking for money. Save some here, tax deduction there. What makes yours special?"

"It's a lot."

"Mr. Dela—what is it again?"

"Delarosa."

"Delarosa. I don't have time to play guessing games. Tell me how I can help or go on about your day."

For a milquetoast of a guy, he sure could be direct.

"I don't mean to be cryptic, but I don't know much. My client hired me to find some money, gave me your name and told me to start with you."

"Who's your client?"

"I can't tell you that." And I couldn't. All I had to go on was my client's name and wasn't even sure that was real. He studied me for a good thirty seconds, sizing me up, or searching his mental files trying to figure out whether my face or my name was familiar.

"How much?"

"Two million."

He put the pencil down on the ledger and sat back a bit in his chair. "Did you say two million?"

"Yes."

His entire appearance changed in front of me. He morphed into a cadaver of himself. The last bit of color in his pale skin drained away. He shrunk back into his chair.

"Is your client a woman?" His voice cracked.

"Maybe."

"About thirty-five. A redhead?"

"You're on the right track," I said.

"I'm sure she's quite beautiful by now." He put his hands in his lap, hung his head and sat there for a good minute not saying anything.

"Mr. Bocci? You know my client?"

"I do...been a long time. I thought this day would never come." His voice was soft and weak. I slid my chair forward so I could hear him. "I can't believe it."

"Believe what? What's this about?"

He looked up at me and I saw a tear roll down his cheek. He took a handkerchief from his back pocket, removed his glasses, and wiped his eyes. He spoke slow and deliberate. "What's it about? It's about trust. It's about greed. It's about loyalty. It's about family. And it's about love." He cleaned his glasses and put the hanky back in his pocket. He adjusted the glasses on his face. "I always wondered how this would end. Who would be here? I always dreamed of seeing her again, too."

"Mr. Bocci, fill me in. I'm sure we can work out what you want."

"Too late for that." He took a slip of paper from his desk and wrote on it. He closed the ledger and then took the pocket protector from his shirt and put the pens into a holder on the desk. He opened the drawer again, put in the pocket protector and pulled out a 9 mm Glock and placed it in front of him on the desk.

I instinctively slid the chair back from the desk.

"Mr. Bocci, hold on now." The last thing I thought this little man would take out of the desk was a gun. I stood.

"Sit back down. Our business is not complete." He placed his hands on the desk with the gun between them.

Sitting put me in the worst position to react. I was at a disadvantage and needed options

"Okay." I slowly sat back down. "Is the gun necessary? I only have a few questions."

"It is necessary. Two things first, Mr. Delarosa, if you would indulge me."

"Sure, anything." I kept my eye on the gun and his hand. He could get his hand on the Glock much quicker than I could reach around to the Beretta in my waistband.

"Make sure she's taken care of is one, and, second, tell her I kept my promise."

"Okay, I'm happy to do that."

He stared at me for a few seconds; it seemed like he calculated something in his mind. Then he said, "I'm ready now."

"Well, thank you. Do you mind if I take some notes – "

Before I finished my sentence, he picked up the gun, shoved it into his mouth and pulled the trigger. His brains hit the wall behind him as I flew back in my chair. I landed on my back and scrambled to my feet only to see a mess of blood and gore on the wall and Bocci lifeless in the chair. The gun was still in his hand.

My hands shook; him blowing his brains out was the

last thing I thought was going to happen. It took a minute for my heart rate to settle down and to regain my composure. The gun blast would attract all kinds of attention, so I needed to get out in front of the barrage of questions headed my way. I picked up the slip of paper he wrote on before he ate lead. A ten-digit number. *A phone number?* I shoved it in my pocket and scanned the room. *Did I touch anything in here?* No need for me to leave fingerprints and incriminate myself any more than what was going to happen. He killed himself with me in the room. I just became suspect number one.

I took another look at the little man in the chair and wondered whether he just took the easy way out.

7

"SO YOU'RE TELLING ME THAT WHILE YOU'RE interviewing the guy, he takes out a 9mm Glock and blows his brains all over the wall?"

"That's what I'm saying."

"Jesus, Johnny, man, you got to give me more than that." Detective Marco Matera hovered over me with his six-foot-two, two-hundred-and-thirty-pound frame. He and Mike shined as the starting defensive tackles for Central Catholic for three years. They both went to Whitman State on football scholarships and after two years of hard partying, convinced themselves they weren't college material. They came back home and joined the police force. Mike and I are close, but Mike and Marco, one Irish, one Italian, are forever brothers.

Uniformed cops swarmed over the office, now a potential crime scene. Two TV crews had set up in the parking lot for the evening news. Forensics was photographing the inner office, and I scouted around for something to wipe off the chair in Bocci's outer office but had to settle for a dusty seat. The dust bothered me more than the interrogation. "I'm telling you, it happened. We talked about my case, and something about it must've struck him. He got real quiet then pulled the gun from his desk. I begged him to put it away but he didn't."

"Let me guess. You are now going to say you can't tell me what you were talking about."

"Marco, c'mon."

"Well, whatever you said, you certainly scared the shit out of him."

"Or the brains."

"Funny." He lit a cigarette and leaned back against one of the filing cabinets. "Johnny, you need to give me something. I can't go back saying the guy was depressed and you just happened to have an appointment when he decided to pull the trigger."

He was right. I needed some time to piece this together and figure out what the hell happened. I looked at him and remembered him from his playing days. Young, fit, and all muscle. Now the muscle was a gut, the hair gray, and the cigarettes were stealing years from him. The booze didn't help, either. "Marco, can you give me some time? Some latitude?"

Two guys from the coroner's office came up the stairs with a stretcher and a body bag. The lead guy asked Marco, "Can we take the body?"

"Yeah, sure, all set," said Marco, coming back to the present situation. They went into the inner office and Marco got up and closed the door behind them.

He pulled a chair close and sat next to me. He didn't care about the dust. "Time for what?"

"I need to talk to my client."

"And I need some answers. Look, if the guy was here by himself and decided to off himself, it would be a suicide. Shit, are you looking at this place? I'd shoot myself, too. But that's not the case. You were here with him. You're a part of this. Start talking."

He'll never let me leave without me saying something. "I was hired by a client to find some money. Money that was stolen."

"And...?"

"The only thing the client had to work with was Bocci's name. So I started here."

"How much money?"

"I'd rather not," I said.

"I have a dead accountant in there and I have to figure out why he's dead. How much, Johnny?"

I lifted my hands in protest and he cocked his head and raised an eyebrow. "Two million."

"Two million?" I could tell his mind went somewhere else, like Bocci's did. *Two million* must be the magic words today. Marco got up from the chair. He dropped his cigarette to the floor and crushed it with his shoe. He shook another one from the pack and lit up.

"Marco?"

"What exactly did Bocci say?" He sat back down.

"Not much, really. I told him I was looking for money and that the client gave me his name."

"Client a woman?"

"Yeah, why?"

"How old?"

"Thirty or so."

Marco leaned back in the chair and stared at the ceiling. "Wow. Wow, wow, wow."

"Marco, what?"

"Johnny, what did you say to the two uniforms who were first on the scene?"

"Same as what I told you."

"Okay, I'll talk to them. If anyone asks you, you showed up here and found him dead. Capisce?"

"Yeah, capisce. What is it?"

"I'll stop by the bar tonight. Make sure you're there. I'll buy you a day or two."

"Marco - whatever you say."

"Make sure you're there."

"I will."

The door opened and the coroner guys wheeled Bocci out in the body bag. Marco nodded toward the stretcher. "You know he was mobbed-up, right?"

"I didn't know but got that impression." I stood and brushed the dust from my clothes. "You got me real curious."

Marco took a step closer to me. "Johnny, I gotta ask. Am I going to find your fingerprints on the gun?"

"No, Marco, no."

He slapped me on the back a couple of times. "See you tonight."

8

I ALREADY HAD A DAY TO REMEMBER WITH MY VISIT to Tony the Scar, Bocci blowing his brains bye-bye, and being interrogated by Marco. But, the day was long from over. The mention of two million made each man react, with Bocci's reaction getting the prize. The suicide, old mobsters, and missing money sure had my curiosity – and adrenaline - on overdrive.

I walked into McNally's along with the happy hour crowd. Mike had his hands parked on the bar as he stared at the television screen and the early news. A local reporter was doing a live stand-up from in front of Bocci's office. He saw me and pointed to the screen. "Are you the unidentified person who was in the office?"

I stopped to look at the screen. The young, blonde reporter relayed the facts "*as we know them at the moment. We're waiting for a statement from the police.*"

"Yep. And we have work to do. And I need to talk to my client. Whoever the hell she is." I poured myself a shot and threw it back, poured a double and headed back to my booth.

Mike slid in opposite me. "Jesus, Johnny. The guy blows his brains out in front of you?"

"I brought up the two million, his demeanor changed. This little pipsqueak of a guy and he gets all wimpy and writes this." I handed Mike the piece of paper Bocci gave me.

Mike looked at the paper. "Ten digits—so not a Social. Could be a phone number?"

"Right. But, he says "*make sure she's taken care of and tell her I kept my promise.*" And blam, he eats the lead."

"Just like that?"

"Just like that."

"Now the case is on the news. Can you draw any more attention?" Mike turned around to keep an eye on the bar just as Carlos came in. Carlos Suarez tends bar for us part-time and I was glad he was working tonight. I needed to strategize with Mike. Carlos is a cop, and a good one. Clean-cut guy, family man, tough, with great street smarts. He rode with Mike for two years before Mike retired.

"This goes beyond the money. When I brought up the two million at Tony's, he got weird. I hit a nerve."

"Sammy there?" asked Mike.

"Slow Sammy, yeah, he was there. But get this, Marco shows up at Bocci's and questions me."

"Thank God for Marco, right," added Mike.

"I agree. But, it was weird—he softened up on me right after I mentioned the money. I'm telling you, we're stepping into something here. Not sure if I like it. He gave me time to talk to Claire and said he's coming by here tonight," I said.

"You tell Marco about this number Bocci wrote?"

"Of course not."

He nodded. "Well, ain't this some shit?"

"We need to talk to Claire. I called her number while driving back here and no answer."

Mike was never the most patient cop and still was the kind of guy who couldn't sit around and wait for something to happen. He needed to make it happen. "All we have is the info on her car. Let's run with that. I'll start with her phone number and you go to the address on the registration. And this bullshit of her only contacting us is over."

And just like that—as if Mike willed it to happen—Claire appeared beside our booth. We both looked at her, looked at each other, and then back to her. "Sit down."

She sat beside me. Not the glamorous-looking Claire from yesterday, though. Today she wore jeans, boots, a black T-shirt with a black blazer. Her eyes were red, as if she'd been crying. She wore no makeup and her hair was pulled back in a ponytail. Still, her natural beauty showed through. The freckles on her face—yesterday, covered with makeup—made her look younger.

"I saw on the news about Mr. Bocci." She sounded defeated and her voice quivered. "Did you talk to him?"

"I was in the office when he did it."

Her hands quickly covered her mouth. "Oh my God, don't say that." Her emerald eyes darted to Mike and then back to me. "You were there when he shot himself?"

Again, I nodded. "Sitting across from him." Her eyes welled up. A tear spilled down her cheek.

"I can't believe it. When I saw it on the news, I had to come right over." Mike went to the bar and brought back some napkins for her to dry her eyes. "Thanks. That poor man." She wiped at her eyes.

"How did you know him?"

"I didn't. When my mother talked about the money, she always said the same thing. That I should go see Mr. Bocci and that he'd help me. I've had his name drilled into my head since I was in high school. I can't believe this." She dabbed at her eyes again, took a breath, folded her hands in her lap and looked at me. "What did he say?"

"Why didn't you go see him?"

"What?"

"If your mother always told you to start with Bocci, why didn't you?" Mike and I spent years interrogating suspects and we became quite good at reading body language, listening for inflections in voice tone, looking for nervous tics and tells, and noting any shift in demeanor. When I asked the question, she failed to hold my gaze. Her eyes went down, usually a quick sign of guilt or embarrassment—or unease—and slowly came back to me.

"My mother always said it would be better if I had a professional help me. Like a lawyer, or a private detective."

I glanced at Mike as he studied her and I knew he was making his own assessment. If she was lying, he'd know. "Did he say anything? Did you ask about the money?" she said.

Mike, holding back as long as he could, chimed in. "Ms. Dixon, how did you find us?"

"My mother kept a paper in her nightstand. Instructions on what to do when she died. *Johnny Delarosa* was written on her paper. Not sure why."

"What's her name?"

"Jackie. Jacqueline Dixon. Grew up here in the city. I guess some bad things happened and she took me when I was five and moved away. To Philadelphia. That's where I grew up."

"Your father?"

"Never knew him."

"You know his name?"

"Donny Dixon. Sometimes I would ask Mother about him and all she would say was that he was not a very nice man and that the best thing she ever did was move away."

"The name sounds familiar."

"Really?" she asked.

"I got to give it some thought," Mike said. "Long time ago."

"Probably twenty-five years. We moved when I was five."

"You're sure this money exists?"

"No. My mother was always sure. I never thought Mr. Bocci would kill himself either. What does that tell you?"

Was that a challenge or a question? "It tells me we opened a box that should've stayed closed."

"My mother obsessed about this. I have to see it through. I promised her."

"Bocci's dead because I walked into his office asking about two million. You need to tell us everything or we can't go on."

"I did tell you everything." Mike and I stayed silent. *First one to talk loses, right?* It was awkward, but after a minute, she spoke again. "She also told me Donny Dixon—my father—did time in jail and the money came from something he did."

"We figured that," Mike said.

Her faced flushed.

She tried to recover a bit. "I can't even speculate about the money. It could be in a bank, invested somewhere, hidden. My instructions were to start with you."

"How did she know Bocci?"

"She never said much, but she did tell me they were friends from childhood."

No need to look at Mike to understand what he was thinking: *Now we're getting somewhere.* He also understood what I was thinking. *Don't say a word.*

Mike's phone rang and he got up to take the call.

"It's been a long day," I said. "How about we pick this up tomorrow?"

"Sure, Mr. Delarosa, I understand."

"Please call me Johnny. Okay?" She nodded and smiled. "And answer the phone, too. I need to be able to get a hold of you."

"Sure, of course. I'm sorry I missed the call earlier."

"Where are you staying?"

"I'm at the Marriott. On Washington. Room 503."

"Okay. Get some rest." We both slid out of the booth. She put her purse on her shoulder and threw her arms around me in a hug.

"I'm sorry about what you went through today. I feel responsible."

"Part of the job. I'll do what I can to help you."

Mike watched us from the bar. She let go of the hug but slid her hands down my arms and grabbed my hands.

"I'm glad you're okay." She gave my hands a squeeze. "Tomorrow."

"Have a good evening."

She left, giving Mike a little wave on her way out.

Mike came over. "Interesting."

"Yeah, it was, wasn't it? Not sure what to make of that."

We sat back down in the booth. "That was Marco on the phone. He wants to meet us at Nancy's in thirty minutes," he said. "We have some big questions here, brother. If her grandfather was Joseph Aletto, then you're looking for mob money."

"And she wants me to turn over the rocks."

"Exactly. Big retainer, gets a little friendly…I'm not trusting her."

"Yeah, and if she's right, and there is two million out there somewhere, she won't be the only one looking for it. And two million is plenty of motivation to make normal people do crazy things."

"Like blow your brains out?"

"Like blow your brains out."

9

When Mike and I got to Nancy's, we found Marco waiting for us at a back table. Nancy's Diner was an old-style diner that served the best greasy diner food in town. Breakfast all day, great coffee: it was our go-to place. Cops and commuters kept Nancy's afloat. She and her husband Bill bought the place when he was just a rookie on the force. She ran it during the week and they both worked it on the weekends. As fate would have it, and because bad things happen to good people, after ten years on the job, cancer grabbed Bill and left Nancy with a pension and a restaurant. So the restaurant became her life. She came over with three coffees. "You boys ever go home?"

"Waiting for you to take me home." Mike winked.

"You hit the lottery, we can talk."

"My girl…!" added Marco.

"Any food tonight for you big handsome hunks?"

"Coffee, for now," I said.

Nancy walked off and when she was out of earshot. Marco piped up. "Delarosa—you might wake up the dead on this one."

"Talk, Marco, talk."

"I was just on, still a green rookie and got assigned to the docks. I learned pretty fast that the mob ran things. All the cops there—all were on the payroll. Most of them resented me from the start. Last thing they wanted was a new guy to screw up their arrangement."

"Aletto the big boss then?" said Mike.

"Oh, yeah. Old man Aletto was the don. Controlled everything. But I learned later the only reason I was assigned the docks was 'cause I'm Italian and they all knew my old man. They all figured I'd just blend right in and be one of the boys. And I did. Mostly. I was smart enough to keep my eyes open and my mouth shut. I did the right thing and gained their trust. Both the cops and the mob."

"Marco, we don't need your resume," chided Mike.

"Shut up and listen. There was a young punk hanging around all the time. Donny Dixon. Not Italian but thought he was. They would give him small jobs on the docks and small jobs working for Aletto. Collections, enforcement. He got good at it and started running numbers. They gave him a part of the city all to himself. He proved himself; made them money. But he didn't make the same mistake most guys make. They start to make money and think they're king shit. Flashing money around, expensive car, designer suits, girlfriends, hookers. Dixon didn't. Stayed in his crappy apartment, drove a junky VW Bug. I'll never forget. Dressed in the same jeans and T-shirt every day. Looked like a pot-smoking hippy from the sixties."

Marco stopped for a sip of coffee, and then revved up again. "He pals up with two other low-lifes, Tony the Scar, and a guy named Jimmy Rosso. All three were making their bones with Aletto when he decides to expand his bookie operation. So he lets these three run the book. They're naturals. Making a fortune. Control the entire city's bookmaking. Tony and Rosso become made men. Dixon can't be a made guy because he's not Italian. He resents it but keeps his trap shut."

I interrupted the history lesson. "How do you know all this?"

"Johnny, like I said, I kept my eyes and ears open. Plus, guys would talk. The low-level goombahs liked to brag. Anyways, the story goes that they start to skim and over about four years, they squirrel away about two million."

"Aletto doesn't get wise to this?"

"Not at first. This is where Donny Dixon screwed up. Couldn't keep his mouth shut. He couldn't live by the omertá any longer. The thought of the money waiting for him was too much."

"And…"

"Aletto investigates and can't find anything. Calls all three into a meeting. They all deny skimming off the top. He lets them go and they think they're clean. But Aletto's not satisfied and sends a message. Two weeks later, some kid fishing off the Twenty-Third Street pier hooks Donny Dixon's head on his fishing line and reels it in. Aletto's boys did everything but water- board Tony and Rosso, but they never cracked."

"Never found the money?" I asked.

"Nope—but here's the real kick in the ass. Along the way, Dixon married Jackie Aletto—the old man's daughter."

"He whacked his son-in-law?"

"Yep—that's the story. Remember, Dixon wasn't Italian. Urban legend—or I should say mob legend—now. The two million went missing with Dixon."

Mike let out a long, low whistle. Marco said, "My turn to ask. What's your client's name?"

After all that, I couldn't hold back. "Claire Dixon."

His eyebrows shot up. "Damn. She's gotta be Jackie's daughter. She's got you looking for the long-lost money?"

"Something like that. What about Rosso and this guy Bocci?"

"Rosso disappeared. Maybe he took the money." He shrugged. "This guy Bocci—all I know is he worked for Aletto way back when. He's going down as a suicide, so you're good."

"Marco, good news. I didn't need to be jammed up in that."

"That might be the least of your problems. If Tony and these guys think mob money is floating around, wise-guys will be coming out of the harbor with their cement shoes on."

We laughed at his line but he was right. *What Pandora's box did we open? Or did my client open?* I could walk away at this point—even give back the retainer—but Bocci killing himself lit the fuse.

Marco got up from the table. "I'll poke around a bit on Bocci. And Johnny, tread lightly."

"I hear ya. Thanks again."

He turned and left.

I sipped my coffee. "Keep going on this?"

"Hell, yeah," Mike said. "Could be a nice payday."

"Already have one dead body. Don't want any more. Especially mine."

"The woman dropped twenty grand on you. She's serious, right?"

"Right."

"Marco remembers the missing money, right?"

"Right."

"So go find it. Do what you're good at."

"It's the client who has me concerned."

"So she's a mystery, plus she's drop-dead. What's not to like?"

"Dead bodies, the mob, missing two million. Recipe for violence, wouldn't you say?"

"And…?"

I pushed away my coffee cup. "I'm gonna need something stronger than coffee."

10

I GOT TO CITY SALVAGE MID-MORNING AND LUCKY for me, Tony's Mustang was not in the lot. I went in to the smoke-filled office as Sammy was finishing up with a customer. He saw me come in and it flustered him because he gave the guy the wrong amount in change. He straightened out the money and sent the guy on his way with a pair of used brake calipers.

"Hey Johnny, twice in one week, huh?"

"You guys ever open a window in here? I can't even breathe."

Sammy tapped the end of his cigar on the counter to knock off an inch of ashes. They fell to the floor, blending into the dirt and grime. "Kind of get used to it."

"How's business?" I waved a path through the smoke.

"Car parts. People always need car parts."

"Yeah, I guess you're right."

"Your clubs seemed to be doing okay."

He chuckled a bit. "Naked women. Men always need to fool with naked women. I guess we fulfill needs."

"You're the smartest guys in town."

He shrugged. "So why are you back here?"

"A couple more questions. From the other day."

The sports page covered the counter and he went back to the box scores. Sammy lacked a full-tank when it came to brains, but he was smart enough to not talk to me. "Tony should be back in a few minutes. He went to pick up some things."

"Tony? Why do I need Tony?"

"You need to talk to him. He remembers all the old stuff."

"What stuff? I thought you guys always worked together."

"Tony did all the hustle. I was the errand boy."

"I'm hearing all these crazy stories about when you guys worked the docks and stolen money and a guy named Donny Dixon."

He glanced up and huffed. "Dixon. Going back some years."

"You worked with him?"

He folded the newspaper. "Like I said, I don't remember. It was a long time ago. I got some inventory to do." And he was saved by the bell—or more like the rumble of Tony's Mustang. "There's Tony now."

Sammy retreated to his inventory and Tony came through the door flinging sarcasm. "Johnny, back for another drink?"

"Tony, not a very warm welcome. What if I'm a paying customer?"

"Are you buying something?"

"We had such a pleasant visit the other day. I can't stay away. Plus, you never called me. I waited by the phone all day."

He put two bags of office supplies on the counter and then unwrapped and lit up a new cigar. "Yeah, about that. I got busy." He blew his cigar smoke in my direction.

"Happen to see the news two nights ago?"

"No, can't say I did. I don't like to watch the news. Depresses me."

Sammy snickered.

"Didn't hear about Carlo Bocci?"

"Who?"

"Bocci. Carlo Bocci. The CPA who blew his brains out."

"Guess he was watching too much news."

This time Sammy let out with a hard laugh. Even Tony chuckled at his own joke.

"Problem is, I watched him pull the trigger."

"You were with him?" I nodded. "Wow. They wrap you up as a suspect?"

"For a minute."

He leaned back against the shelves and crossed his arms. "Is this supposed to mean something to me?"

"Remember I said my client gave me two names? Tony the Scar first, Carlo Bocci second. Why would that be?"

He shrugged. "Got me."

"You ever meet him? Think back?"

"Hell, no. Why would I?"

"Joseph Aletto is how."

"Aletto? Jesus, Johnny. You're going back some years, now."

"Aletto, you, Donny Dixon."

The door opened and a customer came in. Tony nodded toward the door and we moved outside to the parking lot.

"What are you looking for?"

"My client is looking for some old money. She gave us your name. I asked a few questions and we come up with Aletto and a couple of goons. Dixon and some guy, Jimmy Rosso."

He shook his head and smiled. "They're both long gone. Congratulations. You uncovered an old rumor."

"What happened to Dixon?"

"Disappeared."

"You guys were all partners, right?"

"Something like that."

"C'mon Tony. I know who ran the book. Good cash rolling in. Dixon help himself to a bit of the cut?"

"If he did, I didn't see him."

"You guys weren't taking a little slice off the top and Dixon couldn't keep his mouth shut?"

"Like I said, rumors."

"Why did you ask about my client? Her age?"

"Why you doing this?"

"Tony—I'm not a cop. Client hired me to dig around in

some family lore. I don't know if it goes anywhere."

"Man, I haven't thought about this stuff in years."

I let him ponder the past for a second.

"Why'd you ask about her age?"

Tony drew in off the cigar and then slowly blew the smoke up to the sky. "This is irritating. And I don't want you talking to Sammy." He pointed the cigar at me to emphasize his order.

"Deal," I said. "Entertain me a bit and I leave Sammy out of it."

He shook his head. Scuffed at the dirt with his sneaker. "Donny was married to Aletto's daughter. Jackie. They had this cute little girl. Redhead. I guess five at the time. It's got to be her."

"Is there long-lost money buried somewhere?"

"What do you think?"

"My client thinks there is."

"Aletto got it into his head we were skimming and wouldn't let it go. Me and Jimmy took a beating but Donny ended up in the harbor. We were made guys but after that, Aletto kept taking work away from us. When he got whacked, the new guys pushed us out."

"Where's Rosso?"

"No idea. Skipped town."

"And if there was money, it went down with Dixon?"

"It sure didn't come my way."

"Bocci had an interesting reaction."

"He felt guilty. You pushed him over the edge."

"Never deal with him?" I asked.

"Let's say I never made it into the corporate office."

"Well, I got to admit, I was skeptical at first. Then Bocci blew his brains out. Now I'm real curious."

"Johnny." He took a step closer to me. "Do you think if Aletto and his boys thought I took two million of his money that I'd be standing here?"

"Good point."

"I got work to do." He walked back into his shop.

I opened my car door thinking I'm still curious and he didn't give me all the sordid past. Nor did I expect him to.

11

THIS CASE NEEDED STRUCTURE. SO IT WAS TIME TO create a file for Ms. Claire Dixon. I sat in my office-booth with a corned beef sandwich and a beer and put the facts on paper. I made a list of the players. The breathing ones: Claire, Tony the Scar, his brother Sammy, and Elena Garver. The dead ones: Carlo Bocci, Jackie Aletto Dixon, Donny Dixon, and mob boss Joseph Aletto. The unknown: one Jimmy Rosso who blew town years ago. What ties them together? The alleged missing two million dollars. What ties me to this? The twenty grand dropped on me as a retainer and the mystery of my client.

We also had the ten-digit number Bocci left. Ten digits said phone number but Mike tried every variation and came up with nothing. A bank account, but which bank? Or a corporate tax ID. But when Junior searched the state records he came up empty. I thought of asking Marco for access to Bocci's files but it was senseless. I was convinced Bocci had the answers—all now buried and waiting to be unearthed.

I finished the beer and grabbed my keys and phone. No case ever got solved by sitting in a bar booth.

The McDonald's parking lot on Harbor Boulevard took on a quite different persona at ten o'clock at night. Two homeless men sat next to the door of the restaurant with a paper cup outstretched to any customer brave enough to go inside. Three drug buys went down twenty feet from my car. Suburban white guys in expensive cars coming in for their fix. I watched a tall, skinny hooker—a black chick with a pink Afro wig, a pink bikini top, a white micro-mini skirt, and six-inch stilettos—get picked up and dropped off twice within thirty minutes. Either she had mad skills or the johns were quick on the trigger. She came up to my window insisting I needed a date. She said twenty dollars for a trip around the world. I told her I wasn't in the mood to travel. The drug dealer then slinked over to my car. I shook my head. He shrugged and wandered off. Twenty minutes later a group of five teenagers appeared from an alley. Gang-banger wannabes. They weren't doing anything but hanging around in the lot bothering the hooker. She told them no matter how much money they had it would never be enough. Then they spotted me in my 2005 Buick LaSabre. My surveillance car.

All five came to the car. "White dude. Sharp ride." They snickered and surrounded the car as I inched my Beretta out of the holster. "How about we cruise for a little?" I reached into the glove compartment and pulled out an old police badge I kept handy for occasions like this. The lone girl in the group hopped up and sat on the hood of the car. A bigger kid with long dreads and a New York Yankees ball cap came up to the window. *'Must be here for Pinky. She only like white dudes.'* I lowered my window.

The big kid said, "Yo, dude. You lost?" I held the gun in my right hand and the badge in my left and brought them into view. "Shit, dude. You undercover. Our bad. We just lookin' out for our neighborhood. We're the neighborhood watch. Keeping the streets clean. Know what I'm sayin'?"

"Go home."

"Yeah, man. No problem. We cool." They all moved back from the car. He yelled to Pinky. "Yo, dude's bad. Undercover." *Now I got respect.* They walked backward and eyeballed me as they left. Out of the five, one might make it out of the neighborhood and into something meaningful. The other four, it would be a fight to stay alive.

While I was dealing with the creatures of the night, I did not see the Audi pull into the parking lot of the Harbor Court. My intent was to keep an eye on the client and so far, I missed her come in. I was beyond annoyed with myself; I had allowed the upstanding teenagers to distract me. A light was on in Room 112 but the shades were drawn.

Half an hour went by when a Toyota compact pulled into the motel lot and stopped in front of Claire's room. A small Asian guy jumped out. Chinese food delivery. He rapped on the door and Claire answered. I wanted a glimpse into the room but she stayed in the doorway and paid the driver as he handed in two bags of food. She closed the door and he hurried off.

We all have cravings for Chinese late at night. I can do some damage to General Tso's chicken and a couple of egg rolls during a late-night binge, but Claire received *two* bags of food. To me, two bags equals two people. *Who else was in the room with her?* Furious I didn't see her coming in, I waited another hour but the door never opened.

I lowered my window and called to Pinky. She came over. "I knew you couldn't resist this fine ass. What'll it be, baby?"

I handed her two twenties. "Get something to eat."

"Huh?" I put the window up and started the car. "Hey, no date?"

I checked my rear-view mirror as I pulled away and caught Pinky blowing me kisses.

12

I SLID OPEN MY BALCONY DOOR TO LET IN THE COOL night breeze. The clean, crisp air came in off the ocean and chased the stale air from my condo. I grabbed a four-year-old cabernet and a glass.

My thinking spot. Late at night with a glass of wine. I stretched out on the balcony chaise. My way to wind down to solve the problems of the day. Or the problems of the case. I filled the glass, took a sip, and allowed the wine to work. I let the facts settle. I learned long ago to not overthink. When I do, I tend to miss the obvious and make the case difficult.

If there is long-lost money, the answer lies in a bookmaking operation from long ago. *Follow the money* is more than an adage in this business. It's a starting point. However, on this case, working backward was the smart tack to take. Where did the money finish? The money started with the guys on the street. Guys running numbers and taking bets. From there, the cash flowed to Tony, Dixon, and Rosso. They set the odds, ran the book, collected, and then what? The cash went from those three to where? Aletto? Who handled the cash for Aletto? Bocci was Aletto's accountant but did he ever handle the cash?

Logic dictates the less number of people who touched the cash equaled less opportunity for sticky fingers. Aletto was as smart and as ruthless as they came. His reputation was legendary as a man who ran an efficient, organized—albeit illegal—business based upon structure, loyalty, family, and a commitment to punishing anyone who did not abide by the rules of the organization. With no exceptions. Example: his son-in-law Dixon. The Aletto family lived by omertá—the code of silence. Anyone who broke the rules, talked, got greedy, or thought he could do better on his own by running his own game and competing with Aletto, would soon find himself at the bottom of the bay. Aletto was the last of the old-school Mafioso in this town. It would take brains and balls to steal from him and expect to get away with it. If Tony, Dixon, and the boys had such a good thing going, why take the chance?

I got a blanket from the bedroom and went back to my chaise and my balcony safe haven. The night air was too good to waste.

My condo was four stories high on a busy street. During the day, the sound of glass breaking and a car screeching on the street below might not attract my attention. But at three o'clock in the morning, the shatter of glass and squealing tires jerked me from my sound sleep. I got up and looked over the balcony. Nothing— nobody below. I decided my bed would be a better option at this point. I picked up the wine bottle and glass when I got a whiff of the smoke. I looked over the railing again; heavy smoke billowed up the outside of the building. My phone rang - it was the alarm company reporting an alarm at the restaurant. I closed my phone, closed the balcony door and pulled on my shoes all at the same time. I hurried out and down the steps.

I got to the street to find the front window of McNally's broken and flames shooting up the outside of the building. I went back inside and pulled the apartment building fire alarm to alert the other occupants, and then called 911. Next, I went into the bar to try to put water on the fire from the inside. Most of the flames were on the outside of the building at this point, but some flames flicked in through the broken plate glass and tickled the wood work inside. This was an old building with a brick façade and my fear was if the fire got inside, the entire structure would go up in seconds. I grabbed a bucket from under the bar and was able to splash some water on the wood frame around the window.

I went back outside to the street as sirens approached. The fire spread out on the sidewalk. *Did someone throw a*

Molotov cocktail at my building? Were they aiming for the window and came up a little short? My apartment building neighbors came out onto the street, along with residents of the adjacent building. Everyone was asking what happened. Even though I had a suspicion, I chocked it up to gang members with nothing better to do.

I called Mike as a Port City fire engine pulled in front of the building. The guys were out of the truck with water on the flames in a minute, only causing the fire to spread along the walk. They determined an accelerant was used to start the fire and doused it with a chemical mixture, which extinguished it within seconds, leaving a charred window frame and scorched bricks.

Thirty minutes later, Mike arrived. I was inside assessing damage and sweeping up glass and bits of wood and ash.

"You're kidding me, right?" He stood in the doorway with his hands on his hips. "Fire-bomb?"

"Would you believe, good ol' Molotov cocktail? That's my guess. It broke on the sidewalk and most of the fire stayed outside. Different story if that bottle came through the window."

"Jesus." He came over to what was left of the window. "How bad?"

"All things considered, not too. We'll get insurance out later today but we can board this up and open by evening. I'll find a fan to blow out the smoke."

"This could have been a disaster. Did you give a statement?"

"Told them the glass breaking woke me up. I didn't see anyone. Heard a car."

"What do you think? Warning shot? Stay away from mob money?" He picked up a broom and began sweeping.

"Yep. Or somebody we put away and now they're out." My cell rang. "Unknown Caller" appeared on the screen. I showed Mike and then answered. The line went dead.

"Well, isn't that interesting," he said.

"I've only talked to Tony and Sammy. You think they would do this?"

"Two million dollars will make people do crazy things."

"Like throw fire-bombs?"

"Like throw fire-bombs."

13

THE INSURANCE ADJUSTER ARRIVED AT TEN AND set to work. He confirmed what I suspected—the fire could have been much worse. He didn't find any structural damage, classified it as an act of vandalism, reminded me of our deductible, and said we had our choice of contractors to do the repairs. He agreed that we could open today, even suggested we advertise a fire-bomb happy hour. He also commented that what we served last night should be removed from the menu if we got that type of reaction. I do appreciate a good joke, but I didn't share his sense of humor. Not today, anyhow.

I thanked him and as he left Marco walked in. "Boy, you sure are one PI who likes to attract attention. I'm having my morning coffee and there you are, on TV again. You're getting to be a celebrity PI. Reality show in your future?"

"Are you done?"

"Yeah, I think."

"Good. How about finding out who did this?"

"Already started. Nearest camera is at the intersection two blocks west. Couldn't see anything. Forensics said they couldn't lift any prints off the broken glass, either. Your fire bomber wore gloves. Any disgruntled customers? Employees?"

"Only me and Mike. And we stay disgruntled."

"You stir up the Mafioso?"

"Maybe." My phone rang. The screen had "Unknown Caller" again. I pointed it out to Mike and then answered. "Hello?" The phone clicked off. "Third time since this morning. I don't think it's a telemarketer, either."

He shook his head. "Be careful, that's all I can say at this point. You talk to Tony the Scar?"

"Yes, and only him. I don't think he would send a signal like this, though."

"Somebody is sending a message. And it wasn't that the front window needed to be cleaned."

"Everyone is a comedian today."

Mike pulled up in front of the bar and a truck pulled up behind him. Two workers unloaded a sheet of plywood and began to board up the window.

"Adjuster didn't object to us opening later."

"Good," Mike said. "Need to get the smell of smoke out of here. The guys will grab a couple of fans." He looked at Marco. "Anything?"

"Not yet."

"I didn't think. Definitely not random, though."

"I think Johnny's made some new friends," said Marco. "And ones who don't play nice. Call you if I get anything."

"Marco, wait," I said. "The guy Rosso, remember anything on him?"

"Like I said before, he disappeared after Dixon got whacked. Word at the time was he took off."

"Did Aletto think he had the money?"

"Nah—not smart enough to pull that off. They all thought he got scared and ran."

"Hey, ever work with a cop named Worthington? On the docks?"

"Yeah, yeah. Big guy, right?"

"Even bigger than you."

"He was before me. He was stand-up. Seemed okay. Beer taps work?"

"Help yourself." He went around the bar, drew off a half a glass and drank it down.

"All right, back to work. Good luck here. I'll be in touch."

I went back to sweeping and wiping down the tables. Mike went out front to help the two workers. My phone rang again. This time it was Claire.

"Claire."

"Johnny. I'm so sorry. I saw this morning about your bar. Do you think this has anything to do with my case?"

"Most likely."

"Oh God, I feel responsible. First Mr. Bocci, then…"

"Why don't you stop by here tonight? We need to talk."

"I don't know if I can..."

"Tonight at seven." I ended the call.

14

MIKE AND I GOT THE BAR SWEPT AND CLEANED AS BEST we could. The workers boarded up the window and fans were blowing to clean out the smoke. As I got close to City Salvage, I spotted Tony next to his car. He was on his cell phone. He always parked his car next to the fence that borders his property. I pulled my car behind his at an angle and blocked him. I had questions and needed answers. He closed his phone and put his hands on his hips.

"Come on, Johnny."

I got out of my car. "I made the news again, Tony."

"You must have a lot of enemies."

"Son-of-a bitch, Tony. What are you doing?" His face turned red and he moved around his car, headed my way. He couldn't catch me but if he did, I doubt I'd stand a chance.

"You accusing me?"

"Somebody is trying to tell me something."

"It ain't me and I don't appreciate this. You and me have always been cool and this is not right. This is all because you got my name from something that was thirty years ago? Doesn't sit well."

"I understand that, but you're the only one around who knows what happened way back when."

"I told you what happened. Nothing."

"Then why does Bocci kill himself and somebody throw a cocktail at my bar?"

"Coincidence," he said.

"I'm not buying it."

"Ask your client. She's the one who wants to dig up the past. And do you really think I set your bar on fire?" He was now in my face and his cigar breath insulted me.

"Take a step back." Something told me I needed to keep Tony on my side. Deep down, I knew he didn't take a shot at me last night. He didn't move, though. "Tony?"

He stepped back. "I don't need this."

"I don't either. But I got a dead body on my hands and a fire-bomb thrown at my bar. Tell me more about Dixon and Rosso."

"I have an appointment. Move your car."

"What about Rosso?"

"He cut and run. Donny got whacked and he ran. That's it. Now move." He opened his car door.

"Never heard from him?"

"Nope—I always wondered. I liked the guy. We got along good."

"And you never suspected him with the money."

"Delarosa, I already told you. He wasn't smart enough to pull that off. Now if you don't move your car, I'll make sure you end up like Jackie Aletto." He got into his car, closed the door and started the engine.

"Tony, what did you just say?" I went up to his car door. "Tony?" He lowered his window.

"What?"

"Jackie Aletto—what did you mean?"

"You don't know?" I shrugged. A smile crept across his face. "She had an accident and got both legs broke. Surprised your client didn't tell you that."

"An accident?" I said. He put up his window and revved the Mustang's engine. He pulled his car forward a few feet, giving him room enough to back up, cut the wheel, and pull forward to squeeze between my car and the fence. He stopped as he got to the road and then floored it and spun out of the lot, throwing dust and stones at me and my car.

I waved the dust from my face so I could breathe. I guess there were a few things my client left out of her story, and I couldn't wait for the meeting I demanded for later in the evening. We had a lot to talk about.

15

CLAIRE ARRIVED AT SEVEN AND TURNED EVERY head in the bar. She wore a dark-blue knit number that hugged every curve of her long body and stopped a few inches above her knee. The auburn hair fell around her in a fire burst of color against the dark dress. Her heels made her about five ten and a striking presence in any room. I stood behind the bar and she came over.

"Hi, Johnny."

"Hi. Want a drink? We can go to the back booth."

"Sure. Red wine?"

"Meet you in back." I poured her a cabernet and a bourbon for me. Mike was serving the tables tonight so I motioned to him as I headed to the back. I slid into the booth opposite her.

"I'm sorry about what happened here with the fire. Do you think that has anything to do with my case?"

"I'm hoping you tell me."

"How so?"

"Do you think the money exists?"

"My mother always said…"

"No, you. Not your mother. You?" I said.

She sipped her wine and took a deep breath. "I believe my mother. It sounds far-fetched, the silly fantasies of an old woman. She talked about this money ever since I can remember. Something happened way back when. She believed it and so do I."

"Tell me about Donny Dixon."

"My father?" She swirled the wine around in the glass. "I don't know much. Only what Mother told me. I was four when they killed him."

"Aletto?"

"I guess."

"Aletto thought Donny skimmed money?"

"That was the rumor, but Mother always said my father didn't do it."

"Somebody took it? Or else we wouldn't be here."

"You're right, but she maintained my father's innocence until the end."

"Jimmy Rosso? Did your mother ever talk about him?"

"A little. Only that he was one of the guys."

"And he disappeared?"

"According to my mother, after they pulled my father's body from the harbor, he left town, scared for his own life."

I took a drink of the bourbon. "Are you hungry? Want a menu?"

"No thanks, I'm fine."

"I need to check the bar. I'll be right back." I wanted her to sit and think for a while. I wanted it to be awkward for her. I went behind the bar and talked to Mike for a minute. About nothing. He asked whether she added anything new and I told him she rehashed what we already had.

"She's driving the Audi. Parked up the street," he said. "Make her squirm."

"Exactly."

I went back to the booth. "Claire, Bocci is dead and someone threw a fire-bomb at our bar. You need to give me more. What else would your mother say about their life?"

"Always on the edge. She would say they got into arguments about my father going straight. Even though she grew up in the life, she always feared the worst. And the worst happened."

"Did your mother think her own father had her husband killed?"

She shrugged. "Not sure what to say about that."

"He suspected Donny?"

"Sure." She uncrossed and crossed her legs. Shifted in the booth. "My father told my mother that money disappeared but he didn't have anything to do with it."

"Then who?"

"My mother always said Tony."

"Tony denies it, and I believe him. That leaves Rosso."

"Yep."

"Who split when all this went down?"

"Yep."

"Claire—I need to be sure what we're looking for is real."

"I believe my mother. I believe it's somewhere. You sure about Tony?"

"If he knew there was money, he would've searched long ago."

"I really thought Mr. Bocci would have the answer."

"Why didn't you tell me about your mother's legs?"

She had the wine glass to her lips. "You know, huh?" I nodded. She set the glass down. "Didn't think it mattered at this point."

I leaned forward in the booth and put my voice up an octave. "Everything matters. Bocci's dead and my building was torched since you walked in these doors. If you want me to do this, you can't hold anything back."

She shifted in her seat. I could feel her temperature go up from my side of the booth. She took a deep breath. I could tell we hit an emotional trigger point.

"They thought my father gave the money to my mother."

"Who is they?"

"The guys, the mob. Tony. Any of those low lifes." She paused, irritated. Ran her hand back through her hair. I stayed quiet. "After my father was murdered, they came after her. My mother—who had nothing to do with this. But they were convinced she did and when she didn't have any answers..." Her face turned as red as her hair. "They broke her legs." Tears filled her eyes. "They pulled her out of her bed, broke one leg with a baseball bat, pushed her down the stairs, broke the other leg. Then, while she lay on the floor, they smashed her knees and hips with the bat. Spent the rest of her life in a wheel-chair." She took tissue from her purse and dried her eyes. "She was a dancer before she married my father."

"Were you there?"

"Hidden away in my bedroom. I can still hear her screams."

I gave her a second and she sipped the wine. "Did she blame her father for Donny's death?"

"If she did, she never said it. She would never side against her father. She was loyal to the family."

"Your grandfather didn't go after the guys who put his own daughter in a wheelchair?"

"He started to, that's when Rosso left town. Then, a short time after that, my grandfather was murdered. Nobody left to avenge what happened to my mother."

"I see. She went through a terrible ordeal."

"These men are scum. They'll shoot first then ask questions. That's why you—we—have to be careful." She reached across the table and put her hand on mine. "Okay?" She gave my hand a squeeze and then pulled away.

"I'm always careful. But I don't like surprises. That's why I need as much information from you as possible. At first, I was skeptical about any money at all, but after Bocci and the fire bomb, it must be more than family legend."

"I know it is. Trust me."

"What did your mother do for income?"

"Inheritance kept us comfortable. Plus she received some disability. I went to public school and got scholarships and grants for college."

"Did you receive a degree?"

"Criminal justice. Pre-law." She smiled. The irony filled the booth.

"Any man in your life?"

"No. Spent the years since college taking care of my mom."

"Noble. You did the right thing. Was she bitter? About what they did to her?"

"I'm sure. She put up a brave face for me, but as she got older, it was all she talked about. It became harder to take care of her but I'm glad I did. Yes, I sacrificed, but she's my mother. If I could prove her right about the money, I'll be justified."

I nodded but didn't believe a word. Cop instincts kicked in. Did you ever meet someone you liked but always felt you weren't getting the whole story? Something doesn't seem right—an underlying mistrust. Claire gave me that feeling. "Why didn't you give me this background at our first meeting?"

"I worried you wouldn't take the case. The whole thing sounds crazy so I tried to be tough, coy, drop a big retainer, get you hooked. Never did I think what happened with Mr. Bocci would happen."

"Yeah, losing Bocci hurt."

"What's next?"

"I do some research. Talk to some guys who were

around way back when. See who remembers what."

"I just wait?"

"Yep—and keep your phone on."

"Okay." She pulled her purse to her lap. "Johnny—you have kind eyes."

I didn't expect that. I blushed, much to my regret. "Oh?"

"Yes, kind eyes. Warm. You're the man in my life—at least for now." She smiled and got out of the booth. I followed and she gave me a hug and held it for a moment longer than I expected. I saw Mike watching with raised eyebrows. "Thank you again."

"I'll be in touch," I said. She left and I went behind the bar.

"Got yourself a girlfriend, huh?"

"I'm not sure what I have," I said. "But I'm not getting the whole truth and nothing but the truth, either. She's sold on the money, though."

"And...?"

"I need to go back in time. Thirty years."

16

I MADE COFFEE, OPENED THE BALCONY DOOR TO LET in the morning air, and fired up my lap top to check email. I had two new ones that mattered and a lot of junk emails that didn't. The first one was from Cara—my girlfriend—sort of. Cara Silverberg was forty years old with a body that defied her age by at least ten years. She was five five with perfect curves, sparkling brown eyes, and light-brown hair that fell to her shoulders. She had a young face, no laugh lines or wrinkles creeping in yet, and when she pulled her hair back into a pony-tail, she could pass for twenty-five.

I met her when she hired me to follow her husband. Charles Silverberg, a tall, overweight lumpy guy with a half-attempt at a comb-over, was a partner in a large downtown law firm and sure enough, Cara's suspicions were correct. I photographed him and a short, pudgy woman going into and coming out of a hotel for three days in a row. I gave Cara the pictures and she confronted him. He later confessed the woman fulfilled him emotionally. It must have been true. The woman was as wide as she was tall so I couldn't imagine her being a party in the sack.

He apologized and begged her forgiveness—and to my surprise—she forgave him. I think she had a hard time letting go of his five-hundred-thousand-dollar-a-year salary plus bonuses. She got her own secret vengeance, though—me. I became her side guy. At first I thought I was a revenge affair, but we've been seeing each other for two years now and it works out perfect for both of us.

Her email was to say hello and to tell me her husband had an upcoming business trip over the weekend, which meant she wanted to come over. I'd email her later.

The second email was from my ex-wife Kelly. There was some weird karma thing about getting an email from my ex-wife and my girlfriend on the same day, but my head would explode if I tried to figure it out. We'd been divorced for ten years but still co-own a beach cottage on Crescent Beach. We bought the property twelve years ago in a subconscious effort to save our relationship. Fissures in the marriage began to appear after Kelly had three miscarriages in four years. The beach house became a hobby and consumed us for a while, but it was no substitute. We were so disheartened by not being able to have children, it was as if we failed each other. We focused on our careers and drifted into separate lives. My life as a cop—and my drinking—only added to the disillusionment.

We only used it one summer before placing it with a management company as a vacation rental. We never talked about it, but having the house kept us connected—avoiding the inevitable finality of the relationship—until now.

Kelly was marrying a suburban endodontist and it did not sit well with him that she still owned a property with me. I was happy for her; she was now going to be a step-mom to his two teenagers and experience a bit of motherhood. She deserved it, but everything had to be bigger and better with him; he had his own beach house with three decks and a private pool. She wanted to either sell the cottage or wanted me to buy out her half. Now that Claire dropped some dough on me, my first thought was to figure a way to buy it. I responded, asking for a day or two to think about it.

I opened the case file on my kitchen table and worked through my notes. I compiled a list of the banks in town, plus stockbrokerage firms, investment firms, any type of financial institution capable of holding two million dollars. I wrote out a timeline starting with Dixon's death up through Aletto's death. I studied the names over and over, creating different scenarios and relationships. I kept moving the pieces around, seeing who would fit where or what would spark an idea. I worked for two hours and put on another pot of coffee when Mike called, asking me to come down to the bar. He said it was urgent.

Mike was behind the bar. "What?" I said. He nodded to the back booth. For the second time in less than a week, an unidentified female appeared in my office-booth. "Who is it?"

"Hell if I know." This time blonde hair cascaded down and as I approached the booth, a feeling of familiarity set in. I faced her.

"Mr. Delarosa!" Katie Pitts jumped up and threw her arms around me.

"Hey, wow, this is a surprise." I knew I would see her again. The gut is always right. She unwrapped herself from me and slid into the booth as I sat on my side. If I ran into her on the street I don't think I would recognize her, though. Instead of the black streaks on her face and the dirty, matted hair, today she was the all-American girl from an affluent neighborhood. I'm not complaining. She wore a short, black skirt and a green blouse unbuttoned just enough to reveal cleavage that already caught my eyes. Her long hair fell around her, curled in flowing waves and she had it pulled back from her face by two small braids that tied in the back, revealing bright, sparkling ice-blue eyes. "What are you doing here?"

Her purse was on the bench beside her and she folded her hands in front of her on the table. "Well, I came to thank you."

"You didn't have to. Your father tell you where to find

me?"

"Mr. Delarosa, I need to say thank you again. What you did was incredible. I can't stop thinking about how you saved me. And of course he did."

"It's just that I like to keep things quiet..."

"Oh, I know. He told me. You're a very private private investigator."

"Something like that."

She smiled, revealing a perfect line of straight, Hollywood-white teeth. I'm sure the work of the best orthodontist in town.

Mike appeared beside the booth and had that twinkle in his eye that I knew so well. He was loving this. "Excuse me, can I get you a drink?"

"Oh, yes," she said.

"Mike," I said. "This is Katie Pitts from the job we had a few nights ago."

"Oh, nice to meet you." Mike shook her hand. "You had quite an ordeal. Glad to see you're doing okay. I hope those bastards get what they deserve. Excuse my language."

"No, they are bastards," she said. "And thanks to Mr. Delarosa here, we did get a few shots in." She slammed her hand on the table. "I should've kicked them in their balls. The little pricks. Excuse my language."

"Excused," Mike said. "You have every right to feel that way. You know what we used to do? When we were on the job. To send the little gang-bangers a message?"

"No, what?" Her eyes grew big with rapt attention. He sat down beside her and leaned in close, probably for dramatic effect but knowing Mike, he was peeking down her shirt.

"They all wear those chains they attach their wallet to their belt loop. Know what I mean?" She nodded. "We would rip off the chain, yank down their jeans, bend them over a table, then wrap the chain—".

"Mike!" Their heads snapped at me. "Get her a drink."

He collected his better judgment, and remembered some stories are better left untold. "Yeah, okay. Maybe later." He stood. "What'll you have?"

"Vodka tonic. With a twist of lemon."

"Vodka tonic it is. Mr. Delarosa, how about you?"

"My usual is fine, Mike, thank you," I said dryly. The waiter Mike went off to fetch our drinks.

Katie looked at me, still enthralled with my partner. "Wait a minute. You guys worked together?"

"Partners on PCPD for fourteen years. Now we co-own this."

"Oh, freakin' cool. So you guys are ex-cops—now private eyes—who work out of a bar. This is like crazy Raymond Chandler stuff on steroids."

"You read Raymond Chandler?"

"English major. Spent one year into old detective fiction. *The Big Sleep, Farewell My Lovely.* Read Mickey Spillane's Mike Hammer books, all that."

"I'm impressed."

"I love the genre." In her best deep radio announcer voice, she said, "When the men were tough and the women just got in the way." She laughed at her line. I laughed too but I kept going back to when I took her out of the warehouse. I still had the vision of her in her underwear stuck in my head. She was cute and sexy and now funny. "I do have a question, though." She straightened her posture, folded her hands in front of her again and got serious.

"Okay," I said.

"I came here to thank you for what you did, but I've been thinking." She paused, and then leveled her gaze at me. "I want to work with you."

"What?"

"I want to work with you."

"What are you talking about?"

"I want to do this. Private investigator."

"No…not a good idea."

"Why not? I think I would do a great job."

"I work alone."

"Then you need some help. Think about it. Think how I can help you," she said.

"I prefer to work alone."

"Mr. Delarosa, please. Hear me out. I understand I can't walk in and think you'll give me a job. I want to prove myself. I'll do anything. And money is not important—I mean, I need money but I'm not desperate. Daddy, and all…"

"Katie…"

"Don't say no, not yet."

Mike came back with our drinks. "Here ya go. Vodka tonic and a bourbon, no ice."

"She wants a job." I took a healthy sip of the bourbon.

"Oh, yeah?" He turned his attention to Katie and I knew what his warped mind was thinking. "I could use an extra hand on Friday and Saturday nights. Ever tend bar?" We did not need an extra hand.

"A job as a private investigator," I said.

"Huh?"

Katie jumped in without hesitation. She was assertive, I'll give her that. "Yes, as a PI. I asked Mr. Delarosa if he would consider bringing me on. I realize you might not be hiring, but I'm willing to learn, work hard, and take low pay to start."

Mike looked at me like, "*What the hell is happening?*"

"Katie, most guys in this business are cops first. This is not something you learn in a couple of weeks."

"I know. But you said most guys. I can do this. I'm smart and I learn fast."

The eyes are the problem. It's hard to look into those eyes and not be sucked in. The call of the siren. *What was it about good-looking women and their power over men?* "This is not like what you read in detective novels and definitely not glamorous and exciting. Quite boring most of the time."

"It wasn't boring when you rescued me. *That* was exciting."

"Your situation was different. Usually I'm sitting in my car for hours at a time, watching middle-aged married guys sneak into motel rooms."

"Do you take pictures?"

"Yes, sometimes."

"I can do that. I even have my own camera."

Mike, not helping, offered, "Really—what kind?"

"Nikon. The expensive kind. With three lenses and I took a couple of photography classes."

"Katie…"

"What about interviewing suspects? I minored in journalism so I can handle that." She was so jazzed she couldn't even sit still. "Mr. Delarosa…"

"Please call him Johnny. He's never been called Mr. Delarosa in his life," chimed Mike.

"Okay, stop, both of you. Katie, we run a bar. The PI work comes to us by word of mouth, mostly from old police connections. It's not like we have a load of cases we're working. And you don't have any experience."

"Think of it like this—I'm a clean slate." The blue eyes darted back and forth between Mike and me. "I don't bring with me any…any…preconceived ways of doing things. You can teach me, mold me into what you want. Use me for whatever you need." *No way I could look at Mike after that line.* "How many women PIs are there in this city?"

I sat back in the booth. "I can't think of any."

"See, perfect. You can use me on jobs and nobody will ever suspect I'm an investigator."

"She's got a point there, boss."

"Katie, I never work with anyone but Mike, and we handle things all our own way. Our experience came from our days as cops and years on the streets. I appreciate your enthusiasm, but I don't think." She sank back in the booth. I turned to Mike for some help.

"Johnny's right," he said. "You need a police background. Plus, it's not normal work. A lot of it is at night and in some not-so-nice places with not-so-nice people. You're intelligent. You should be looking for a regular job in some company."

She took a deep breath, let it out. As nice as it would be to have her around to look at, I hoped she was letting go of this idea. Instead, she geared up for round two. She looked at Mike. "Would you mind sitting down?"

"Of course not." He slid in beside me.

"I understand what you are saying, but do not allow my looks or my age to fool you. I learn fast and I'll only do what you say."

I got to give her credit for her determination, but her motivation was all wrong.

"Katie—when I got you from the warehouse, yes, it was exciting—your adrenaline was pumping—"

"—I know. It was incredible—seemed like something out of a movie—"

"—they're all not like that. We were lucky it didn't go bad. People get hurt in those situations."

"He's right," Mike said. "Most kidnapping victims are not recovered. You were lucky. What happened with you is one in a hundred."

She went quiet again, but only for a few seconds. She took a sip of her drink. "Ooo—good vodka tonic, sir." Mike elbowed me. "Okay, I understand it can be dangerous. I knew that before I came here today." She reached into her purse and put a copy of her resume on the table. "Would you consider this—you said need some help at the bar on Fridays and Saturdays…"

"Well, I can use someone," stammered Mike.

"Okay, I'll work on the weekends and you let me intern during the week. I can start with little small jobs as I learn. An internship. You won't have to pay anything."

Intern. That's all she had to say for Mike. "Well, there's an idea. What do you think, Johnny? An internship."

I sat back without saying anything for a good minute. I think she could tell I was getting a bit exasperated with this conversation. I drummed my fingers on the table, took another sip of bourbon. "Katie, why do you want this? I mean, what's the real reason?"

"All my friends, they all have boring nine-to-five jobs. Offices and cubicles. Being an office drone is not for me."

"Does your father know about this?"

"I'm twenty-four. I'm my own person. I want a job then my own place."

"Have a boyfriend?" Mike asked.

"No. I broke a guy's heart down in Florida. He came from this rich, stuffy family and it was a turn-off. I know I don't look the part—but I'm not one of those country club princesses looking for a doctor or lawyer, either." She sat back, done making her case.

Mike and I both knew this was a stupid idea.

He broke the ice. "I'm fine with you coming in and working the bar on the weekends. If Johnny can use you in some way, it's up to him. But what he says goes."

She focused on me.

Damn the blue eyes. The long legs. The curves and the breasts that sat up high. This could rank up there with some of my dumbest ideas. Although, the gut told me this would be okay. I nodded. "Maybe we can find some little things to start with."

"Seriously?"

"Come back tomorrow," I said, very matter-of-fact.

"You won't regret this. I promise!" She was so excited the entire booth was bouncing. She grabbed her purse and tried to stand but bumped her drink. I caught the glass before too much spilled. Mike steadied the table. "Oh, sorry, sorry. I'm so stoked. Is there anything special I should wear? Anything I need to buy…?"

"Katie," I snapped, my voice deep and stern. She stopped and stared. "Sit down." She did. "Have you ever read about, or seen on TV or in the movies, a private eye acting the way you are acting now?"

She got it immediately. She gathered herself, sat back in the booth, put the purse back on the bench, and folded her hands on the table. "No."

"I don't need the flighty country club princess. I need a real private dick who will get the job done." Her cheeks got red. The giant blue eyes were wide and fixated on me. I glanced at Mike and he was biting his lip. I stared at her. "Do you get it?" She nodded. "Come here." I leaned across the table and she slowly leaned toward me. So close I could smell the scent of her shampoo. I put my hand on her forearm and squeezed a bit. Physical contact makes it real. She glanced at my hand and then back to my eyes. "This is for real. Do you get that? Life-or-death real." She nodded again. I squeezed harder. "I need to hear you say it."

She swallowed hard. "Yes, I get it. This is real."

Neither one of us blinked. I had her attention. "Your first lesson." I slowed my speech. "Play it cool. Okay? Play it cool." I let go of her arm and sat back. She did too. She didn't say anything. Just looked from me to Mike. He crossed his arms in front of him and cocked an eyebrow. "Tomorrow. Ten a.m."

She kept nodding but it was if she went into slow motion. Her movements were deliberate. She reached into her purse, and—as cool as the coolest—put on her Donna Karan sunglasses. She slid out of the booth, stood, smoothed out her skirt, slung her purse over her shoulder, and turned toward the door. Mike and I sat in silence until she left the bar.

"Are we out of our minds?"

"Did you see the body on her?"

"We're breaking our own rule," I said. The rule was to never hire any good-looking women. We already learned our lesson on that one.

"I don't care." He got out of the booth. "Just don't get her killed."

"Thanks, buddy."

"Play it cool? Really?" He walked to the bar, laughing. Then he stopped, turned back and pointed at me. "I'm proud of you!"

I threw back what was left of my bourbon in one gulp.

17

TEN P.M. AND TIME FOR A SPIN THROUGH THE LUSH surroundings of the Harbor Court Motel. A light drizzle was falling, which was good. It kept folks off the streets. I turned right off Harbor Boulevard into an alley that ran along the right side of the building, and then a ninety-degree turn left into another alley that bordered the back length of the motel. The back alley dumped me out to Fourth Street and a left turn there took me back to Harbor.

I drove around the block a second time, only much slower. Three trash Dumpsters in the back alley made it barely wide enough for my car to squeeze through. Large gray rats scurried across the alley and were in and around the bins. When my headlights lit up the trash bins, the rats stopped—stared at me for a second—and then went back to their scrounging. *City rats all right. No car would interrupt their dinner.* Each room had a small window that faced the alley. Lights were on in half of the windows which, in the rain, cast a pale yellow sheen to the mist.

After the second reconnaissance trip around the building, I parked in the McDonald's lot to gauge the scene. Claire's Audi was in its spot. I connected a 70-300mm zoom lens to my Nikon and zoomed into the front office. A telephone pole blocked part of the view but I noticed a hefty-sized black guy behind the front desk. The long-haired, aged hippy was not on duty. Leaning on the counter was a rent-a-cop security guard. The desk clerk looked to weigh at least two fifty and I bet the security guard had a good fifty pounds on him. *They must take turns going across for Big Macs and shakes.* A TV in the corner had a ball game playing and had their attention.

I watched for thirty minutes and nothing happened. I thought I'd find Pinky on the job but the rain kept the street vermin indoors. Anyhow, time to move closer. I convinced myself someone else was in the room with Claire and had to find out who it was. *Damn my curiosity.*

I put the camera equipment on the floor of the car and threw a blanket over it. With my gun tucked into my waistband, I walked halfway up the block, away from the motel, crossed Harbor and then walked back down on the motel side of the street, out of the line-of-sight of the front office. I wore my black jeans and black jacket and pulled a cap down low so I blended into the shadows. I walked up to Claire's car and put my hand on the hood. It was cold; the car hadn't been driven in a while. I went to the door of room 112 and stood and listened. A TV played the evening news broadcast but I couldn't hear anything else. I stayed for another minute, listening for a voice or two, but I feared someone would come out of a room on a late-night run to the snack machines and spot me lurking.

I went to the side alley and around to the back. Claire's room was fourth from the end so I counted four small windows and realized the first trash bin was perfect for me to boost up and peek into the window. The shade was drawn down to about two inches from the bottom. Judging from my height, the windows were eight feet from the ground.

The trash bins had sliding doors on the side to throw in garbage. I slid the door open and it screeched—causing a tom cat to come screaming out—bounce off my chest—and scamper away down the alley. I'm not sure who was more startled, me or the cat. I took four good deep breaths to slow my heart rate and leaned back against the building to gain my composure and make sure I didn't wake the entire neighborhood. My night as a peeper was off to a bad start. I heard the rats rummaging. I faced the most hardened criminals over my career but there was something about rats—a lot of rats—being three feet away that gave me great pause.

I grabbed the top of the bin and pulled up to where I got one boot on the open door. From there, I could reach left and put a hand on the window sill to steady myself. I leaned left and only had a glimpse into the motel room's bathroom. A lady's hair brush and a tube of toothpaste were on the sink. *That's not going to blow the case wide open.* The corner of a motel dresser was visible through the bathroom door. The lights were on in the main room but unless I stayed in my precarious perch all night, I wasn't going to discover anything.

"Hey!" A man's voice sounded from the opposite end of the alley. The security guard. I don't know whether someone saw me or whether he was on his normal rounds. I hopped down and took off toward the side of the building, only to step back to avoid being hit by a car coming down the cross alley. The car swerved and missed me by inches. It straightened itself and I darted out behind it. It turned in to the motel.

I got down to the intersection and stopped. I glanced back to the motel lot only to see Claire get out of the car—a Lincoln, but I'm not certain—and go into her room. At the same time, the security guard rounded the corner and yelled. At forty-eight, I'm not as fit and fast as I used to be but I'm damn sure faster than his three hundred pounds. I ran two blocks before I stopped and turned around. The guard lumbered back to the motel. He gave up after less than a block.

I walked another half-block for good measure and then crossed Harbor to the McDonald's side of the street. I took off my black jacket and cap. That left my white T-shirt and jeans – in case the security guy was keeping an eye for a man in all black.

I got back to my car and started the engine. I sat for a while, disappointed in what transpired. *Did Claire see me?* I doubt it with the rain and my cap pulled low but that was too close. My intuition was right. Unless she went out and left the TV and lights on, someone else was in the room and it bothered me. *And who dropped her off? A friend? A lover? An accomplice? Somebody who knows where the money is but can't access it?*

I smacked my hand on the steering wheel—frustrated. Most cases, I know what the client wants: Is my spouse cheating? Is someone embezzling from my company? The target of the investigation is clear. The execution of the investigation is clear. On this case, there was thirty years between the missing money and the investigation. Nothing was clear and memories could get selective over thirty years.

The one person who I needed to remember was Carlo Bocci. Him killing himself bothered me, saddened me, and made me real curious. He held the key. I knew it. *Why did he kill himself? What did he want to avoid?*

18

RESEARCH WAS ON MY MIND THIS MORNING. AFTER last night's almost botched fiasco at the Harbor Court, I needed a fresh head to begin the day and went for a much-needed run. Not only to loosen my aging muscles but to clear my brain. The rain stopped overnight and the morning was cool and crisp. The temperature had dropped and much of last night's humidity had blown out to sea. The three miles went by quickly and I ducked into the bar before going upstairs to shower and change.

Katie Pitts was there, sitting at the bar. I forgot about her and was annoyed with myself again.

"Hi, Mr. Delarosa!" She jumped off the stool when she saw me.

"Katie."

"Out for a run, huh? Good for you. A beautiful morning, too. Do you think I'll have a set schedule? Nine to five or something like that?"

Oh boy. Mike had a grin on his face as wide as the bar itself.

"You're here. I did tell you ten, didn't I?"

"Yep, and I'm ready to start. I brought my camera and laptop, too."

"She got here before me," Mike said.

"I didn't want to be late on my first day."

"No, of course not," I said. "Punctuality is important. We don't tolerate tardiness here, do we, Mike?" She wore a short jeans skirt, a white T-shirt, sandals, and her hair pulled back in a ponytail. *Did I need a dress code?*

"Nope."

"What happened to the window? Fight or something?" She flashed the gorgeous pearly whites.

"I wish it was that simple." She had her computer on the bar. I hoped she was as good on the computer as I was bad.

"I tell you what. Set up in the back booth. You can plug it in back there. I'm going upstairs to change and I'll be right back."

"You live here too?"

"Condo on the fourth floor."

"Cool."

"While I do that, I have your first assignment. Some research." I wrote our Wi-Fi access code and "Donny Dixon" on a note pad.

"I want you to find news articles on this guy. He was murdered and his body pulled out of the harbor thirty years ago. Try the *Herald* archives first."

"Sounds like a juicy mob hit."

"See what you can find. I'll be back."

Mike gave me a thumbs-up as I left. I went up to the condo, showered and changed. I still had reservations about my distraction of an intern, but if I could figure ways to use her—computer research, for example—it might be nice having someone handle the mundane stuff I hate.

I got back to the bar and Katie was tapping away on the laptop. She had a coffee beside her and some notes on the pad. I poured myself one and I slid into the booth. "Anything?"

"You need to create an account with the newspaper. No charge, but I didn't know what name I should use."

"I don't want your name out there. I'm the licensed PI so we use my name." I wrote my info on the paper. "But stop for a second."

"Sure."

"That broken window in the front—somebody threw a small fire-bomb at it two nights ago."

"Really?"

"My point is this. We run across people in this business who don't like us snooping around sometimes. You must realize there's a dark side in this work. A dangerous side."

"Oh, I do. I'm aware."

"I need you to understand that."

"I do. I understand."

"Good. It's important. What did you tell your father?"

"I told him you needed help in the office and I'm working at the bar part-time."

I nodded. "Perfect. I need help with the computer and I'm sure your skills are better than mine. My skills are on the streets, not in an office."

"Do you have an office?"

"You're sitting in it."

"Oh."

"You didn't want a normal sit-in-a-cubicle job."

"I know. And I love it, but I thought you must have a desk or an area?"

"Nope, just work from here. We'll think of something. Mike will give you some employment forms. You are technically an employee of the restaurant."

"Yes, sure. I get it."

"Keep digging on Dixon. And by the way, the work you are doing now, the research, that's ninety percent of your job. Got that?"

"I got it."

"I need to make a call."

I walked over to the bar to call the Marquis and asked for Worthington. He came on the line and agreed to see me in an hour. I told him I had some questions about when he worked on the docks and he jumped at the chance to talk.

I went back to Katie.

"I found his obituary," she said. "Here, look."

"That was fast." She spun the computer around and showed me an obit for Donald Francis Dixon. We read through it. *Tragic boating accident. Survived by his wife, the former Jacqueline Aletto, one daughter, Claire Elena*

Dixon. Funeral Mass to be held at St. Anthony's. "Your first task as an employee of Delarosa Investigations and you aced it. Good job. It would've taken me three times as long to find that."

"Thank you, boss."

One reason I was successful as an investigator was that I never forgot anything. I could always remember names or how I knew a person. I could remember the guys I put away, when they got out, and when I put them away again. I remembered who ran with what gang and what they sold, stole, pushed, or trafficked. My memory solved more cases than the investigative techniques I had learned. These days, I can't remember where I put my phone or where I left my reading glasses. But, I can still remember names. Elena is not a common name and now I heard it twice within a week. *Elena Garver and Claire Elena Dixon.*

"Katie, let's go for a ride."

19

IN THE ALLEY BEHIND McNALLY'S WAS A TWO CAR garage that I rent. I pulled up the door and there were my two darlings: the BMW and the workhorse, the Buick.

"There's the BMW you used to bring me home. I asked my dad if I could get one but he ignored me. I love this car." Katie went to the passenger door. "Can we put the top down?"

"Wrong car, I'm afraid."

"What?"

"We're taking this."

She pointed at the Buick—repulsed at the affront to her social status. "That?"

"Welcome to the glamorous world of the private detective. Still want to go?"

"Of course I do."

"Hop in. Oh, the AC is on the blink but we can roll the

windows down."

She opened the door but brushed off the front seat before she got in. I pulled the car out of the garage, stopped, hopped out and pulled down the door. I got back in and we headed out of the alley.

"They make electric garage door openers."

"I know," I said.

We were on our way to the Marquis. Katie's short skirt was even shorter as she sat in the car. Much to my dismay, I did need a dress code.

"The purpose of the car is to not attract attention. I use it when on surveillance or if I'm tailing someone. Everyone will remember a Z4; nobody will remember this."

"Ah, I see. Do not attract attention." The enthusiasm that waned by having to ride in the Buick came back. "Sort of undercover, aren't we?"

"Well, kind of. But, on the subject of attracting attention, I want you to think about how you dress."

"How I dress? What's wrong with how I dress?"

"Nothing at all. But if you walk into a hotel – like we're about to do – and you're wearing a short jeans skirt, every guy in the place will be bug eyed."

"So I need to blend in instead of stand out?"

"Exactly." Easier than I thought and it would be less distracting for me. "Many times I must be invisible, and if you're in the field, it will be the same for you."

"Hmm, I didn't think about that. Now I'm stoked. Ever wear a disguise?"

"Sure."

I filled her in on the basics of the case on the car ride to the Marquis. Being hired to find money that disappeared thirty years ago, Donny Dixon, Claire booked into two hotel rooms, and Bocci offing himself. She took it all in, made some notes. One thing I learned: when Katie got excited, she talked. Nonstop. She quizzed me about my life, my years on the force, my marriage, my ex-wife, whether I had any kids, whether I had a current girlfriend, my most exciting case, whether I ever shot someone—*yes*— if she will get a gun—*no*—what kind of food I like, what kind of women I like—*quiet ones, but I dodged that one*—and finally, did I think I would ever get married again. It was an interrogation, not a conversation.

Worthington met us in the lobby of the hotel and took us to his office on the ground floor. We crowded into his cluttered office. Twelve security monitors lined the wall, each one focused on a different area of the property. He squeezed into a chair behind his desk and we sat in two chairs opposite. I introduced Katie as my associate.

"Associate, huh?" He looked her up and down.

"Handles a lot of the research and back office work."

"Back office work—is that what we call it now?" Katie stiffened and I didn't react. His face got red. "Sorry. How can I help you?"

"Think back to the olden days on the docks. Ever remember a guy getting whacked for stealing two million from Aletto?"

Katie flipped open her note book and started writing. "Was that Dixon?"

My head snapped to her. “I’ll ask the questions.”

“Sorry.”

“I don’t recall. How long ago?” he asked.

“Thirty years. The story goes that some of Aletto’s soldiers were handling his bookmaking operation and skimmed two million. One of the guys, Donny Dixon, took a swim in the harbor for it. Never found the money.”

“Boy, I don’t know.”

“Ever run into the Scarazzini brothers?”

Katie was scribbling away now.

“Tony and Sammy? Yeah, those scumbags. I know them.”

“They’re tied into this somehow.”

“Really? Wouldn’t surprise me. Those two were into everything way back then. They still own Stiletto’s?”

“Yep.”

“I remember Sammy. A little on the slow side. They’d had him doing all the dirty work.”

“Oh yeah?”

“Rumor was he clipped one of Serrano’s boys. Couldn’t prove anything.”

“Michael Serrano. He became boss after Aletto?” I asked.

He nodded. “Didn’t command the respect Aletto did, though. The made guys started running their own business. Serrano couldn’t control them and the docks fell apart. Russians moved in. Serrano couldn’t compete. Then he disappeared.”

“Russkies string him up?”

"Supposedly."

"Ever hear of a Carlo Bocci?" I asked.

"I remember the name. He was an Aletto guy. Lawyer, I think."

"CPA."

"Yeah, right. CPA. Word was he and Serrano didn't get along." Every time Katie put her head down to scribble notes, Worthington would sneak a peek at her legs. That bothered me and I was afraid to think why.

"So after Aletto got whacked, Bocci stayed active?"

"Well, they would still talk about him when I was there twenty years ago. They said he was the brains and Aletto handled operations."

"Remember a Jimmy Rosso?"

"Rosso? No, never."

"Back to Tony and Sammy. Do you think they could've siphoned off two million and kept it quiet?"

He shook his head. "No way. Tony was a big talker. If he had that much cash, he would have shown his hand."

"Yeah, I agree."

"One last question. Nobody knew who hit Aletto, right?"

"Nope. Every guy who was around at the time had a different theory. Most thought it was Serrano on a power play, but no one could prove anything. Serrano was the only one who had anything to gain—and that didn't work."

"Well, I think we got enough." I looked at Katie. "Shall we?" She nodded, afraid to say anything at this point, I guessed.

I shook hands with Worthington. "Thanks. Appreciate your time."

"Hey, anytime. If I can help out any way, let me know. Love to take a break from here for a while."

"I'll keep it in mind."

He extended a hand to Katie. "Nice to meet you." She politely shook it but didn't say anything. "If I think of anything else, I'll call."

We got a few steps out of Worthington's office when he came out behind us. "Delarosa. You might want to come back."

We hurried back in.

"Take a look." He pointed to a monitor. There was Claire in the restaurant at a table by herself. "Isn't that your girl?"

Katie and I took up a spot at the bar. My same spot from before. "That's our client."

"By herself, huh." She made a notation on her pad and jotted down the time. "This is interesting. Who is she meeting?"

The bartender came over, the same guy as last week. We both ordered drinks and sat there, watching. Claire had lunch, by herself. Every so often she would text someone on her phone. An hour passed and nothing happened. She got up and left. We each finished a second drink.

"Welcome to the world of private investigation," I said. "At least you got a look at our client."

"I did and I got good notes from today, too. We'll solve this mystery, right, boss?"

"No doubt."

We got off the bar-stools and Katie swayed a bit. She grabbed the stool to steady herself. "Whoa. I guess I'm not used to two vodka tonics before lunch without any food."

"Let's eat then. Not here—this is too fancy."

"Do we always drink while on the job?"

"We try."

20

WE DROVE OVER TO NANCY'S DINER FOR LUNCH and on the twenty-minute ride I again became the focus of the Katie interrogation machine: How long were you married? How long have you been divorced? Why did you separate? Do you miss her? Do you think you will ever remarry—*the answer was no on that one*—. What about growing old with someone?"

"Katie…!"

"Yes?"

"Can we talk about the case and not about me?"

"Oh, sure."

"Good. I love your inquisitive mind, but save it for the job."

"I want to get to know you."

"This is only your first day."

We parked in an alley along the side of the diner. I

waved to Nancy as we went in and led Katie to a table toward the back. Nancy came over with menus.

"Katie, meet Nancy, the most wonderful woman in all of Port City. She's the love of my life but won't have anything to do with me."

"Sweetie, he had his chance way back when and blew it."

"Don't remind me." They shook hands. "Katie is helping me out—my new computer expert."

"Hey, I don't blame you. I have trouble turning mine on."

I ordered a cheeseburger and fries and Katie ordered a salad and garlic bread.

"Best food in town."

"Good, I'm starving."

Nancy brought two iced teas and while we waited for the food, I gave Katie an index card with the number Bocci gave me.

"Your new assignment. Figure out what it is."

"Phone number?"

"We tried. Could be a bank account, but which bank? Corporate tax ID number—but couldn't come up with anything."

"Where did this come from?"

I explained the case in greater detail: Claire dropping the big retainer, Bocci killing himself, Tony and Scar and his brother, the fire bomb at the bar. She was enthralled. And now the number from Bocci and the message—his dying words—that he kept his promise.

"He kept his promise to whom?"

"Not sure."

"Must be Claire."

I shrugged. "He also said it was about greed, family, and love."

"Oh, man. This is good!"

"Remember, not all cases are like this."

"He was in love with Claire, wasn't he?"

"All the cases are about love. Usually love gone bad, or the love of money and that always turns out bad. But, Claire was five when the money went missing—according to her."

"Oh, yeah," she said, but I could see her gears churning in her head. The food came and we both dug in. This girl was feminine to the max when it came to her style and manner of dress, but she plowed through her lunch as though it were the first meal she had in weeks. She talked through each bite. I've seen groups of cops at a FOP dinner with more table manners. She picked up the card.

"This number holds the key to the case."

"It is the key to the case. We hope. At first I thought I was chasing an old rumor, but why would someone drop that kind of retainer? What does Claire really want? I think that is the question."

"You mean more than the money?"

"If a woman hires me to follow her husband because she thinks he's cheating, and I discover that he is, most times the real problem is the trouble in the marriage. The affair is a product of the real problem."

"So what's the real motive?" She wrote that in her

notebook. "This is incredible." She put her pen down and swallowed the bite of food in her mouth. "I know this is my first day and all, but thank you for giving me a chance. I knew from the moment we met—when you rescued me—that you and I were meant to do something. I realize that sounds like the romantic musings of a young girl, but I had this feeling…a passion. I'm embarrassed now." She gulped down the iced tea.

I thought the same thing. I knew that night I had not seen the last of her—I never thought she'd be an employee, though. I not sure what I thought she would be. "Don't be embarrassed. You found something that appealed to you and you decided to explore it. You have an inquisitive mind, right?"

"Yes!"

"That's what we need in this business. Remember, not all jobs are like this."

"You guys keep telling me that."

"It's true. Boring."

"Okay, got it, boss. Okay if I call you boss?"

"Sure, just don't call me Mr. Delarosa. Makes me feel older than I am."

"How old are you?"

"Back to the case, please." Nancy cleared our plates and asked whether we wanted dessert. Katie looked at me wide-eyed and three minutes later we both had a slice of apple pie in front of us, hers with ice cream.

"Big eater, huh?" I said.

"I was starving. I think the drinks stirred my appetite."

Nancy gave me the stink-eye as we left the diner. The guys at the bar would never believe my twenty-four-year-old golden-haired research assistant was only an employee. But, I'm a modern man and an equal opportunity employer and if I want to hire an assistant who looks like a beach volleyball player, that's my prerogative. *Yeah, right.* This will test every fiber of my being.

The target of the investigation cannot know they are being investigated or it would not work. I need the element of surprise. When I investigate a cheating spouse, they are shocked when I throw down photographic evidence of their illicit behavior, and when I provide evidence that the employee was embezzling from the employer, surprise works to my advantage and the employee has no way to weasel out. In cop terms, I get the drop on the bad guy.

This case was the opposite and it betrayed my basic cop instincts. Things were happening *to me* that didn't make sense. Claire coming in with the large retainer, Bocci's dramatic exit, and a fire-bomb at the bar all have me off balance.

We left the restaurant and turned the corner. We both saw it at the same time and stopped. Scrawled in red spray paint, across the passenger side of my beautiful vomit-colored LeSabre were the words: *Warning #2.*

"Oh my God," she said.

I pulled the Beretta from my waistband. "Go back into Nancy's."

"What?"

"Go back into Nancy's—now!"

"Okay, okay." She ran back around the corner. Two women walking toward noticed the gun in my hand and turned and hurried away.

Son of a bitch, I could not be surprised like this. This case was controlling me instead of me controlling the case. I scanned the street and there was nobody else around. We were in the restaurant for at least forty-five minutes. Whoever did this vanished by now.

I tucked away the gun and got on my back to look under the car. The paint on the side might not be the warning, but if someone could throw a fire-bomb at my building, they could sure as hell stick a bomb under my car. I couldn't see anything on the passenger side of the undercarriage or in the wheel wells. I got under the driver's side and sure enough, there was an oblong black box, maybe ten inches long, with two wires on it strapped to the undercarriage.

I got up and there was Katie beside the car watching me. "Go back to the restaurant, now!"

"What is it?"

I grabbed her arm and walked her back to the restaurant. "When I tell you to do something, you do it. Understand?" I let go of her arm; I was squeezing harder than I realized. She had tears in her eyes. She nodded and went inside.

I called Marco.

Eighteen minutes later, seven police cars and a bomb squad truck surrounded my Buick. I stood on the corner watching. Katie stood across the street, with Nancy and all the other patrons from the building who had been evacuated. A bomb squad technician came up from under the car. He waved me and Marco over.

"This is a fake." He had the black box with the two wires sticking out in his hand. "Looks like someone wants to keep track of you." He held up his other hand, which held a small black device. "GPS tracker. Stuck under your fender." The bomb squad technician chuckled a bit and then saw I wasn't amused. He called it as a false alarm and they packed up their gear. A TV news crew pulled up; they heard the report of a possible car bomb on the scanner. I motioned for Katie.

A GPS tracker is a helpful little gadget and one I'm using more often. It tracks in real time and the battery can last for days, plus it has a strong magnet to hold it in place. Katie came up to us. "Tell that news crew it was a false alarm. We don't need them around here." She ran over to the news truck. My phone buzzed—a text. I showed Marco. Second warning. "Can you trace the number?"

"I'll try," said Marco, sensing my frustration. He jotted down the phone number. "This case got you, doesn't it?"

"Someone's watching." I scanned the crowd, which was quickly dispersing.

He nodded toward Katie, who was now in a conversation with the young male reporter from the news crew. "Who's your girlfriend?"

"Not my girlfriend. Tell you later."

"Later then."

"Sorry about all this."

"Hey, better off safe. Be careful, okay?" He lumbered off and dismissed the other officers. I headed to the news truck to grab Katie.

I was afraid to find out what she told him.

21

KATIE WAS QUIET FOR THE FIRST FEW MINUTES OF our ride back to the bar. If she didn't believe the seriousness, the absolute inherent danger of the case and of this type of work, she now understood. I asked her what she said to the news crew.

"That it was a false alarm. Someone played a joke on you."

"Did he ask who I was?

"Yes. I said you own a bar and that I work for you."

"Excellent. Good girl."

"That's sexist."

"What?"

"Saying, 'good girl.'"

"Oh. Okay—good job, then."

"Thanks."

She took out her note pad and started to write. I called

Mike to tell him what happened, and then Marco called me to say he couldn't find a traffic camera aimed at the street beside Nancy's, and that none of the surrounding businesses had outside security cameras. I parked in the perfect spot for my fake bomber-miscreant to tag my car.

We pulled up to my garage and I backed in the Buick, and pulled the BMW out, left it running, and opened the trunk. Along with the extra clothes I stashed in the car was a small fishing tackle box I used for my gadgets. I opened the box and pulled out a small black device, about the size of a cell phone, and switched it on. "Watch." Katie came over. "Have to keep the car running." Sure enough, after a few seconds, the device beeped and a LED turned green. These guys did not disappoint. "GPS detector. Picks up GPS signals being sent from the car."

"Wow, they got both cars."

"Yep."

"They could follow wherever we went."

"Or if I followed anyone." I got on the ground, searched under the car and found a tracker under the front left fender.

We went into McNally's and she set up her work station in the back booth. I tossed the second GPS on the bar. "Found that one in my Z4." Mike picked it up and shook his head. "Check your car."

"I told you. Don't get her killed," he said. I smirked. "How was she out there?"

"Talks too damn much."

"She'll work in here from now on."

Mike put a shot in front of me and I threw it back. "Either my client is tracking me, or someone else who knows we're out looking for this money wants to keep tabs. Right?"

"Right." Katie walked over with her notes and sat beside me. Mike pointed at her.

"Umm, can I have a ginger ale? My stomach's a bit on the queasy side."

She opened her pad. I said, "So the obvious person would be Tony."

"Yeah," said Mike. "He has guys who would do the dirty work." He gave her the soda and she sipped at it while tapping her pen on the notepad.

"Or, it's Claire," I said.

"Our own client?" asked Katie. "Why?"

"Ah, and that's not even the big question, is it?"

Mike leaned on the bar and we watched her. After a moment, she realized we were quizzing her.

"Oh, okay. Somebody is tracking the cars. They want to know where you are and who you're talking to." She hopped off the stool and paced around. "Okay, I can do this. The first guy, the Tony guy—it could be him because he wants to know if you find the money…but, but, that's too easy."

"I agree. But think through today."

"We go to the restaurant, come out, the car is painted…wait, what made you check under the car?"

"The paint on the car tells us we were followed. They knew I'd figure out a tracker was used and search the car."

"Why tell us?"

"To tell me what they're capable of."

"Confirming the money exists. Right?"

"Don't know." I had Mike pour me another. "They tipped their hand on purpose. That's the curious part. That's the big question."

"Right, why a fake car bomb and why throw the fire bomb two feet short of the building so it does minimal damage?" Mike asked. "They want to scare you but not too much?"

"Nothing is normal with this case. Either way, you are working from here. No more outside work."

"What?" Katie said. "Today was incredible. A little scary, but I'm stoked."

My phone rang and I held the screen up for Mike and Katie to see: CLAIRE DIXON. I answered and walked to the back of the bar for privacy.

The call only lasted a minute and I came back to Katie, who moved back to her booth. Mike was in the front with a customer.

"I changed my mind. Are you doing anything this evening?"

"Really? I don't have any plans."

"How about I buy you dinner?"

"Sure, okay."

"Head home and I'll call you with details."

"Great, thanks." She gathered her things and hurried off.

Two can play the GPS game.

22

CLAIRE CALLED TO INVITE ME TO DINNER. SHE SAID she wanted to make up for the trouble that happened since she hired me. She asked that I recommend a restaurant because she was not familiar with Port City, so I offered Martino's at seven o'clock. By allowing me to suggest the location, it gave me an advantage, like playing on my home court. But her playing as a visitor in this game did not make her less of an opponent. Remember the gut feeling I had about her when she walked into McNally's? More and more I felt I was up against a calculating female with an agenda.

I called Katie and told her the plans for the evening and apologized for not being truthful when I told her I would buy her dinner. I'm buying dinner all right; we're just not eating together. I told her to meet me at six thirty in the Martino's parking lot and to find a friend to join her there at seven thirty.

Martino's is not the fanciest place in town but it is one of the best Italian restaurants in the city. White tablecloths, only men as servers, great homemade pasta and sauce, and an excellent wine list. I showed up fifteen minutes early and slipped the maître d' a twenty and selected the table I wanted. He agreed without hesitation. I took a seat at the bar and ordered bourbon on the rocks, and kept an eye on the door as a piano player in the corner began his set of Sinatra classics.

Claire arrived right on time. She wore a black cocktail dress, black heels, a gold necklace, and carried a small, black clutch. Her hair flowed behind her as she made a head-turning Bond-girl entrance. Two waiters almost collided watching her as she walked to the maître d' station.

I stood and waved. She flashed a smile as we exchanged a polite greeting. No doubt the other men in the restaurant were focused on her. *Eat your hearts out.* The maître d' did his job and we sat at the prearranged table that gave me a view of the bar area.

I complimented her, which was easy, and ordered a bottle of Chianti.

"Thank you for meeting me," she said. "I am making a formal apology for any problems my case caused. I guess I'm responsible in some way for the fire at your business."

"Don't apologize. It's part of the job. I mean, we always run the risk of that kind of thing happening."

"I never thought about the potential danger."

"Been shot at more than I care to think about, chased by a car, bit by a dog, and the worst of all—sued in court."

She laughed and remarked my job must be exciting. I told her most days are mundane at best. She went on about her life and how she put things on hold so she could tend to her mother and now the business of her mother's estate. She asked me questions about my life: whether I'm married, do I have children? I had the same interrogation today with Katie but her line of questioning differed from Claire's. I believed she worked with a motive in mind; Katie was only curious about her new employer.

Our food came, lasagna for me and veal parmesan for her. We went through the first bottle of wine and ordered a second. The conversation became fun. She laughed at my old cop stories, the ones I could tell, and she didn't seem too shocked or offended at the un-politically correct way of how cops did business before every left-wing action group took on the role of police brutality watch-dogs.

Katie came into the restaurant with her friend, a black-haired young woman about her age, and they took seats at the bar, which signaled to me that she completed her task without incident. When I looked over Claire's left shoulder, I was in direct eye-line with Katie. They ordered drinks; I saw the friend turn around to look at our table. Katie must have pointed out her new boss. *Not cool in this circumstance.*

It reminded me of a comfortable first date. Claire was quite enjoyable to talk with, not to mention gorgeous, and any man would be sucked in fast. She would twirl her hair around one finger, laugh, and tell a funny, self-deprecating story that made her down-to-earth in an unexpected way. I told myself there was more to this dinner than an apology. *An agenda, Delarosa; she is working an agenda.* This was the woman who booked herself into two hotels. This was the woman who dropped a twenty-thousand-dollar retainer. Carlo Bocci killed himself at the mention of this woman. *Keep the guards on duty.*

My phone buzzed in my pocket. Normally, I would not bother while at a dinner like this but Claire heard it, too. "You better answer that."

"I'm sorry." I took out the phone and it was a text from Katie.

She's into you.

"Just Mike." *I'm going to schedule a lesson on investigative trade craft for Katie.* "Where were we?"

"About to ask for the check and I'm paying." She waved to the waiter. "Do not argue."

"Not me, I'm a modern man. If a beautiful woman wants to buy me dinner, I'm all for it." My phone buzzed again. "Gosh, I'm sorry." A second text from Katie: *She's hot for you.* I put the phone away.

"You know, Johnny, I said you have nice eyes." She reached across the table and took my hand in hers. "Well, I like your eyes, and I like your smile, too."

I blushed, but her come-on to me was not a surprise. "Claire. You're a beautiful woman—but you're the client."

"So?"

"Business and pleasure—you know." It's never a good

idea to sleep with a client, but it's a horrible decision for me to sleep with *this* client. The waiter came with the check and it gave me a moment to recover. I looked at Katie; she had one eyebrow cocked and her arms were folded across her chest.

Claire finished up with the bill. "Shall we?" she said.

"Sure."

We left and I let her lead the way across the lot to her Audi. She turned to me. "Well?"

"You hired me. I can't believe I'm saying this, but it's not a good idea."

"Mr. Delarosa, are you sure?"

"We've had too much wine."

"Okay, then." We hugged. She came in for what I thought was going to be a kiss on the cheek but she planted it on my lips. "You'll regret this." She grabbed my hands.

Why did I feel like Fredo getting the kiss of death from Michael? She smiled and got into her car. I waited while she pulled off and waved as she left. I sent Katie a text and she came out in less than a minute.

I met Katie at six-thirty that evening in the parking lot and gave her a GPS tracking device. I also gave her a hundred dollars for their dinner. The technology delivered a convenient efficiency—maybe not always legal—to the private eye biz. I told her to wait in the lot and keep a look-out for Claire. I gave her the make and model of Claire's car, along with the license plate number. Once Claire parked and went into the restaurant, Katie was to stroll past the car, pretend to drop her keys, and then stick the GPS under a fender.

"Any trouble?"

"Nope. Perfect."

"I think you're a natural at this business. Go home and get some sleep."

"She wanted you to go back to her hotel, didn't she?" I shrugged. "Don't shrug it off. She did. It was obvious."

"Go home. See you tomorrow at ten." *Having a female mind around might have some advantages.*

"Okay, stud."

She went back into the restaurant. I got into my car and sat for a second before I started the engine. The kiss was quite pleasant but I was proud of my will-power. Going back to her hotel would be a colossal bad decision and would compromise the entire case.

But yeah, she's right. There's not a man alive who wouldn't regret it.

23

MANNY GONZALES WAS THE MOST HONEST MAN I ever met. I helped him with his citizenship papers and he still thanks me every time I see him. He's been my mechanic for over fifteen years and always discounts my repairs. I made arrangements for Manny to pick up the Buick to have it repainted.

McNally's opens at eleven, so I met Katie at ten to let her in. If this worked out, I would make her a key. She went to the booth and opened the laptop and the tracker app. "This is cool—according to this, the car is on Harbor Boulevard," she said.

"That's the other motel."

I brought two coffees to the table. "You're to monitor this all day. Plus, I want you to start on the mystery number I gave you." I gave her the case file. I compiled a list of banks in town and made some calls. I gave her the paper. "I marked the ones I already called. Tell them your grandmother died and you found this number and you think it might be a bank account. Your goal is to find out if the number belongs to that bank. If the bank won't give any information, just move on to the next one. Don't use your real name."

"Cool."

"It could be an account with a stock-broker, too, but start with the banks. Keep good notes. Always. Notes are part of case work-product and can be subpoenaed. A lot of my work comes from law firms and I've had plenty of cases end as law-suits. They required accurate, detailed notes."

"Got it."

"I'm going up to my condo. Call me if the car moves."

"Will do."

"I was worried you wouldn't come back. After yesterday."

"Are you kidding? Yesterday was incredible. Last night with the GPS—what a turn-on. This is the best job ever."

Turn-on? "Well, it worked out and you did great, but your days will be like today. Research."

"I understand."

"Call me with anything."

I took my coffee and was at the door when she called out. "Mandy thinks you're cute."

"What?"

"Mandy, my friend from last night. She thinks you're cute. Said you have sexy Italian hair."

I had to hear this so I went back to the booth. "What

are you talking about?"

"She said Italian guys are either bald or have a full head of hair. She liked your hair."

"Oh. I'll give her a call."

"Funny."

I went into my condo with Bocci on my mind. He needed to be the order of the day. With Katie on research, that freed me to hit the streets. Bocci held the clues and I had to figure a way to pry them from his cold, dead fingers.

I checked for any new email and realized I never responded to Cara telling me the moron—she refers to her husband as the moron—was going to be out of town over the weekend and she wanted to come over. It'd been a stressful week and spending some time with her could be a nice stress reliever. I sent a quick reply: Dinner will be ready at seven on Friday.

I had an email from an attorney, Jim Rosswell. He's a partner in the firm Rosswell-Ward, and I work for them on occasion. He asked me to give him a call. *Why do people email asking you to call them? Why don't they just call?* So, I wrote back, telling him I'm on a job and will call as soon as time permits.

I packed some of my tools of the trade into a leather brief-case, including my mini digital camera and a small, portable drill with bits, and my Beretta. I put on my blue suit, a white shirt, and a gray and blue striped tie. On my way out of the condo, I stopped in the bathroom and took a look at my hair. Most of it was still black.

Mandy was right.

My ego stroked.

The outer street door to Bocci's office was locked. I walked around the strip of stores, looking for another way into the building and only found the rear doors of the retail stores. Back around front, it was lunch time with a lot of traffic coming and going. Most folks went into the Chinese restaurant or liquor store.

I went into the liquor store and an older, Middle Eastern gent manned the counter. I told him I was an insurance adjuster investigating the death of Mr. Bocci and was to meet a police detective in the office, and we needed the outer door opened. He sent me to the Chinese restaurant. Said they owned the entire building.

I gave the same story to the owner of the restaurant, talking to him between calls for take-out orders. He kept repeating, "Bocci dead, need paid rent." I tried to convince him I'm the guy who can get him his rent money, but I needed a key to the outer door. "Bocci dead, need paid rent."

A young Asian woman stood in line behind me waiting to place her order. She came to my rescue but I'm sure hunger motivated her act of kindness. Sometimes you need a little luck. She explained to the owner in Chinese that I needed access and that I would get him his rent. That did the trick. He gave me the key and I thanked her and paid for her lunch. She was all smiles when I left. I told her to tell the owner I'd bring the key back in a few minutes.

I opened the outer door and went up the flight of stairs to Bocci's office. I took the pick set from my brief-case. The lock on Bocci's door had to be fifty years old and it took me less than twenty seconds to open it. I went inside. Nothing had changed since my first time here. The pens were on the desk, his glasses in their place. The mess on the wall behind his desk was there and brought back the nightmare.

Conspicuously absent from this office was a computer and that was a good thing. Old school Bocci must have refused to enter the cyber age, which left the two old, wooden filing cabinets that sat along the wall. One labeled Personal and one Corporate. Both were locked, and I had no luck with the pick set, so I used my drill. The bit easily went through the soft metal and I had the cabinets open in seconds.

Files and more files. Each one with a client's name on it. This was the haystack and I didn't even know what the needle looked like. Aletto's name was on a few files, but primarily personal finances from what I could determine.

I didn't recognize any other names and started in on the corporate clients. Nothing stood out to me. No companies I recognized.

My phone buzzed. A text from Katie: *The car is moving.*

I called her. "What road is she on?"

"Umm...she left Harbor and it looks like she's heading

downtown."

"I'm going to put you on speaker."

"Okay, she's getting onto the highway. The interstate—I think."

"The roads will be marked. You'll see."

"Yes, it's the interstate."

"Tell me when she gets off the highway."

"Is this legal?"

"Is what legal?"

"Putting a tracking thing on someone's car?"

"We'll talk about that later." I went back to the corporate files and looked for anything that seemed relevant. Nothing did. I took the files out one at a time, flipped through it, and then replaced it. Each cabinet had six drawers, so my search was pointless without a name or lead. I guess somewhere in my brain I thought I was going to find a file labeled, "*Secret Two Million Dollars.*"

"She's turning off the highway," said Katie.

"Where?"

"Umm…it looks like Western Boulevard."

"Western—are you sure?"

"Yes, wait…yes, it's Western."

"That's where I am."

"What?"

"I'm at Carlo Bocci's office on Western."

"Oh my God…she's going to where you are?"

"Katie, where is she, what is the cross street?"

"Umm…hold on…Twenty-Fourth Street. I think."

"Okay, she's about two miles—I'm at Western and

Third."

"Get out of there."

"No, no. Just keep giving me updates..."

"Okay. Damn, this is exciting."

"Katie, stay focused."

I closed the file cabinets and scanned around the room. *Did I touch anything else? No. Do I stay and surprise her or get out and observe? How will she get into the office? I have the landlord's key to the street door and had to pick the lock to the office. What is she up to?*

"Western and Tenth," Katie said. "Eighth...Seventh...she stopped."

"Must be at a light."

"She going again...Sixth...Fifth...Fourth. She stopped. She must be there."

"Okay, I'm hanging up." I closed the call and slipped the phone into my pocket. The office had two windows but they faced the back of the building. I locked Bocci's office door. The downstairs door was unlocked—a blunder on my part; I should have locked it behind me—so I made it easy for her. This would be interesting. I stood beside the filing cabinet that was farthest from the door. Whoever came in would not see me until they made their way to the middle of the room. *Advantage Delarosa.*

The office was quiet. I heard a car door slam and I heard the lower door open and close and then footsteps on the stairs. I grabbed the Beretta from the briefcase. The person was now in the outer office. The doorknob jiggled...locked. A key went into the lock—the knob shook again—the door didn't open. A moment passed; a second key went into the lock and this time the door opened. *She has a key?*

Claire stepped into the office and the mess on the wall behind Bocci's desk stopped her. She stood there for a moment, taking in the scene and I hoped the magnitude of the situation. The man killed himself over the mention of the money. Her actions were the direct catalyst of his death. She picked up his glasses and held them for a second, studied them, maybe trying for an insight into the man, and then gently laid them on the desk. Was she paying her respects, feeling his spirit, or apologizing? Or was she here for the same reason she hired me – to find the money?

"Hi Claire."

She spun around, startled, and reeled back into the desk knocking the desk backward and sending the glasses and the pencil holder to the floor.

"Ahh—Oh my God, you scared me." She doubled over, and then stood up with her hands to her chest. She paced around the office, heaving, gulping in breaths.

"Johnny—frightened me. I didn't know you were here." She put her palms on the desk, leaned forward, her hair falling around her.

"I'm sorry I scared you but you sort of startled me. Why are you here?"

She paced around, patting her hand on her chest. She couldn't get words out yet. She plopped down in the chair and put her head between her knees. I let her recover. I put the gun and drill back into the brief case.

"I didn't think anyone was here." She gasped for breath.

"Why are you here?

"I…I wanted to see his office. I feel…"

"Responsible?"

"No…I mean…no…I don't know. You really scared me."

"You have a key."

"What?"

"You have a key. Why do you have a key to Bocci's office?" She kept breathing deep. To stall? *Is my client investigating behind me or is she way out in front of me? And if so, why? If she has a key, what else does she have?*

"I forgot we had these…"

"We?"

"My mother and I. She always said Mr. Bocci gave her keys. I found them in her things when she died. I remembered last night and thought to come out here today."

"Why didn't you say something?"

"My mother's instructions were for me to hire you." She stood, her breathing back close to normal. She slid the desk back in place and then leaned back on it with her hands folded across her chest. *Defensive posture?* "I got curious and decided to look around. I didn't know what I would find, if anything. I didn't even know if the key would work. The downstairs door was open so I came up."

"Good way to get yourself killed."

"I didn't…whatever."

My phone buzzed with another text from Katie. *U ok?* I sent a—*yes*—back.

"Why didn't you tell me about the key? Would have made things easier."

"Wait, how did you get in?" she asked.

"Let's stick to the subject. You hired me to investigate this for you. I can't have you running your own investigation. This guy killed himself over this. Somebody threw a fire-bomb at my bar. We've opened the box on this and if certain guys out there think there is money here, they'll be relentless. Killing you—or me—is no big deal for them."

"I'm sorry." She knew I had her and she went into recover mode. "I got curious. That's all. Mother talked about him, and I wanted to…I don't know…feel him…feel his spirit or something. Thought maybe I could find something that could help. I guess you had the same idea?"

"We better get out of here. I didn't find anything, and you should have told me about the key. I don't understand…"

"Johnny, I'm sorry." She came to me and put her arms around me and her head on my shoulder. "You really scared me."

I pushed her an arm's length away from me. "Claire." I didn't need to say anything else. I had a client who had motives only known to her. She knew she made a mistake. How big of a mistake was yet to be seen. "Let's go."

I made sure Bocci's office door was locked and then the outer door. Claire got into her car and drove off. I returned the key to the restaurant owner, thanked him and bought two lunch combos.

I called Katie as I left to make sure she monitored Claire's car.

If the heat wasn't already turned up on this case, it was now on high.

24

I HURRIED BACK TO McNALLY'S AND KATIE WAS IN her spot, on the phone with a local bank. I put the food on the table and grabbed a couple of sodas. She gave me a thumbs up.

She ended her call. "I'm starving. Thanks."

"I scared the hell out of her. She had a key to his office," I said.

"Why was she there? What was she looking for?" She spooned the fried rice and beef and broccoli on a plate.

"That's what you are going to find out."

"Man, that was like—"she shoved a fork-full into her mouth—"like right out of *Mission Impossible* or something."

"It's not like the movies. This job is ninety-percent research."

"You keep saying that, but that was nerve-racking." She

talked and ate at the same time.

Table manners?

"Any luck with the banks?"

"No, OMG—some people wouldn't even talk to me—said I have to come in. Other places they were nice, had no problem talking to me, but the numbers did not match anything. Oh, and some guy stopped in looking for you. He talked to Mike. Creepy-looking."

"What did he look like?"

"Fat, bald, smoking a cigar. Gross."

"Tony?"

"That was Tony the Scar? Didn't look too happy."

Carlos had come in to work the lunch shift. "Where's Mike?"

"Bank and errands."

Katie had the full case file with all my notes. "Keep going on the banks—start going in person if you don't come up with anything. In the file are two sites where we can do background checks. I have subscriptions and I wrote down the passwords for you. Run everything through—all the names I have listed. Even the dead ones. Bocci, Dixon, everything you can find. I want news articles from thirty years ago. We know when Dixon was found - search around that date. And everything you can find on Claire."

"My pleasure. Looks like a bitchy skank to me."

"Umm, I'm not sure about that but your opinion—"

"He's back."

I turned around and Tony had come in. I got up and motioned him to the bar. We sat and Carlos came over.

"Two bourbons." Tony took the cigar out of his mouth and leaned into me, his face bright red and ready to explode.

"What the fuck, Delarosa?"

"Tony..."

"Somebody fuckin' spray painted '*Where's the money?*' on my Mustang." He jabbed the air with the cigar. "I told you not to do this. See what the fuck you started."

"Okay, first, where was the car? Any security cameras?"

"At the club. Only cameras are out back. My car was in front."

"Maybe there's a street camera. I'll work on that."

"Damn right – somebody needs to." He was so mad he couldn't stay on the stool. He got off and stood and then got back on the stool and then got off again.

"Tony, what did I start? Tell me what happened?" Carlos brought our drinks. Tony threw his back and I told Carlos to leave the bottle. I poured Tony another.

"Me, Dixon, and Rosso had the bookmaking by the balls. Rounded up all the small-time guys so everyone was working for us. Money up to our asses. All of a sudden, there's a rumor of two million missing. We denied it—I still deny it—but Donny gets whacked. Jimmy splits town.

"Rosso?"

"No way."

"Dixon?"

"He was always a guy who did right by the family. He liked being the boss's son-in-law. Was proud he was accepted. Kind of guy you could count on. Was good to Jackie, never a goomah. No way. He didn't take anything."

"Leaves you."

"What, I took two million dollars thirty years ago and tucked it away for my retirement?"

"Somebody thinks it could be you."

"You start asking questions, all of the sudden people remember what they want to."

"Many guys still around from those days?"

"Sure, they're around. Lot of them gone straight—like me." He poured another drink. His blood pressure came down a bit. "Ever hear of Alberto Brindisi?"

"No."

"Big Al Brindisi. Was a lawyer but also a silent partner of Aletto. He died about a year after Aletto did, but he had a son, Little Al. A real piece of shit. Aletto wanted us to work with him, give him jobs as a favor to Aletto. He was a worthless putz, though. We all wanted to turn him into fish food but he was protected. Thought he was God's gift, you know. Women hated him – he was the only guy I knew who got turned down by hookers." We touched our shot glasses. *Salute!*

"I remember he would never stop talking. Always running his mouth. Annoying little wop. Anyhows, I heard at the club the other night that he was around town. It would be like him to get wind of this money and show up..."

"Brindisi. I'll check him out. Who knows?"

"I told you guys will come from everywhere if they think that kind of cash was laying around. They'll all lay claim."

"Tony, is the amount realistic—could someone siphon

off that much?"

"Hell, yeah. We'd do fifty thousand dollars on football weekends. It would take a couple of years to do it, but yeah."

"What happened with Jackie Aletto? Who thought she had the money?"

He looked at the floor for a minute and then huffed. "Not my shiniest moment."

"Yeah?"

"After Aletto dies, Rosso comes back into town and he has it in his head that Donny did take the money and he must have given it to Jackie." He pours what little was left in the bottle into his glass. "He wants to take some guys and put pressure on Jackie to talk. I refuse, I want no part. He keeps pushing and pushing, swears he won't hurt her. Wants to scare her into talking. I give in and they go to her house one night and get carried away…hurt her real bad. Rosso left again and never came back. Cops liked me for it but there was no proof. Not too long after, Jackie took her daughter and left town." He downed the rest of his drink. "I'm not happy, Johnny. Put a lid on this."

"You'll be the first to know."

"Somebody's gonna pay for my car."

He got up and waddled his unmistakable round body out of the bar. I poured myself another. Katie came over with the folder. "What happened?"

"They sent him a message." I watched through the window as he got into an old, primer-gray pickup truck and drove off. *Are the sins of the past coming back to haunt him?* They always do. I almost felt sorry for him in a way. He made a lot of money over the years, but money made by illegitimate means never lasts. Yep: sins of the past, karma, whatever we want to call it—the universe has a way of squaring the deal. Nothing in life is free; we all pay our way, eventually.

"We got work to do."

25

TONY LEFT AND KATIE AND I WENT THROUGH THE file to review her notes, and nothing reached out and talked to me. She had a sheet of paper for each name we'd come across during the investigation, and I leafed through the stack, looking for something I had not seen before: some aspect of their background that would provide an insight, a clue, anything to link them with the events of thirty years ago.

My gut instinct, my trusted friend, twitched when I got to the sheet with Elena Garver written at the top. Jackie Aletto's sister, daughter of Joseph Aletto, the mobster. Philanthropist, lives in an expensive condo on the Silver Strip with husband number three—real estate developer Martin Garver—and had to be around thirty years old when the business of her sister being attacked and maimed for life happened. Katie's notes did not indicate whether she had any children and a *Herald* newspaper profile, done a few years ago lauding her for her charitable work with Children's Hospital, said she was a private person who enjoyed a group of select friends and traveling with Martin. *Time for a visit.*

"You only have Ocean Palms as an address for Elena Garver?"

"Umm, yeah, let me see." She picked up the info sheet and went through her notes. "No criminal record. I couldn't find any phone numbers, nothing in a reverse directory, but we don't know her condo number. The general background search only listed her husband. I'm getting better at this, though. You should see what I found on Tony and Sammy. Wow. Those guys were busy."

"Let's stay on Elena."

"Okay, okay."

I called Worthington at the Marquis to see whether he could dig up a phone number for Elena, remembering he mentioned she holds her fund-raising dinners at the hotel. He put me on hold for five minutes before coming back with the only contact number they had on file. I thanked him and dialed. A woman answered, identified herself as the housekeeper. I told her I was a detective with PCPD and asked to speak with Mrs. Garver. A minute went by before Elena came on the line.

I told her I was an ex-detective and I was writing a book about the history of the Port City and want to interview her about the political and business climate in the city thirty years ago. She balked, said the housekeeper told her I was a detective. I apologized and said the housekeeper must have misunderstood. I praised her charitable work and said how I would love to have the thoughts and recollections of such an outstanding and prominent leader of Port City. I told her the book would not be complete without her and her husband's input.

She softened a bit and then said she and her husband were leaving in three days for Italy and would agree to meet me when she returned in a month. I explained about my publisher's deadline, and after extolling the contribution she has made and how I would value having her as part of this project, to live in the history of the city forever, she agreed to give me one hour in one hour.

Katie had on jeans and a T-shirt. "You have any other clothes with you?"

I handed her the eighty dollars that I had in my pocket. "Can you go get something more business-like and be back in thirty minutes?"

She counted the money. "For eighty dollars? I'm going to need shoes, too."

I grabbed the cash back and gave her my credit card. "Go."

"Where are we going?"

"Go!"

Thirty-five minutes later, we were in my car and she looked as if she spent the entire morning getting ready. She wore black dress slacks, a cream-colored blouse, black heels, and had her hair in some combo of half-pulled back and half-down.

"I'm impressed. You look great."

"Thanks. I'm a professional. I'm not used to the time crunch, though. The store clerk thought I was nuts when I came out of the dressing room with all this on. I told them I had an emergency job interview."

"I want you to keep some clothes with you. For different situations."

"Like you do in the trunk."

"Yes. You never know when you have—"

"—to blend in."

"Now you're getting it."

I filled her in on how we would approach Elena but it was a flimsy scheme at best. My hope was to garner new information. Anything that would give us another path to work.

The doorman at the Ocean Palms had our names and he asked for our IDs. He took them to a small office off the lobby and made copies. He came back and directed us to the elevator and said she's in number 1200. The elevator opened into a small foyer and we faced a door marked 1200. We both realized she had the one and only apartment on the twelfth floor. We knocked; the housekeeper answered and let us into the condo.

The style was a classic modern design with nautical themes that reflected the ocean front location. A wall of windows overlooked the beach and opened to a large balcony. Inside, the furniture sleek and minimal, dark browns and tans with light-blue and green accents—nothing garish or overstated. A single painting hung on each wall—they looked like originals to me—all with a beach motif.

We were ushered into the great room and took seats on a brown leather sofa with a coffee table in front of us. The housekeeper asked whether we wanted a drink and we both said yes to water. Moments later Elena Garver came into the room and we stood as she greeted us. We got through a few pleasantries, including complimenting her condo and the furniture, and then sat back down. She wore blue slacks with a white top, a blue beaded necklace with matching earrings. Slender. In her mid to late sixties. Her smartly styled brown hair—the work of a high-end salon, along with her smooth skin—a little nip and tuck?—shaved off a few years. She had minimal makeup and was truly an attractive woman.

I thanked her for seeing us and introduced Katie as my writing partner.

"Are you published, dear?" she asked Katie.

"No ma'am. I just graduated from college a few months ago."

"What school?"

"Florida State."

"Oh, a state school?"

I thought I needed to intercept this before Katie figured out she got insulted. "She's a very talented writer. Graduated with honors."

"Uh huh."

Katie shifted in her seat. She opened her notebook and took a pen out of her purse.

"Mrs. Garver, I'm concentrating on the impact of organized crime in Port City. We're going back some years—things are different now—but organized crime had a definite influence on the city, especially the shipping industry in the harbor."

"I'm not sure what I can add there."

"Well, again, we are going back many years, but I wondered if you could talk about your father. It was public knowledge about his involvement in organized crime."

"Mr. Delarosa, my father was a successful business-man in this town. Very successful."

"I don't mean any disrespect, but I spent many years in law enforcement. I'm not judging, but what happened, happened. This is not meant to disparage your father in—"

"He was a respected businessman who gave freely to his community."

"Yes, and I don't mean any disrespect—"

"He practically paid for the altar in St. Anthony's on Twenty Fourth Street. You can put that in your article. He also gave over two hundred thousand dollars to the initial funding of Children's Hospital to start the construction. That was a lot of money back then. Equivalent of millions today. You can put that in your article."

"Nobody is disputing that, Mrs. Garver."

"Good. I guess we are done." She stood.

"Mrs. Garver, I didn't mean any disrespect. Please. Can

I ask you about some other names we've run across from that time? I promise, another minute?"

She sat back down. "One minute. I'm packing for our trip."

"Thank you. Your sister, Jackie."

"Jacqueline."

"Yes, Jacqueline. We heard a story of how she met with some tragedy."

"She did. It was a shame. Beautiful girl, and a talented dancer. She gave up a promising career for some thug."

"Didn't he work for your father?"

"I don't know who worked for my father. I was out on my own by then. Jacqueline was always enamored by a certain type of man. I would talk to her about it. I wanted her to move with me to New York. Start a life there."

"Was she married to Donny Dixon at the time?"

"Yes, Dixon. Good old Donny. She loved him, for some unknown reason. What did it get her? A life in a wheelchair."

"What happened? Is it true there was missing money?"

"I have no idea. I can't imagine anyone taking money from my father. Is there anything else? I don't feel comfortable with this conversation."

"Mrs. Garver, I don't want you to be uncomfortable. I want to portray Port City in the most flattering light as possible while being honest with the past."

"Well, in that regard, I wish you success. The world of my father and my sister was a long time ago and a world away. My housekeeper will show you out." She got up and walked out of the room.

The housekeeper came within seconds and showed us to the door. Neither of us said a word until we got to the car.

"She was annoyed, to say the least," Katie said.

"The last thing she wanted to talk about was the past. Probably reminded her of a time she's ashamed of. I'm sure many in her current social circle don't know who she really is. She is an Italian girl from the Twenty Fourth Street crime family who happened to marry big."

"What do we do now?"

"You know what to do."

"Find out everything I can about Elena Aletto Garver?"

"Exactly. But again, you only have a state school education. It might be tough for you."

She punched me on the arm.

26

IT WAS TIME TO VISIT MY NEW, FAVORITE STAKE-OUT location, the Harbor Court Motel. Katie was eager to ride along. It had been a long day but she couldn't get enough of the work—her curiosity about the case brought a fresh perspective and exuberance.

The case had a mystery to it and her constant questions kept the ideas flowing. Working with her, having to explain procedures and techniques, sharpened my mind to different possibilities and angles. When I was stumped, I would pace around my condo asking questions out loud. Over and over, I would ask the same question, hoping an answer would fashion itself from the atmosphere. Her curiosity replaced my pacing. I quizzed her about the case in order to spark a thought, and she would come back with an answer that generated a new question. If the investigator could keep asking questions, the solution would appear.

The night was warm and the boulevard pulsed with heavy traffic. Street creatures slithered along the sidewalks looking to do business with anyone any way. Pinky was working her corner, wearing a long, white, skin-tight dress that went to the ground. It had a split on the left side that came up to her hip, revealing her entire leg, and a plunging V-shaped neckline down the front that revealed everything else.

The McDonald's lot was busy with legit customers and illegitimate ones. I parked near my usual spot, not an ideal vantage point but I had a view of Claire's room and the motel office. But we were in my Z4, sticking out like the proverbial sore thumb. I glanced at Katie and her eyes kept going from Pinky to the activity in the lot. She checked the door to make sure it was locked.

"I take it you don't visit this part of town very much," I said.

"Uh, no."

"Interesting, huh?"

"That hooker has been picked up three times since we've been here."

"Uh huh."

"Gross."

The black guy from my botched surveillance night manned the front office desk. I wanted the name of the day shift clerk, the man with the gray pony tail who went into Claire's room the first day I sat here.

I had brought my camera and Katie kept an eye on the office. "Only the one guy and he's watching TV. Every now and then he gets a call. Why can't you go in as an investigator and just ask for his name?"

"He would be suspicious. An investigator would not normally come at this time of night. Plus, he'll be hesitant to give out the other guy's name."

"So we need another plan, huh?"

"And, there's the security guy who chased me the other night. Yes, we need another plan."

She used the camera to scan the front of the motel. "No sign of the guard. So you think the day guy knows Claire?"

"He knows something. He spent twenty minutes in her room."

"Hmmm…very interesting," she said. "Maybe he's the one who did the paint job on your car? Or threw the fire-bomb? Sounds like a job for Investigator Pitts."

"I don't think."

"I'll get his name."

"How?"

"The same way I got into every bar in Florida before I was twenty-one."

"Oh, yeah?"

"Have clothes in the back?"

"Of course." I popped open the trunk and she got out and rummaged around and came back into the car with one of my old dress shirts. She began unbuttoning her blouse.

"What are you doing?"

"My job," she said. I sort of turned my head but it was hard to not peek. She stripped off her slacks and blouse and put on my shirt, leaving most of it unbuttoned. She slipped into her heels and took the belt from her slacks and fastened it around her waist. "What do you think?"

"What I think is—I'm not letting you out of the car. We need to talk about this first."

"I'll be fine." She got out and headed across the street, in my shirt and three-inch heels. The shirt tail barely covered her butt; two cars slowed down to gawk at her as she crossed.

Pinky also took notice and yelled at her. "White ho? Why you on my corner?"

I picked up the camera and focused on the desk clerk as she got to the office. She pressed a button to be buzzed in. The clerk's eyes got wide as she entered. All he saw was blonde hair and an unbuttoned shirt revealing most of her bra. I didn't know what she was telling him but all he did was nod his head and smile. She kept leaning up on the counter, putting her breasts on display. Every time she did, the shirt would flip up in the back giving me a cheeky peek. *Of all days for her to wear skimpy underwear.* I didn't know whether to be happy or embarrassed. I couldn't help myself and snapped a few pictures, to hell with my morals and integrity.

A few minutes went by before a car pulled into the motel lot. The security guard—the guy who chased me—got out, carrying a pizza. He went to the office door and had to knock twice before the clerk took his eyes off Katie and buzzed him in. He went behind the counter with the pizza box and took a position next to the clerk. They motioned to the pizza; she shook her head. The clerk wrote something on a piece of paper and handed it to her.

She waved to them as she left and trotted across the street, teetering a few times on the heels. Pinky was ready for her this time.

"Yo, whore. You lost? This is my corner, you hear me?"

Katie ignored her and kept coming to my car. Pinky didn't let up, defending her claimed turf. "That's right, bitch. Keep your lily-white ass going."

I reached across and had the door open for her. She plopped in. "There you go. One Karl Boyd."

"You got it?"

"Yep. Nice set of tits works every time."

Truer words were never spoken and she was only twenty-four. I guess women learn they have a built-in advantage at an early age. "What did you say?"

"That I was there earlier in the day and the guy working said I could rent a room for the week for one-fifty. Maurice, the guy there now, said, '*Karl told you that?*' I said, yep. We went back and forth. I pretended I was a bit drunk; he said they couldn't rent a room for that cheap for the week; I told him he had a cute smile; and then finally I got Karl's last name out of him. We left it that he could work a deal much better than Karl's. Men are pigs."

"Well, you were half-naked."

"Your point?"

"Never mind—good job on getting the name, but we don't act impulsively. We need to think these things through." I paused when she took off my shirt so she could put her clothes back on.

"It's okay, you've seen me before."

"That was a little different... Anyhow—I had no way to contact you. I appreciate what you did, but let's be smart."

"Sure, boss."

"Claire's car never moved. I guess we can pack it in." My phone rang.

"Hey, Tony."

Nothing but screams. *"He's dead. This is your fault. He's dead!"*

"Tony? Who's dead? Where are you?" The call dropped. I started the car.

27

KATIE AND I GOT OUT TO CITY SALVAGE AND emergency vehicles were everywhere. I got as close as I could and then got out of the car and walked. I told Katie to stay in the car but she got out and followed me.

"Go back to the car." I turned and walked her back.

"But I want to see—"

"We don't know what happened and if they tie me to this, I don't want anyone knowing your name, let alone seeing you. Stay in the car." She got back in and I continued toward the salvage yard. I got about a hundred feet away before a uniformed cop stopped me.

"What happened?"

"Accident. You need to stay back," he said.

I pulled out my PI license and my retired cop ID and handed it to him. "I'm working with these guys. I got a call from Tony. One of the owners."

"You know them?"

"Yes, Scarazzini. The two brothers."

He gave me back my ID. "Bad news. Looks like a hit-and-run. More like a hit, if you ask me."

"Yeah?"

"Guy got run down right in front of the place. Deliberate, but that's my opinion. You didn't hear nothing from me."

"Can I get closer?"

"Stay out of the way."

I edged along an ambulance and another police car and got within thirty feet of the scene in front of City Salvage. Two white tarps were spread on the ground—covering two bodies. Three officers surrounded Tony in front of the building. He was inconsolable—screaming, cursing, swearing revenge on the bastard who did this. I didn't have to ask; I knew it was Sammy. But the other sheet—who was the other person?

I spotted a lieutenant—Franklin was his name; I knew him some years back—and called him over.

"Delarosa. What are you doing here?"

"Tony called me. Screaming—so I came over."

"Why would he call you?" asked Franklin.

"We've been working on something. I saw him earlier today."

"Oh yeah. Can you add anything to this?"

"I don't know. What happened?"

"Sammy comes out, and best we can figure, somebody runs him over."

"Who's the other person?"

Franklin looked at me, realizing I didn't know. "Sammy. Both are Sammy."

"Oh, Jesus."

I took a step back; the impact of what happened hit me in the gut. I had seen many horrible sights throughout my career in the department—drowning victims, a dead child, people burned in house fires—but seeing Sammy in two pieces punched me hard. The bile came up in my throat and I swallowed it back down.

I said to Franklin, "Anything on the vehicle?"

"Nothing yet." He pointed toward the convenience store. "They have some cameras, so we'll see if they picked up anything. Whoever did this sure hit him hard. No skid marks, didn't even try to stop."

"Son of a bitch."

"You're working with Tony? On what?"

"Something with his club."

"These guys didn't have any family, did they?"

"No," I said. "It's been just them for years. Tony always took care of Sammy. I don't know what he'll do now. But I do know this—he'll be out for revenge."

"Yep, I'm sure he will." He gave me a slap on the back. "Delarosa. Don't leave town either."

It sounded as if he was kidding but he wasn't. He'd want to talk again. I wanted to go to Tony and help, but I feared he'd launch in on me and the case. He said through his screams on the phone it was my fault and I prayed he would keep his mouth shut. He would be crazy mad, but if

I knew Tony, I was confident he wouldn't give the police anything. He'd take this personally and would damn sure avenge his brother's death. He'd give his brother a proper Catholic funeral and burial, and then, out of respect to his brother and his own grieving process, he'd wait until the right moment.

After that, he would come with all guns blazing.

28

WE GOT BACK TO McNALLY'S AT ONE-THIRTY IN the morning. I walked Katie to her car and thanked her for a job well done and told her to get a solid night's sleep and not come in until noon. She didn't say anything on the ride back to the bar. I think the gravity of the situation, somebody dying—being murdered—made it all real for her.

I got up to my condo, stripped, showered, wrapped a towel around me and opened a bottle of cabernet. I wasn't in the mood for music so I skipped it and took the wine to the balcony and sat there, contemplating Sammy. I was sorry for Sammy and the way his life ended. Who deserved to go the way he did? My heart broke for Tony—he took care of his brother, protected him his entire life. Tony was the smart one, the enforcer, the protector; he devised the schemes, hustled the streets, with Sammy, two years younger, always in tow. The teachers in school considered Sammy slow. These days, he would have a learning disability, but back then the teachers told their mother he was destined for a life of menial jobs and to "*not expect too much.*"

Sammy was in fourth grade—two years older than the other kids in the class—when a classmate, Dominick Ponzelli, made a fateful decision that changed life forever for Sammy and Tony. Ponzelli called Sammy an "*overgrown stupid retard*" and pushed him to the ground and kicked him in the ribs a couple of times while they were on the playground. Tony heard of the incident and beat Ponzelli to within inches of his life. The Sisters of Mercy, the teachers at St. Anthony's Parochial School, got Dominick patched up and pulled both boys into the principal's office. It was Tony's word against Dominick's; when the sisters questioned other boys in the class, they all sided with Tony. They were glad the bully Ponzelli got what he deserved. From that day forward, Tony realized he would be Sammy's guardian, protector, brother, and friend for life. The beating of Ponzelli sent a message to the rest of the school and the neighborhood to not mess with Sammy Scarazzini. And nobody ever did.

I finished two glasses of wine while thinking of Tony and Sammy. The night breeze blew away the humidity and the cool air put me to sleep.

Claire came out onto the balcony. She was wearing my shirt, the one Katie wore earlier into the Harbor Court, unbuttoned to reveal her breasts, and she knelt beside my lounge chair and removed my towel. She pulled her auburn hair around her and let if fall onto my chest; slowly and carefully, she dragged it up and down my body as if she were painting me with her hair. She kept saying, "*You know you like me*" while brushing and tickling the hair over my body. "*You know you like me.*" I tried to put my arms around her to pull her close but I couldn't move them, as if they were tied to the chair. The hair teased my body; my arms were pinned. "*You know you like me.*" Her dazzling smile. "*My arms,*" I said and she laughed. I was aroused and she gripped her hand around me and said, "*Tell me you like me.*" "*I do like you but my arms.*" She smiled, took her hand off me and moved her face close to mine. *A kiss?* Her hair fell in front of me. I wanted to kiss her but I couldn't see her face. Then a gun came through her hair, the 9mm Glock Bocci used, and she shoved it into my mouth. "*Tell me you like me.*" I felt the cold steel in my mouth, the oily metal of the barrel on my tongue. "*Now who's in control?*"

I jolted awake on the chair, so startled I knocked the wine glass to the floor and it shattered. My heart pounding, my breathing fast and hard, I went inside to regain some composure. I poured myself a bourbon and swallowed it. I tried to shake the dream from my head but it was still there. I could still taste the gun in my mouth and feel the caress of her hair on my body. It was too real and too scary. *Was my subconscious giving me answers to the case?* I went to the bathroom and splashed cold water on my face to help snap me out of the daze. I pulled on jeans and a T-shirt, grabbed the broom and dust pan and cleaned up the balcony. The red wine left an all too real blood-like stain on the concrete balcony floor.

I put on a pot of coffee and let it brew while I opened my laptop to a local news site. An article about a hit-and-run accident on Lincoln Road was on the front page, but it did not identify the victim.

The coffee was ready, so I poured a cup and went back to the balcony. The night sky was clear with billions of stars in view. Questions pounded at my brain. I blamed myself. My decision-making of late was less than stellar. I was responsible for Bocci's suicide and Sammy's murder. That is what it was: murder. Someone could make a case that Bocci was depressed and would have killed himself anyhow. Or some gambler, upset over his losses and blaming his bookies, sought revenge by running over indefensible Sammy. Sure, they were possibilities but I knew what happened was the direct effect of what I started. Bocci's death affected me; I could still see him pulling the trigger and the image would never leave my mind. It would stay tucked away in a little box in my head where I keep the traumatic, horrible, heart-pounding, soul-shaking events of my life. Things I hope I never have to think about again. But sometimes, when I least expect it, the little box opens and one of those memories creeps out and stabs at my soul. Sammy covered in two pieces of tarp would now go into the box.

Not vetting Claire as a client was the first poor decision I made with this case. I allowed the fantasy of my client to cloud my judgment and it proved fateful. I should've done background checks on her and her family before accepting the job. The dramatic dropping-the-cash retainer in front of me sure did block my common sense. My years of experience never had a chance against the auburn hair and the cash. Shame on me.

The second poor decision I made was allowing Katie to talk her way into my employ. What was I doing? I admit it was fun having her around, but I had to be smart before Mike's words—*just don't get her killed*—came back to haunt me and she took a place in the little box in my mind.

I abandoned the coffee and balcony and went back inside. I downed another shot of bourbon, and then two more, and then stretched out on my bed. I knew sleep would not come that night. The little box was wide open and images of Sammy and Bocci flashed violently in my mind.

29

I FELL ASLEEP BUT NOT UNTIL 4:00 A.M. THE SHOTS of bourbon did a good job of knocking me out and blocking any more nightmares. The demons in the little box in my mind were kept away by the demons from the bottle.

After stopping by the hardware store, I got to the bar at noon. Katie was in her booth—it was now her booth—tapping away on her laptop.

"Hey, you're here," I said.

"Good morning. I got here at eleven."

I put two keys on the table. "This one is for the front door here—I'll give you the alarm code—and this key is for my place."

"Oh, okay. Thanks," she said.

"I have a couple of filing cabinets upstairs so we'll keep all files in the condo. Anything new this morning?"

"No. I did a background on Mr. Bocci and nothing looks out of the ordinary—from what I can tell." She turned toward me and noticed my bloodshot eyes and unshaven face. "Didn't get any sleep, did you?"

"Nope."

"That was a tough night. You were friends?"

"Yeah, grew up a couple of streets from each other. They were older than me but we were all from the neighborhood. Tony will be out of his mind."

"The news said it was a hit-and-run."

"More like a direct hit. You are not to leave this booth."

"Why?"

"I have bodies piling up over money that might not even exist. You're not leaving this spot."

Mike came out of the back room and wandered over. "Sammy?"

"Somebody ran him down. Gut tells me it has to do with this case."

"You don't know that. They had plenty of enemies," Mike said.

"Yes, but nobody local would do this and not expect retaliation. They had respect from the streets and from us. Can only be an outsider and the only outsider is Claire."

Four guys came in and took spots at the bar. Mike went over to take their order. I turned to Katie. "Well, since you've done such a great job in your short time here, I decided to give you a promotion. You are officially the head of research."

"Is that right?"

"Yep. Head of your own department." She smiled and it lightened the mood. I went behind the bar and poured two coffees and came back to the booth. "Let's pull up the GPS and find out where our friend is."

She opened the app and it pinged on the Harbor Court Motel.

"Still at the motel."

"Okay, in that case, I want a peek inside her room at the Marriott. I still don't understand the two hotel rooms."

"To throw people off, like you said. No one would think about her at the skanky place."

"Still, I'm going to figure a way in. Keep the GPS app open and tell me if the car moves. And, do some background on Elena Garver. That old broad knows more than she's telling."

"I want to come with you." She folded up the laptop and her files. "We can follow the GPS while in your car."

"How do we do that?"

"We can use my phone as a hot spot."

"No, wait—I just said I don't want you in the field."

"You're going to the Marriott. How dangerous can that be? Besides, won't it make sense if we go in together instead of you by yourself?"

"Katie—so far this is working much better than I imagined. But after last night, I'm not sure about anything. I want you here, doing research."

"Are you going to go in and just ask for the key?" She turned up her palms. "No. We go in like we're going to lunch—and then we'll figure something out."

"That's the plan?"

"C'mon. I'm dying to see inside the room, too."

She had a point. It would be better for the two of us to walk in. Men would notice her and ignore me. Sexist, sure, but this was a life-and-death case and I needed answers. "Get your stuff together."

"Yes—you're the bomb, Johnny D."

On the ride over to the Marriott, I had Katie call the hotel and ask for room 503. No answer. She connected her phone and the computer so we had wireless in the car. Claire's car was still at the Harbor Court. We parked in the hotel parking garage and went to the lobby and sat for a moment while she linked to the hotel's wireless. I wanted to keep tabs on the Audi. It didn't mean Claire didn't have any other means of transportation, but I needed to cover all angles.

We took the elevator to the fourth floor and then walked up the stairs to the fifth. A tiny bit of tradecraft—I wanted to approach the corridor from the side stairs and not come out of the elevator and be surprised by Claire or anyone else. The hotel was built in the shape of an *L*. The stairs brought us into a small alcove in the short corridor, thirty feet from room 503. The hallway was empty.

"The GPS," I said. She checked; the car had not moved. "Stay here and call the front desk and ask for her room."

She dialed as I went to the door of 503 and listened. A moment later, the phone rang. After five rings it stopped and I went back to the alcove. "Okay, nobody's home. Don't move."

I went down the hallway to where it turned left into the long corridor. I peeked around the corner and as I hoped, a housekeeping cart sat in the middle of the hallway. I came back to Katie. "You wanted to be in the field, so here you go. The maid is around the corner about four rooms down—"

"—Way ahead of you, boss." She gave me the laptop, pulled off her T-shirt, handed it to me and then trotted down the hall in her bra and jeans. I've seen her in her underwear more times than I saw my ex-wife in hers during the last year of our marriage. She turned the corner and I could hear her talking to the maid. *"Miss, miss, can you help me?"* I heard the maid giggle and a few seconds later, they came back around the corner, the maid laughing and Katie carrying on about how dumb she was to lock herself out of her room. The maid unlocked the door and Katie went inside, thanking her.

I waited in the alcove until the maid went back to work and then walked down to 503. *Open the door, Katie.* Ten seconds passed, and then another ten. I did not want to knock—horrible scenarios began to form in my head. *Did someone grab her as she went into the room?* Ten more seconds passed so I tapped on the door. It opened and the expression on my face said it all.

"Oh, sorry," she said, as I went into the room.

"Nothing."

The room was clean, the beds made, no clothes hanging in the closet, no toiletries in the bathroom. Our intuition was correct: Claire had this room only as a diversion. But if a person thought to rent a second room as a diversion, why not make it look lived in? In case the private investigator you hired might wonder why you rented rooms in two hotels? Or, better yet, what if one of the scum bags you resurrected came looking for the money?—you just exposed that the room was a false front. Now they'll search for you elsewhere. An oversight by the calculating Claire?

"Let's go," I said to Katie.

"My T-shirt?"

"Sorry." I handed her the shirt and she slipped it on.

We stopped at the door and listened. A door opened and closed; it sounded as if the maid was still working in the other corridor, so we opened our door and went out just as the door to room 502—directly across the hall—opened. Out stepped a tall, well-built black guy, about my age, and a young blonde, about Katie's age. He looked at me and I looked at him; he looked at Katie and I looked at his girl.

We both nodded at each other and he said, "My man." *Solidarity, approval.* They went to the elevators and we went to the stairs.

"That was interesting," said Katie.

"Take it as a compliment."

"You need to take it as a compliment 'cause it looked like you're an old man who scored some young hottie. I know I can get any man…"

I stopped halfway down the first flight and turned back to her. "Stop talking. We are still in the field and you need to stay focused."

"Sorry."

"Check the car." She opened the laptop; the Audi had not moved. "Remember, just because the car is there, doesn't mean Claire is."

"Got it."

"And thanks for what you did. And last night, too. I never intended for you to keep getting, you know—…"

"—getting undressed. It's fine. Whatever it takes, right?"

"Not always."

"It's cool. Really."

"Fair enough." I took a step down and then stopped. "And I'm not old."

"Stay focused."

30

MARCO CALLED AS WE DROVE BACK TO McNally's. "We finished the investigation into Sammy's death. From what the forensics guys figure, Sammy was standing in the lot when the car plowed into him."

"So he came out of the office and somebody took dead aim?"

"Yep, he never had a chance."

"Thanks. That was quick."

"Hey, we can get stuff done when we want to." He ended the call.

"Her car is moving," Katie said.

"Okay, keep an eye on it." I pulled into the alley behind McNally's to park. Mike called my phone.

"Where are you?"

"In back."

"Stay put."

I parked the car in the garage. Mike came out through the back door and met us in the alley. "Some dirt bag inside asking for you. I don't recognize him."

"Yeah?"

"Wouldn't give me his name."

I said to Katie, "Go around the front and up to my place. The wireless code is the same as down here." She sensed Mike's suspicion and didn't argue. She went off around the building and we went in.

Sitting in my booth was a short, bone-thin man, wearing black jeans with a black T-shirt, and a black leather jacket. He had four gold chains around his neck and his thinning hair was slicked straight back on his head. I sat down across from him. He was older than me, somewhere in his fifties, dark circles around his sunken eyes, his face pock-marked with red splotches on his cheeks and nose. Either a drunk or a junkie or both.

"Can I help you?"

"You Delarosa?"

"Yes. Who are you?"

"Name's Brindisi. Somebody said we might have a mutual interest."

"Who is somebody?"

"Does that matter?"

"It does to me."

He scanned around the bar, drummed his jittery fingers on the table. "Every now and then, I like to get a wager down on the games, you know? I have a guy who can take a bet for me, and he tells me about you looking for information on something that happened a long time ago."

"Is that so?" He turned toward the front of the bar and then back at me. "Nervous?" I said.

"It's not that. I just seen the news from last night and I remember about Sammy and his brother and it brings me back to what this guy was saying."

"Your guy's name is…?"

He shook his head. "I can't tell you that."

"Go on."

"I was around when Donny Dixon got whacked."

"Yeah?"

"Over money that went missing, and Aletto had him…you know." His left hand trembled and he would grab it with his right to stop the tremors.

"That's the rumor," I said.

"What if I have proof?"

"Of Dixon having the money?"

He checked the front again and then focused back on me. "Could I get a drink? Whiskey?" I signaled to Mike for a couple of drinks.

"You not supposed to be here?" He shrugged and sank back in the booth. "Conversation goes no further than this table."

"Dixon took that money and they found out. He gets whacked."

"You know this how?" Mike brought over two drinks. Brindisi made short work of draining his glass.

"Like I said, I was around. Is there someplace else we

can talk."

"I don't think." My phone buzzed with a text message from Katie. *The car is heading our way.* "If you knew where the money was, why not go for it?"

"And risk what happened to Donny? No way."

"You saw the money?"

"Not exactly."

"You and Donny were pals?"

"No, me and his partner, Jimmy Rosso. Me and Jimmy were tight. I would help him out with different jobs."

"So you're not sure if there was money or not?"

"Jimmy always said there was..."

"Where's Rosso now?" My phone buzzed again. *The car is on our street!!! Is she coming here?*

"I can't speak to that." He leaned across the table. "Unless there might be some…some sort of compensation." I noticed the tremors in his hand stopped. The drink did the trick. He's either bluffing and working me for a quick score, or he's hustling for Rosso, or he got wise to all this from Tony, which didn't make sense to me, because Tony would not talk. I don't like the way he showed up here, either. When my gut perks up and sends a warning, I take it seriously.

"Club Cuba. Meet me there at six tonight." I had to move him out of here and go on the offense.

"Club Cuba? Yeah, okay. But what about—"

"—See you at six." He turned to the front again. *Did he know Claire was heading this way?* "Why don't you go out the back?"

"Yeah, yeah..." He got up and scurried through the kitchen and out the back door. I followed him into the alley; he trotted up to the cross street and out of sight.

I called Katie. "Where's her car?"

"Right out front. I'm coming down."

"No—"

"—I want another look at her..."

"Katie—we need to keep you invisible. Do not come down." I closed my phone and went in through the back. I stopped at the kitchen door. Sure enough, Claire sat on a stool near the end of the bar. Mike placed a glass of white wine in front of her as I approached.

"Hi Claire." She turned her green eyes to me but they lacked her alluring sparkle.

"Johnny. Hi."

"What are you doing here?"

"The hit and run accident last night. Does that have anything to do with..."

"With you?" I said. She nodded. "I'm afraid so."

"I never intended..."

"Anybody to die? I'm sure you didn't. But if we keep throwing chum in the water, the sharks will come around."

She sipped her wine and then looked at me with sad eyes, held my gaze, reading me, calculating. I couldn't tell whether she was figuring her next statement or feeling remorseful. I got the impression that she never thought her mission to find this money would produce dead bodies. She turned back to the bar and had both hands around the wine glass, her body language blocking me. "Now what?"

she said, without looking at me.

"Up to you. Do we keep going?"

She swiveled around and faced me, flipped her hair back from her face, opening herself to me, inviting; the body language sent a different signal. Whatever plan was cooking, she knew she needed me to work for her. "Of course we keep going. I'm convinced Mr. Bocci's actions, and now what happened with Sammy, tell me my mother was right. The money is real."

"I have a few ideas and I'm still researching, but I do need to tell you, going back thirty years is not easy. A few people confirmed the old rumors, but they all seem to think the money went down with Dixon."

"My father."

"I'm sorry, yes, your father."

"It's just that my mother was certain…" She trailed off, went back to the wine. I stepped behind the bar, poured a drink for myself and refilled her glass. I stood opposite her and became the wise old bartender who dispenses sage advice.

"I thought Mr. Bocci would tell you everything about this money and what really happened. Mr. Bocci was all she ever talked about," she said.

"Did she like him, hate him?"

"Never expressed any like or dislike. Never a personal comment about him, only that he had the key to the money."

I nodded. No way was I telling her I had information—a number—from Bocci. Not yet, anyhow. Not until I figured out what the number meant and what Claire was all about. I had an inherent mistrust of her and it did not sit well with my trusted friend—my sixth sense, my gut.

"We're looking into everything we can about Mr. Bocci. I agree, his actions are key to the investigation. If your mother was right, we'll find it. Or find out what happened."

"I hope."

"Something will break; it always does. Cases like this, we'll find an answer. Not always what the client is expecting, but… I'll do my best." Mike had wandered over.

"You're in good hands here," Mike said.

She smiled.

I checked the time: 4:30. I wanted to be at Club Cuba well ahead of Brindisi. "I have an appointment. You're welcome to sit here all night if you want."

"No, I should go."

"I'll call you tomorrow."

Her mood seemed to lighten. "Tomorrow."

I went up to the condo. I told Katie to pack it in for the night and she objected.

"I'm on to something."

"You've been at it all day. Let's meet first thing in the morning." I wrote Albert Brindisi's name on a paper. "Priority tomorrow. Go home." She closed the computer and neatly stacked the files. I went into the bedroom and changed and when I came out, Katie had left.

I opened my phone and made a call critical to my meeting with Brindisi.

31

I MET LEAH LOVE—THAT WAS HER REAL NAME—twenty years ago when I arrested her for running a high-class call-girl escort service in the city. She was also the smartest person I have ever met. She was five feet four, with smooth caramel skin, sparkling black eyes, long, silky black hair, and hips that had a sultry sway that could knock a man off balance.

She grew up on an island in the Caribbean and came to the United States on a student visa, receiving an undergraduate degree from Rutgers and a MBA from Princeton, and spent three years working on Wall Street before she made an entrepreneurial move to Port City. Less than three months later, she had a website established for the escort service and the cash poured in.

I booked her on the prostitution charge and she was out on bond in less than a day. She was the only woman I have ever met where I experienced an immediate, undeniable, electric connection. Two days after her release I knocked on her apartment door and didn't leave for three days—except for food and wine. We had a natural attraction that was so palpable, I finally understood what it meant when people talked about love at first site. The problem was Leah was a restless soul and had no interest in a relationship and I was still married to Kelly. After a three-month torrid affair, we both knew it was time to let go and get back to reality.

She had a healthy savings account and used it to open a nightclub, the Cuban Connection. She ran a tight ship; the club prospered and became the place to be and to be seen, but after two years, she made a rare mistake. She allowed Tony and Sammy to buy half the business and with them came an element of clientele who changed the scene. The hip, cool, thirty-somethings drifted to the newest hot spot and Tony's network of domestic-beer drinking, gambling, sports-loving, good old boys, who had no interest in reggae music or Caribbean cuisine, moved in.

Business dropped off seventy-five percent in less than a year. Leah kicked herself for bringing in a partner, but re-grouped, sold her half for pennies on the dollar to Tony, and reinvented the original club at a new location.

The birth of Club Cuba. Leah applied her magic: live Afro-Cuban jazz bands replaced reggae, she brought a chef in from New York City to create a trendy small-plate menu, and a world-class bar ran the length of the interior. The restaurant and the chef received four star reviews in the *Herald* and the millennials came in droves.

Leah saw me come in and we embraced. She was stunning in a tight, dark-green satin dress that had a teasing neckline and hugged her in all the right places. Her curves got your attention but her smile and eyes sucked you in. She led me to her back office and closed the door.

"Brindisi, yeah, he comes in here every so often and sits at the bar. Nobody pays him much attention. Julio—my bartender—says he likes to talk. Always rambling about some new job he scored."

"Right down to business, huh?"

"Sounded urgent on the phone," she said.

"It was, but your eyes distracted me."

"They always did."

Being beside her brought back a flood of perfect memories. "Amazing, as usual. How are you?"

She sat in her office chair and crossed her legs. "I'm well. The club is hot, keeps me busy while I wait for you."

"It will happen." I let her spirit warm me for a minute. "I need to come around more, it's been too long."

"Yes it has."

Her phone buzzed. "Julio—says your guy is here. At the bar." She got up and we hugged, and then she kissed me on the lips. "I miss you." She turned me and pushed me toward the door. "Be careful."

"I'll be back."

I went out to the bar and sat down beside Brindisi. He was surprised to see me.

"Oh, hey there," he said. "I guess we're both a little

early."

"That's right, and I want information. Any compensation will depend on the quality of the information and I have a great ear for bullshit. Start talking."

"Damn, brother, I'm helping you out."

"First of all, I'm not your brother."

The bartender swung by. I ordered a bourbon with an ice cube and offered Brindisi another drink. He accepted. His eyes were bloodshot, his teeth a pale yellow and his hand trembled. He was a junkie all right; I've arrested plenty over the years.

"Okay, okay." He scratched at his filthy, scaly neck and leaned into to me and kept his voice low. "I runs into Jimmy Rosso a few weeks back. I ain't seen him in years. Like I said before, we were buddies back in the day."

"You don't have to whisper. Where?"

"Where, what?"

"Where did you run into him?"

"Umm…I don't recall. A bar somewhere. Anyhow, we start talking and he says he has some work for me. I'm always looking for some cash."

The bartender put the drinks in front of us and he took a big swallow of what I hoped was truth serum.

"I thought he split Port City years ago?"

"Me too," said Brindisi. "You can imagine my surprise."

"Uh huh," I said, rather nonplussed.

"He starts talking about the Scarazzini brothers and Donny Dixon and what happened way back when. He tells me he hears Donny's daughter is in town sniffing around about the money that went missing long ago. Hired a private eye."

"I'm listening." My phone buzzed and a text from Leah popped on the screen. *My guys say he came in alone. Nobody following.* He downed his drink and I signaled for another.

"Anyhow, he says if there's money, he's entitled to some 'cause he was part of that crew. But he's not sure. He asks me if I want to help shake things up a bit. Stir the pot, he says, and the money will magically float to the top. So I agree, give him my number, and he never calls."

"Until?"

"Well, a few nights ago, but before that, I hear about the accountant guy and remember him from years back. I used to drop money to him."

"Yeah?"

"Yeah, he worked for Aletto. Now, I destroyed a lot of brain cells over the years, but I ain't stupid. I starts to figure there might be something to what Rosso is saying. First the accountant, then Sammy gets run down."

"Could be coincidence."

"I'm not buying that. Not with Rosso back here," he said.

"How did you find out about me?"

"Rosso told me. Said you were investigating."

"Who told him that?"

He shrugged. "But, I'm thinking I can make a little scratch. I can slide you information. For a fee."

"You're working your own angle?"

"I'm a businessman."

"What if Rosso finds out you're talking to me?"

"I'd rather not dwell on that."

"Tell you what. Let's be smart about this. Why work against Rosso and put yourself at risk?"

He had every brain cell—the ones remaining—working overtime.

"You mean work together?"

"Why not? Rosso might have information I need. Everyone ends up happy. Tell him you and I go way back and you might be able to set a meeting."

He finished his drink. "I'm not sure..."

"Let me ask you a question. You think there is money?"

"I knew those guys. If Donny got whacked, there was money."

"Where do you think it is?"

"Isn't that the two-million-dollar question, isn't it?" He laughed; his lips peeled back to reveal blackish gums and yellow teeth. The laugh turned into a violent smoker's cough and it took him two minutes to get the cough under control. He grabbed a napkin from the bar and held it over his mouth with grimy, stained fingers. The bartender brought over a glass of water and gave us a sideways look, along with everyone else in the place. He sipped the water and the cough slowed.

"Years of cigarettes, huh?"

"Yeah, don't smoke."

"So why wouldn't anyone dig for the money before

now?"

"They all thought Donny hid it, and when he wouldn't talk..." He slashed a hand across his throat. "Then they thought his old lady had it and tried to beat it out of her. That didn't work. No place else to look. Rosso sure as hell didn't have it."

"So then here we are thirty years later."

"Yep. Donny either hid it and nobody knows where it is, or someone else grabbed it."

"And Rosso wants his share?"

"Hell, yeah. Me too."

"Donny's daughter?"

He shrugged. "Why else would she be here?"

My phone buzzed. A text message from Cara: *See you in thirty. Can't wait.* Damn! It was Friday and I forgot about my dinner with her. "So what about the meeting? Me, you and Rosso."

"I got to think about that."

I handed him my card. "Call me—tomorrow at the latest." I threw a couple of twenties on the bar. "Have a few more."

He scooped up the money. "Yeah, thanks, Johnny. Don't worry, I'll call you."

I gripped one of his bony shoulders. "Don't be stupid. We could all come out winners on this. "Tomorrow."

I left and shot a text to Cara telling her I'm running late but would be there. No time to cook; I'll pick up Chinese on my way. I didn't believe a word Brindisi said. My guess was he and Rosso were working together and Rosso sent him to find out what he could.

If Rosso was back in town, then Claire's hunch about the money was correct.

Or did Rosso ever leave?

32

I GOT TO MY CONDO AND FOUND CARA SITTING IN THE hallway with her back against my door. "Nice of you to show up."

"I'm sorry. I got stuck. Have you been here long?" I had food cartons from Royal Hunan and two bottles of chilled Riesling.

"About ten minutes." She got up and kissed me. "Only two bottles? What I'm thinking will require more than two bottles."

"I knew I loved you." The last thing I wanted to do was break the momentum of the case, especially after the meeting with Brindisi, but I also had not seen Cara for a month and looked forward to an evening with her. Plus, we enjoyed each other's company; she had an easy way about her and we talked about anything and everything. We could be comfortable, not worrying about a relationship or commitment: she had no intention of disrupting her gravy train, and I had no interest in anything serious. Cara was well aware that Leah was the only woman who could ever get me into a long-term relationship.

We spread the food out onto the table and opened the wine. She didn't have to work; Charles provided enough money so Cara could maintain her trophy wife status, which I think she secretly enjoyed. But, she loved mocking the bottle-blonde Botox babes at the club, laughing at how they all bragged about their latest affairs, which doctor freely dispensed Xanax, and how the hot, new club masseur slid his hands a little too high on their thighs, and how they wished he would just get on top and get it over with.

But with me, Cara could be Cara Carruthers, the half-Irish, half-Scottish girl who grew up three blocks from me in a working-class neighborhood with a plumber father and a secretary mother, who went to public school, Williams High—home of the Wildcats! —because her parents couldn't afford Catholic school, who went one year to PCCC, Port City Community College, before striking gold in the form of Charles Silverberg. Here, she abandoned any pretense and could laugh, feel good, and make love without being judged or held to the status quo. Somewhere inside, she missed Cara Carruthers.

After dinner, we opened the second bottle of Riesling and got cozy on the sofa. She asked about my latest case and had genuine concern because she saw the news reports. I gave her some of the details and it made for good storytelling: mobsters, missing money, and dead bodies.

What's not to like? Hollywood prospered on it.

She excused herself and I topped off our glasses. A minute later, she appeared in the doorway that led to my bedroom.

"Hi there."

"Well, hello," I said. She was naked except for a necklace and heels.

"Missed me?"

"Oh yes. I missed you." She slowly walked toward me and I let my eyes travel down her body. Her breasts were full and round, her small waist flared to soft, narrow hips, her thighs were long and lean, and her calves shapely, the calves of a woman who played tennis three times a week.

She put her arms around me and we kissed while I stripped off my clothes. I sat down onto the sofa; she kicked off the heels and straddled me with her hands on my shoulders. The night breeze coming in off the balcony was cool, the wine was intoxicating, and the moment was passionate. We settled into a gentle rhythm, as close as two people can be. We kissed and the pace quickened and her breaths came faster. She moaned and I could feel the intensity in her movements. She gasped, gripped my shoulders tight and—the front door opened.

Katie.

We stopped and her eyes met our eyes. "Oh my God." She had a folder in her hand and quickly put it in front of her face. "Oh my God, Oh my God, Oh my God, I'm sorry. I didn't think you were home." She turned around and faced away from us.

Cara jumped off. "Who is that?" She was too startled to remember she was naked.

"My research assistant," I said.

"Your what?"

"My research assistant."

"I'm sorry. I didn't know you were here," Katie said.

"You didn't lock the door?" Cara had her hands on her bare hips.

"I used my key."

"She has a key?" Her stare melted me back like a scolded child.

"Yes, she's my assistant—Katie." I pulled a couch pillow onto my lap to cover my retreating self.

"I don't even have a key. You didn't tell me about her. Did you leave that part out?"

"I just hired her. Nothing to leave out—"

"And who hires an assistant who looks like some bimbo beach volleyball player? Huh?"

"Hey…" Katie said.

"Cara. It's not like that."

"What's it like then? She just comes in when she wants?"

"No. I keep files up here."

"Where, in your bedroom?"

"In the closet," Katie said.

"Oh, you know a lot about the place. How many times have you been up here?"

"I'm sorry. This is embarrassing. Oh my God. I only wanted to drop off a file."

Cara stormed off to the bedroom.

"Well, this is awkward," I said.

She still had her back to me. "I'm so embarrassed. I'll just put this file on the table and we can talk about it tomorrow. I found something."

"What?"

"Elena Garver owns the Harbor Court Motel."

"No kidding?"

"Yes. Garver Holdings is a company…" Cara came from the bedroom, with her underwear and blouse on, holding her pants.

"You're still here?"

"I'm leaving." Katie put the file on the table and ran for the door, letting it slam shut behind her.

Cara hopped around pulling on her pants and heels, and then grabbed her purse. "Research assistant? That's what we call it?"

"Yes, research. Strictly business."

"Uh huh."

"Cara—you're overreacting."

"Overreacting? I was on top of you—naked and having sex. I've never been so humiliated." She slung the purse over her shoulder. "And I had to sit on the floor in the hallway until you got here and she has a key?"

"You're mad because she has a key?"

"Thanks for dinner." She stormed out and slammed the door behind her.

My wine glass was empty so I reached for the bottle. It was empty.

I laid my head back on the sofa.

Oh boy.

33

I READ THROUGH KATIE'S RESEARCH ON ELENA Garver last night and again this morning. If she was hiding behind Garver Holdings, she wasn't doing a good job. My novice "research assistant" had no trouble digging through state records for the corporate information that itemized subsidiary companies, board members, and various IRS and state financial filings.

Listed as a subsidiary was Garver Hotel Properties, LLC, and one of the properties was the Harbor Court Motel. Claire staying at the Harbor Court was no random choice. She booked into the Marriott because that's where anyone would expect her to stay; she booked into Aunt Elena's hotel so she could be close to…what?

It was 8:30 a.m. and I had poured my second cup of coffee when a knock came on my door. Surprise doesn't work for me and I was unsure of everything at this point, so

I picked up my Beretta and went to the door. No peep-hole; I had been meaning to install one. Gun in my right hand, I opened the door an inch with my left. A bag from a bagel shop was in my face. I pulled the door wide. "Why didn't you use your key?"

"After last night? Are you crazy?" Katie said.

"How about we put that out of our heads?"

"Your girlfriend didn't seem too happy." She laid the bagels on the kitchen table along with cream cheese.

"Not my girlfriend."

"Looked friendly to me. Knife?"

"She's a friend—we sort of have an arrangement." I got a knife out of the drawer and refilled my coffee. "Coffee?"

"Yes. Does that mean she's married?"

"Kind of complicated." I poured her a cup.

"That's a yes."

I thought it best to not say anything from this point forward on the subject of Cara. We each fixed a bagel and stood in awkward silence in the kitchen, both looking at the floor as we ate. She giggled. Our eyes caught and I laughed and she laughed and we lost control. We roared, doubled over, both of us wiping laugh tears from our cheeks.

"She was standing there naked…yelling." Katie got the words out between gulping for breaths.

"Oh, *she* has a key…" I mocked. She snorted and we laughed harder.

Five minutes went by before we regained composure and could talk without laughing.

"What happened stays between us," I said.

"Sure, boss. Who would I tell anyhow?"

"I bet you already told your friend, Mandy?"

"I told her before I got to my car last night. She thought it was cute, two old people having sex."

"Old people?"

"Well, older. Don't worry, you're still hot. She thinks you're handsome and wanted to know what I saw."

"And?"

"I told her it all happened real quick and I didn't see anything. You owed me anyhow. You've seen me in my underwear."

"Okay, okay. You're right. A little different, but okay. Can we now get to work?"

We cleared the food from the table and spread out the folders. Her organization impressed me. She had a separate folder for each person we'd come across and another folder with a timeline for the case. She put a folder in front of me but kept her hand on it.

"Did you know we can search marriage records online?"

"Yes," I said.

"Oh, of course you do. Anyhow, this is what I found last night." She opened the folder and removed a copy of a marriage license between Elena Aletto Richards and Francis Rosso. *Frank Rosso.*

"She married Frank Rosso? Which means Jimmy Rosso is her son?

"Step son. Jimmy was sixteen years old at the time she married Frank. And Elena was only twenty-two. The reason I couldn't find anything on Rosso before is because Jimmy Rosso is Martin James Rosso."

"Well, how about that."

"Listen to this. When I do a criminal background check on Martin James Rosso, six pages of records came up. He was a bad dude."

"They're all bad dudes."

"The charges date right up to the time Donny got whacked then stop. Must be when he split town."

I picked up the folder and leafed through Rosso's rap sheet. "This is great work."

"It means that Claire and Rosso are cousins. Sort of. Can you be a cousin with your aunt's stepson?"

"Close enough, I suppose. It also means it was easy for Claire to find him when she put all this in motion. Marco and Tony both said Rosso left town and never came back. But I have a suspicion…"

"Karl Boyd is Rosso."

"You're getting the hang of this."

She beamed; all proud of herself. She got up from her chair and paced around the kitchen. All she needed was a trench coat and a fedora. "So Claire contacts Rosso, he confirms the money, makes him her accomplice, then he's the one running around with the spray paint." She slammed her hand down on the table. "Or he ran over Sammy."

"Or paid a flunky to do the job."

"Right—why do it yourself when you can blame somebody else?" She sat back down.

"Get them to take the fall."

"Huh?"

"Take the fall. It means when you get blamed…never mind. Here's the goal for today. Albert Brindisi. They call him Little Al. He's the flunky who came to the bar yesterday. Says he's working for Rosso, which confirms Rosso *is* back in town. He wanted to put himself in the middle and try to work both sides, but I'm sure he's bluffing." I wrote his name on a pad. "Find out what you can about him. I'm sure you'll need a ream of paper for his rap sheet."

"Okay." She made a note in her book. "What about you? Where are you going?"

"To the Harbor Court for starters." I went into the bedroom and changed. When I came back to the kitchen, she had her laptop set up and had another bagel in front of her.

Oh, to be young and to not worry about the calories.

"Keep an eye on her car. Call me if she moves."

"What happened when she came to the bar yesterday?" she asked.

"Nothing. I'm not sure. She asked about Sammy, remorseful, like it's all her fault."

"It is all her fault."

"True. Keep going on Bocci. He's our unknown."

"Our X factor?"

"Yep." I put my gun into my bag and headed for the door. "Hey, excellent job. You're a natural at this."

"Thanks."

I stopped and turned to her, "Use your key anytime."

"Whatever you say."

"And lock this door behind me."

"You got it, stud." She smiled.

I smirked and closed the door behind me. I waited in the hallway until I heard the click of the lock and then I left. Smiling.

34

I GRABBED A COFFEE IN THE McDONALD'S DRIVE-thru and took up my usual spot. I had a perfect view of the motel office and could see Jimmy Rosso—aka Karl Boyd—working the front desk. Claire's Audi was *not* in the parking lot. I sent Katie a message to update me on the location of her car and reminded her to do a background on Karl Boyd. You never know what could turn up. If Rosso was Boyd, that explained why he spent twenty minutes in her room the first time I set up camp here, and also explained why she got enough Chinese food delivered for three of four people on the second night I observed. And who dropped Claire off on the night of my fumbled surveillance run? Rosso or Brindisi?

If Rosso split town when Donny got whacked, as all sources kept telling me, and mob guys didn't bother to search for him, that means he was protected. If the mob wants you, they will find you. If the feds place a squealer into witness protection, the new identity only works as long as no one talks. The mob had a funny way of finding guys who were supposed to stay hidden. A little cash payment to a mob-friendly fed and suddenly the guy in protection disappears from his new suburban life.

Martin James Rosso was Joseph Aletto's step-grandson and Elena's step-son, so out of respect for Aletto, they left him alone. Didn't try to find him, or they all figured he was too stupid to pull off taking the money and were happy he split town. Tony and his boys had no problem using baseball bats on Jackie; they would have done worse to Rosso if they suspected he had the cash. My guess was the cops turned up the heat for beating up Jackie and he took off to avoid being caught. Now he's back in Port City because ten years ago the Garver group buys the motel and she puts him to work with a new name? Did Elena create her own witness protection for him? Why? A favor to husband number two, Jimmy's father? All that mattered now was his involvement with Claire and what he's doing with the IQ-less Brindisi.

Little Al's visit to me was nothing more than a message from Rosso that he was here running the show. Why? Why would Claire need to use Rosso? Gain access to where? She hired me to dig for the money, wasn't that enough? The involvement of Rosso didn't seem necessary, unless Claire wanted to keep her hands clean.

An old, beat-up black and grey Lincoln Mercury squealed into the motel lot and interrupted my expert analysis of the case. Brindisi got out and went into the office. I picked up my camera and zoomed in. He and Boyd-Rosso—were having a more than animated conversation. Rosso's arms were flailing about while he shouted at Brindisi. Then Rosso went out of the picture and Brindisi plopped into a lobby chair. That lasted for only a few seconds when Rosso reappeared behind the counter and again launched into his tirade. Brindisi cowered in the chair with his head down. What did he screw up?

My phoned buzzed—a text from Katie: *The car is at the Marriott.*

Rosso stormed out of the office with Brindisi following. They went to room 112 and knocked. The door opened and they went in. *Was Claire in the room? If so, then why wasn't her car here? And why didn't I know her car moved to the Marriott?* I became angry with myself for not knowing. When did they move it? *Last night when Cara was riding me like a jockey on a thoroughbred?* Shame on me. This case was twenty-four hours from now on.

They came back out of the room. Brindisi got into the Mercury and peeled from the lot. Rosso went back into the office and picked up the phone. A moment later, Katie called my phone.

"Are you at the Harbor Court?"

"Yes."

"Mike said the TV news is reporting cars on fire in the parking garage of the Marriott hotel."

"You're kidding."

"He said, three cars are burning and all the streets are blocked off."

"Might be nothing to do with us but why do I have one of those feelings?"

"You think it's Claire's car."

"One way to find out." I closed the call. *Did Brindisi go to the Marriott and set Claire's car on fire? Did he torch the wrong car and that's why Rosso was screaming at him?* Katie called again.

"I put the news on and they are saying it looks like arson."

"If my guess is correct, I'm not surprised."

"Wait..." Silence on her end and then I heard my TV in the background. "Unbelievable...at least one was a black Audi. They interviewed the fire captain."

"Thanks." I hung up and sat there. *Why would she have her own car destroyed?* I started my car to head to the Marriott to confirm it was her car. Then I'd confront her.

A cab pulled into the Harbor Court just as I started out of the McDonald's lot. I stopped and reversed back to my spot. It waited a few moments and then Claire came out of her room, wearing jeans and a blouse, and got into the cab. I wished all my clients had vibrant auburn hair. Makes surveillance much easier.

The cab turned on Harbor Boulevard and I slid in right behind it. It wasn't necessary for me to follow; I knew exactly where she was going.

35

I FOLLOWED THE CAB UNTIL IT PULLED TO A STOP three blocks from the Marriott. Claire got out and walked the rest of the way. Three fire engines and several police cars had the road and front portico drive to the hotel blocked. I couldn't get any farther by car so I parked and waited.

My phone buzzed no more than ten minutes later and it was a sobbing Claire. Through her sobs, she told me her car was torched and I needed to come to the hotel right away. She sounded scared, distraught and said she didn't know what to do. What she said and what I thought were two different things. No doubt in my mind that she knew exactly what she was doing.

I hustled the three blocks and as I got there, the firemen were winding fire hoses back into the trucks. People—curious guests, staff—bustled around the lobby but I made my way to the elevators and up to room 503. Two police officers were in the hall and they stepped up to me as I approached. The door was open; Claire must have heard us and called for me to come in. I walked in and I was stunned. It was as if she'd been staying there for at least a week. She had clothes in the closet, snacks and makeup on the dresser, her purse on a chair, shoes on the floor, magazines and a book on the desk, and the bed unmade. Another officer was in the room, asking questions.

"He's with me," she said to the officer. She threw her arms around me and started crying again. "Do you believe this?" She had changed her clothes from what she had on when she left the Harbor Court. She wore sweat-pants and a T-shirt, no makeup, and had her hair pulled back. It appeared she had never left the room.

"Tell me what happened," I said.

The officer interrupted and rightly so. He'd want to ask the questions.

"Who are you?" he said. I showed him my ID and my retired police ID. He identified himself as Sergeant Mooney. "Three Audis were set on fire. Funny thing is, the cars were not next to each other. So, whoever did this either has a vendetta against Audi or didn't know which one to target, so he lit up all three."

Brindisi. Was he stupid enough to do something like that? Claire sat on the bed. "She said you're working with her. Anything to add?" he asked.

I looked at him and nodded to the hallway. "Can we?" He said sure and we went out in the hall and huddled up with the other two officers.

"Domestic case. She's afraid of her ex-husband but I don't think he has the stones to do something like this. The more I get into the case, the more I think she's the one who needs some help. What about the other two cars?"

"One belongs to a doctor who's in town for a meeting and the other car is rented to a guy who's up in the penthouse suite, but he can't tell us what he does for a living," he said.

"Open-and-shut," I said. "Somebody was short on his last payment to his supplier." All three guys chuckled.

"I think you're right." Mooney nodded toward Claire's room. "Why are the good-looking babes always the craziest?"

"Tell me about it," I said. "Wish me luck." We all laughed. I hoped I held them off for a couple of days. Brindisi on a security camera would eventually bring them back to Claire. They said their next stop was the penthouse and we parted ways. I went into the room.

Claire sat on the edge of the bed and I sat down beside her. "What did you say to them?"

"Only that I was involved in an investigation and I think I was a target."

I held her hand in mine. "I realize this is upsetting, but I don't want you talking to the police or anyone else for that matter."

"What would I say?"

"That you have no idea why someone would do this to you. I'm glad you called me when you did. Anything else like this happens, don't say a word."

She hooked her arm through mine and drew closer to me. She put her head on my shoulder. "This is all my fault. I'm aware I started this, but I never expected all this to happen."

"I'm sure you thought this would be more of an investigation with Mr. Bocci and me looking for a bank account." A leading question and I was doing my best to lead. No more surprises.

"Yes, I did." She turned more into me and her hand went on my thigh. Those stunning, green eyes welled with tears. Her other hand slid up my back, onto my neck, and then pulled me to her. Her eyes held mine, our lips closing in.

She whispered, "I don't want to be alone."

"Claire..." *Don't do it Johnny boy—don't do it.* But I have no will-power. This is the last thing that could happen but this woman was irresistible. The hair, the green eyes, the body; there's not a man alive who could say no. We kissed, at first soft, and then harder. It was passionate, magnetic, her hands on me and my hands on her. I pulled her shirt off and we lay back on the bed.

A knock on the door. *Coitus-interruptus twice in less than twenty-four hours. Unbelievable.* "Miss Dixon?" The hotel manager.

"He'll go away. Don't stop."

"Claire, we have to. We can't do this. Answer the door." She pulled on her shirt.

"Miss Dixon?"

"Just a minute," she yelled. "Johnny, please stay. I need you."

"We'll talk later."

She opened the door and the manager apologized for what happened with the car and offered to arrange for a rental. She took his information, thanked him, said she would call him once she had herself ready for the day.

She came back into the room and sat beside me on the bed. "Stay."

"We can't. You're the client. It never ends the right way." *And with this chick, there's no telling how it will end.* "Come to the bar tonight for dinner and we'll talk and see where we are. Somebody set your car on fire. Obvious warning and we need to figure out who sent it. Do not leave this room before then."

She put her arms around me. "Why can't we talk now?"

She kissed me full on. I kissed her back for a moment and then pushed her off. "Claire."

She tugged at my belt buckle. I grabbed her hand and stopped her.

I stood. "Come to the bar tonight at seven."

"I'm scared."

"I know you are. That is why you go from here to the bar. Nowhere else."

"Whatever you say." She stretched out on the bed.

Did she have her own car set on fire and why? Too make it look as if she's targeted and somebody—Tony?—is coming after her? I took a second to take in her long body and the hair that tumbled around her. I was mad that I allowed it to go as far as I did. Claire was a person, a client, who could not be trusted. I knew that. But what still confused me was her motivations. I'm working on finding the money: wasn't that the goal? What did she want and why?

"Do not leave this room. Okay? Take a cab to the bar tonight and don't speak to anyone. We need to find out who did this. Hotel security will check their cameras and I'll stay in touch with the police."

"Johnny?"

I walked over to the bed.

"Thank you. I'm sorry about…."

"No apology necessary. Let's stick to the case and with any luck, we'll find your money."

"Deal."

"See you tonight." I turned and left. Unsure of everything.

36

MY CAR WAS THREE BLOCKS FROM THE MARRIOTT and I was glad because I needed the walk to clear my head after getting tangled up with Claire. Plus, more mind-blowing: her room had clothes and her things strewn about as if she had been there the entire week. *What was the play? When did she move all her clothes and things to the Marriott? Was Brindisi the errand boy?*

When Claire got to McNally's for dinner, we'd rehash what we knew at this point. I called Katie when I got back into my car and filled her in. She was working on Bocci and the number he gave me but had not come up with anything. I also had Mike and Junior brainstorming on the number and they both struck out with federal and state databases. We'd tried everything we could think of. Was it some type of address, storage locker, phone number, stock ID number? We were running out of possibilities.

I arrived at the bar and Katie had moved herself down to the booth. I told her I wanted her back up in my place before Claire showed up. I wanted Katie invisible; nobody needed to know I hired her. Too many mobsters around and I didn't need Katie to be used as a target or a pawn. She was kidnapped once; we didn't need her abducted again and held for information or— let's say—two million dollars.

"But I like working down here where I can be with live human beings."

"I understand, but caution is the word of the day. I don't need any of these guys getting any ideas."

"Fine. Want some lunch? Mike said he'd fix me a sandwich."

"Sure, whatever you're having." She went to the kitchen as my phone rang—Brindisi. I slid into the booth and answered. "Brindisi?"

"I did what you said. Rosso wants to meet. Tonight. Says we can work something out," he said.

"What did you say to him?"

"Just what you told me. That we should work together. Made it sound like my idea."

"Good."

"You'll take care of me, right?"

"Of course. Like I said. If this works, we all get paid," I said.

"Tonight. Eleven. Pier 21."

"Got it." I closed my phone. I'd like to think they took the bait but there wasn't any bait to take. Rosso sent

Brindisi to me, no doubt. Why? To draw me out? To find out what I know and get between Claire and the money? If the money exists.

Katie carried two plates of food, chicken salad sandwiches, which she placed on the table. Mike came over and put a beer in front of me and gave her a soda. Her phone rang and she answered it.

"Yes, speaking." She listened and after a minute her face lit up. I hoped that meant good news. "Oh, that's encouraging. Thank you. Yes, we'll see you tomorrow at one." She ended the call and sat down at the table. "Guess who that was!"

"Well, I'm hoping—"

"Margaret Finley from First National Bank. I talked to her a few days ago and she remembered my story and thinks the number is a safe deposit box. She remembered the safe deposit boxes are all four digits, each with a six-digit passcode. She said there is a box that matches our number."

"You got a lead. Congratulations."

"We go tomorrow at one."

"And?"

"And what?"

"Even if it is a match, don't we need identification? Some sort of document?"

She picked up her sandwich but stopped mid-bite. "Oh."

"If it's Bocci's box, and I hope it is, we don't have any ID and you sure as hell don't look like Bocci."

"I said I was a niece and he passed away. Like you told me to do."

"Then we stick with that story. Good job. At least we have something."

We clinked our glasses in a toast. "I realize you want to be out on the street but these cases are solved with the research. You keep digging until you hit something. Let's hope tomorrow—whatever the outcome—gives us a nugget more than we have now. All we have now are washed-up mobsters running over people and setting cars on fire."

My new concern was the Rosso, or now Karl Boyd, and Brindisi connection and how Claire had brought them into her world. Or, did Rosso orchestrate all this and bring Claire in as a front person? If he's supposed to be in a self-imposed witness protection program, he would need somebody, and Claire would be the perfect person, to begin the search for this money. But why now after all these years? What if Claire's story is legit? Her mother died and she's carrying out the dying wish? She knows the once hidden away Rosso was back and she finds him through Aunt Elena and he happens to be closer than Claire ever expected. Claire pulling Rosso into the gig made more sense. *But she hired me, why the need for anyone else?* That was the nagging question I couldn't answer.

I called Claire to check on her—more like to keep tabs—but she didn't answer and that concerned me. Why not answer? Deliberate, or did something happen? Now with her car, and my GPS device looking like burnt toast, we had no way to track her.

We finished our lunch and cleared the table. I asked Mike to sit in and we talked through a plan for this evening's meet-and-greet with Rosso. *Prepare for the worst and hope for the best.* Mike and I lived by that credo for many years and we were still alive.

I gave Katie the access code for the GPS that was in my car. All I wanted her to do was stay in touch with Mike tonight by phone. Mike had no time for computers and how to track a car with a GPS device. He could operate a beer tap and that's all he ever intended to do. But tonight, I needed him to have my back.

Claire did not answer any of my calls since this morning. I dressed in all black and prepared my duffel with tools I might need for tonight's meeting with Rosso. I left my apartment at nine and went to the Marriott. I got lucky with an assistant manager. I flashed my old police ID and he agreed to go with me to Claire's room. She didn't answer our knock and he opened the door. Nothing had changed in the room except that the sweat-pants she was wearing were now in a heap on the floor.

I thanked the manager and drove over to the Harbor Court Motel and found just what I thought I would find. Nothing. I parked in the side alley, walked up to room 112 and knocked. No answer. No lights on in the room. *Was she missing or hiding? Did somebody grab her because she's the conduit to the money?* A good possibility.

The one I dreaded the most.

37

PORT CITY HARBOUR, A BUSY, WORKING HARBOUR, provided over 5,000 jobs to dock workers, shipping line management, and administrative personnel. Two domestic shipping lines made Port City their base. Automobiles, machinery, sugar, and wood pulp and paper were the major imports. Coal, cars and small trucks were the main exports that constantly moved through the fourth busiest harbor on the East Coast, behind New York, Philadelphia, and Baltimore. Colossal cranes loomed over the piers, ready to load and off-load the massive rectangular shipping containers, some stacked three high, that lined the holding areas of the docks. The containers made for an elaborate maze of small nooks, concealed angles, and narrow roadways that were conducive to illicit deals, secret meetings, and the occasional need to make someone disappear.

I arrived at the harbor at ten o'clock, one hour before the meeting with Rosso and Brindisi. Most weeknights, the docks operate until eleven o'clock, the dock workers on a two-shift day: seven to three, three to eleven. But on a Saturday it was only me, the seagulls, and Harbor security. Pier 21 is the last pier, twenty-one out of twenty-one, and the significance was there was only one way in and one way out. Depending on how I positioned myself, my back could be against the wall, or the water, in this case. Rosso made a smart choice in choosing this location. I needed to make sure I used it to my advantage. Locked gates prevented access to the piers but this meeting, located on the service road, was patrolled by private security. PCPD maintained a presence on the docks during the day, and rent-a-cops kept watch at night.

I parked my car between two containers at Pier 19 and walked along the edge of the bulkhead, the containers providing great cover, except that a full moon hung in the night sky. That was bad for two reasons: it brought out the crazies, and I had enough crazy on this case already, and second, the moonlight shone so bright it cast shadows. I stayed in the shadows of the containers as much as I could. I took a position on Pier 20 that gave me a clear view of the roadway. Anyone approaching 21 had to come past me—unless they came by boat.

Harbor security rolled by at 10:15 and did a cursory drive-by. If memory served, it took them an hour to cover the piers and the surrounding area, and most of their time was spent chasing off drug dealers and couples making out in cars. It was a warm night, so hopefully there would be enough necking teenagers to keep security busy. If Rosso showed up on time, we would have fifteen minutes to discuss business before security came through again.

I found a spot behind an office shed and grabbed an old crate to sit on. I sent a text to both Mike and Katie to let them know I was in position. I told them I would text them again when I saw Rosso and if they didn't receive a message from me within fifteen minutes, Mike was to come looking. Katie sent a text back confirming my location through the GPS in my car.

I participated in plenty of stake-outs in my life, waiting for some low life to show up or for some deal to go down, but I always had the entire PCPD behind me. Tonight it was me and my Beretta and a couple of washed-up mobsters living in the past. My nerves were up and my senses wide awake. I heard every seagull caw, every splash of water as it lapped against the piers, every creak and squeak that you only hear at night. I had the gun in my shoulder holster under my jacket—safety off.

At 10:58, the low whine of a car came up and I peeked around the office shed. It was the old Lincoln Mercury. The headlights blinked off as it went past Pier 20 and then it slowed and stopped at 21. I left my spot and stayed as concealed as much as I could while I made my way to 21. The car doors opened and two guys got out. One was the skinny guy with the gray ponytail I saw working at the Harbor Court. Had to be Rosso, or now Karl Boyd. I did not recognize the second man but he was tall and muscular.

No Brindisi either, which now meant Rosso recruited more goons into the operation. Which meant more men to pay—or promise to pay—which meant more men who would talk, which meant more who need to be eliminated when this all goes bad, or if Rosso doesn't want to share. Not too smart.

They stood in front of their car, silhouetted by the arc lights that lined the roadway.

"Delarosa?" It was Rosso. I didn't say anything for a minute. I was now behind a container and he would see me as soon as I stepped out.

"I thought you left town a long time ago?" I yelled.

"C'mon out. This is a friendly meeting. I want your proposal. About our mutual interest."

I came out of the shadow. "About that. I'm not sure how mutual it is." I moved forward; my eyes darted around to make sure it was only the two of them.

"Oh, it's very mutual."

"I was hired to do a job. That's all."

"That money belongs to me."

"My client feels otherwise."

"Your client is wrong. I was there. The money belongs to me."

"You should have hired me. Or are you mad you didn't think of this first? Is it true you left town with your tail between your legs when Dixon got whacked?"

He took a step forward and his goon put out an arm to stop him. "You don't know what went down."

"Okay. The past is the past," I said. "What are we doing

here then?"

"You find the money; it belongs to me."

"Did you kill Sammy?"

"Why would I do that?"

"Get him out of the way. Is Tony next?"

"I'll take care of Tony."

"He's coming after you."

"You find the money and we'll all end up happy."

"Tony won't be happy."

"Like I said, I'll take care of Tony," said Rosso. "We're brothers. We go back."

"I get you want the money. Money that I have *not* found. But now what?"

"Now what?" He nodded to the muscleman and he went around the car and opened the trunk. He pulled a gagged and bound Claire from the car and dragged her around to the front. Her hands were tied around her back. My worst nightmare was now true. The goon had a fist-full of her hair in his hand and held her between him and Rosso.

My hand instinctively went to my jacket.

"Don't do it." They both had guns pointed at me. She screamed my name through the gag. "Shut up, Claire. Delarosa, hands up."

I put my hands in the air. "Rosso, what are you doing?"

"My insurance. You now work for me. You find the money, she lives."

"We don't even know if the money exists."

"There's money, no doubt in my mind."

"Let her go and we'll figure this out. Claire, you'll cut

him in, right?" I said.

She nodded and tried to say yes.

"Can't take the chance."

The skin on the back of my neck began to crawl. I sensed a presence behind me and took a step to my right, hoping to angle him into my peripheral vision.

"Don't move," said Rosso. "You need to know I'm serious."

A sharp pain on the side of my head and a white-hot flash in front of my eyes and I went down to one knee and put a hand on the ground to steady myself. Then everything went black.

38

I WOKE TO THE SOUND OF TAPPING KEYS ON THE laptop computer. I was lying flat on my back on my sofa, staring at the ceiling in my living room. I raised my head only to be knocked back down by a sharp pain on the right side.

"Welcome back from the dead." Katie was working at the table. She came over to the sofa and I looked up into the mop of blonde hair. "Do you want to sit up? You got yourself a nasty bump and cut on your head."

With her help, I slowly got myself into an upright position. "Did Mike bring me in last night?"

"Yes. Do you remember?"

"Most of it. I think." I put my hand to my head and I had a lump the size of a golf ball. "Damn."

"We had ice on it all night."

"We? You were here?"

"Yep. When you didn't respond, Mike called me for your location. You parked a bit away from where he found you."

"Yeah, I did."

"I called him and he told me what happened and I came over." She went into the kitchen and came back with an ice pack. "Here, hold this on your head."

"What time is it?"

"Nine thirty."

I held the ice to my head and the cold felt good, but then it all rushed back to me. Rosso, Claire being pulled from the trunk of the car, her hands tied and the gag in her mouth, and then my lights going out. Katie sat in the chair opposite me.

"Rosso is holding Claire."

"What? Oh my God. Mike wondered what happened. I wanted to take you to the emergency room but Mike said there wasn't enough blood. Some crazy rule you guys came up with. I sent him a text telling him you are awake."

"Mike's right. Hospital only if the bleeding won't stop." I pushed myself up to my feet, wobbled a bit and Katie grabbed my arm until I was steady. "I'm going to wash up. If I'm not out in ten minutes, come in."

"Let's hope it doesn't come to that."

I took a quick shower to wake up and changed into clean clothes. I got back out to the kitchen to find Mike sitting at the table with Katie, and a bottle of my bourbon and two glasses in front of him.

"Can you believe she doesn't like bourbon?" Mike said.

"Can you get her drunk later. We got problems. Rosso has Claire and wants the money in exchange."

"Well, that's a game-changer."

"I know."

"Call Marco?'

"Who's Marco?" Katie asked.

I poured myself a shot and knocked it back. "Our cop friend and no, we don't call him. We figure this out. I never thought Rosso was behind this, but now I'm not so sure."

"You think he got wind of this money-hunt and just showed up?"

"He got wind of it, but he's been in town awhile. Found out he and Claire have a connection. Sort of step-cousins."

"Interesting. What's the play here, now?"

"If Rosso is the mastermind, and I doubt it, he put Claire out in front so he wouldn't attract attention, right?" I said.

"Doesn't seem likely, but okay."

"I agree. I think Claire started this like she said, but Rosso finds out and moves in."

"And Tony?"

"Rosso stirs things up to draw Tony out?" I paced around the room, my usual thinking process. "No, that can't be right. Tony's name was on Claire's original paper. So Rosso figures out his name is *not* on the original paper and gets bent out of shape. He decides to play his own game."

"You need to round up Tony. Like now."

"Right. I need him on my side of this. Claire's side. I'm headed out to the salvage yard."

"What do you need me to do?"

"Not sure yet. The Harbor Court Motel. Do you want to sit on that for a while?"

"Sure."

"Or Junior or Carlos if they're available."

"Don't forget my appointment at the bank at one," Katie said.

"Right, we need to keep that. I'll meet you there at twelve forty-five. Figure out what we're going to say. Dress professional. Bring a folder and a notebook."

"What is that?" Mike asked.

"A lead on the number Bocci gave us. Lady at First National."

"Damn." He turned to Katie. "Did you find this?"

"Sure did."

"Well. Good job. Let's hope you found the money and we can put this to bed."

"Before someone else gets cracked in the head," I added.

"Description of Rosso?"

"Tall skinny, maybe sixty, gray ponytail. And Claire—well you've seen her."

"Oh, yeah."

"If they're not at the Harbor Court, then—I'm not sure."

"I'm on it. Let me square up things downstairs, first."

"A McDonald's across the street gives you a good vantage point."

Mike left and I went back to Katie. "Okay, I'll meet you at the bank. Keep the GPS app open and an eye on me. Hopefully, Tony won't take a two-by-four to the other side of my head."

"I'm going home to change first."

"Hey, thanks for last night. I appreciate you staying."

"Sure, boss."

"What did you say to your folks?"

"I was at Mandy's."

"When this is over, we'll talk about your hours and duties. You've done an incredible job, but you can't be out all night."

"Okay, Dad."

"Sorry, I didn't mean it that...anyway, you know."

"Just giving you a hard time." She picked up her purse and headed for the door.

"Oh, and Katie, I told you to keep some extra clothes in your car, but you can keep some clothes up here, too. There is some room in the closet."

She turned back to me and I knew that she knew my suggestion was an affirmation of my confidence in her.

"I'm sure Cara will love that."

39

TONY ANSWERED ON THE FIRST RING AND HE WAS jacked up, as I knew he would be. I tried to calm him down enough so we could talk. He said he'd be waiting for me in his parking lot with his friend, which meant his twelve-gauge shotgun. He wasn't kidding, either.

I pulled onto the gravel and there he was, leaning back against his truck with his arms folded across his chest and his gun propped next to him. I got out of my car and he picked up the double barrel.

"You better be here to tell me who killed my brother."

"I have an idea but I want to talk through this with you. You were right. This missing money is making people crazy. Will you hear me out? We'll figure a way through this and get Sammy the justice he deserves."

He didn't say anything but leaned the gun back against the truck. I took a step closer. I had the coiled-up cobra listening to me; I didn't want to provoke it any further.

"You called it when you said Brindisi was back in town," I said.

"Brindisi?"

"He's working for Rosso."

"Rosso is back?"

"Evidently he's been in Port City for some time with a new identity and some shitty job. Staying low and under the radar."

"Where is he? I'm going there now."

"Hold up, Tony—"

"Where is he?"

"Tony, this is what we don't want. Let's talk through this."

He picked up the shotgun and aimed the barrel at my chest.

"Sammy was my only family. I promised my mother I'd look after him. And I failed. It's because of what you started. I told you not to open this."

"I know—"

"Johnny, you don't. He was run over deliberate. His body was in two pieces. You ever see something like that? Huh?" I shook my head. "They made me identify him. My brother. I had to tell the cops that the bottom half belong to the top half. How fucked up is that? Huh?"

"Tony, I'm sorry..."

"It don't matter now anyway." His emotions were all over the place. Grief, anger, revenge; it all flowed from his pores. He jabbed the gun toward me. "Where is he?"

"No idea. But that's why I'm here," I said.

"He'll pay for this. They'll all pay for this. Even you."

"Listen. Listen to me. Let me make it right. Okay? Put the gun down and let's figure this out. I'll give you Rosso. I'll give you Brindisi. I promise. I just need some time."

"I'll give you five minutes."

"Tony—"

"Where is Rosso?"

"I will find him. I don't want them coming for you. If Rosso finds the money, they'll want you out of the way. Guaranteed."

"You don't worry about me."

"Tony. Please. They took Claire."

"The girl?"

"Yes. Donny's daughter. Rosso has her and wants the money in exchange. That's why I need you to work with me. So we all don't end up dead. No doubt in my mind he'll kill us all if he smells a chance at the cash," I said.

"Which you haven't found."

"Right." A car drove into the lot—a customer—and saw Tony holding the shotgun on me. The car backed out faster than it pulled in. "Now you're scaring away customers."

Tony looked at me with such sadness. He was broken, destroyed. He and Sammy were together, hip-to-hip, since childhood. Now they were apart. It will take a long time for Tony to recover. If he does.

"Doesn't matter. I'm going to burn the place down anyhow. Only kept it to give Sammy a legit job. He was a natural. He understood cars better than anything. Had this uncanny ability to remember what we had in inventory without looking at the computer. A knack, any part, any car. Without him, why bother? I'll go back to hustling. Work out of the club."

"I'm sorry, Tony. I really am."

"I want my time with Rosso. Brindisi, too."

"Of course you do." I took a few steps closer to him, hoping he came to a more reasonable position. But I was wrong. He pushed the barrel of the gun into my chest. "Tony?"

Tears filled his eyes. "Go do what you have to do. Now. I want Rosso's location by tonight. Understand?" He pushed me backward with the gun until we got to my car.

"Let me find them and I promise you'll get your piece. Okay?"

He pressed the barrel into my ribs. "How long do you think it will take me to find Brindisi."

"Minutes."

"If I want, that little weasel faggot will be dead before he hits his second martini tonight at happy hour. He'll never see me coming. But I want Rosso first. He's better at disappearing."

"I understand."

"Once I finished with him, you and I will conclude our business."

"Tony – "

"Capisce, paisan?

"Capisce."

He backed down and I decided to not push my luck. I think I bought myself—and Rosso—a few hours. Tony knew everyone on the street and he'd have no problem finding Brindisi and sticking those double barrels up his coked-up nostrils. I pulled out of the lot as Tony stood there with his arms folded around the gun. I truly felt sorry for him. He and his brother did bad things— not horrible things, just immoral things—like hustling bets, hustling girls—but he always took care of his family. Not only his brother and relatives; his family on the street, too. had a big heart in that old, round body. And now it was broken.

40

TONY WAS OUT FOR BLOOD, ROSSO WAS HOLDING Claire, my bar was fire-bombed, Bocci and Sammy were dead, and the money was still a mystery. The only lead we had was with an assistant manager at First National Bank, and this was the most progress I'd made in the case. We needed some positive karma, new mojo, or a leprechaun selling good luck. Tony would find Brindisi. I had to get to the money and Claire before Tony went on his killing spree—and he had nothing to lose. The smart bet would be on the bookie and vengeance.

On my way to the bank, I called Claire's phone again and it went to voice mail, and then called Leah and asked her to make sure her guys keep an eye out for Brindisi. The junkie/drunk would need a fix. He could not hide all day and would likely show up at one of his regular spots. I hoped for Leah's place.

First National was one of the smaller banks in the city and we were to meet at the downtown location at one o'clock. We both parked in a garage across the street and sat in my car to discuss a strategy. She dressed the part with a blue skirt, white blouse, and two-inch heels. Professional and conservative. The last thing we needed was to appear like long-lost greedy relatives showing up to collect a payday after our beloved Uncle Carlo passed away so unexpectedly.

We asked for Mrs. Finley and we were directed to a waiting area in the lobby. Ten minutes later, a tall, linebacker-wide, African-American woman, in a skin-tight black pencil skirt that did no favors for her rolling mounds of hips and backside and a light-blue satin blouse that stretched over a major league bosom that challenged the strength of every straining thread to hold each button in place, teetered over to us on three-inch stilettos that I swore were made of titanium rods or they would have given way to the weight by now, and greeted us with a big, friendly, toothy smile. The scent of gardenias enveloped us like a cloud of toxic gas.

"I'm Margaret Findley." She extended a hand. We exchanged introductions and followed her to a small, private office. The flowery scent of her perfume was so strong the office smelled like a funeral home. She sat at her desk and we sat across from her on two small chairs. The walls were decorated with family photos, notes and greeting cards, and small posters with positive messages about "learning to get back up after falling" and "to persevere is to live," and an odd poster that said "Bankers Do It With Interest." A computer monitor and keyboard sat on the desk at an angle.

"All I could think about was your call and the number you gave me. It kept eating away at me. The number was familiar but it wasn't, know what I mean?" she said.

"Well, yes—" Katie said.

"At home the other evening while making dinner the number still tickled at my brain. You know when a word is on the tip of your tongue? That's what this felt like. I had that number stuck in my head, and then it hit me. Work it like a puzzle."

"Oh—" Katie tried.

"So I did…I got out a paper and a pen and wrote it ten different ways and finally it occurred to me. Our safe deposit boxes are numbered with four-digit numbers and the customer has the option of adding a six-digit passcode. I haven't been in the retail end of our bank in a couple of years or I would have thought of the safe deposit box the day you called."

"We appreciate you taking—" I attempted.

"So sure enough, the next morning I got here early and opened the safe deposit box roster and praise Jesus!—number 1115 with a six digit passcode."

"And it matches the rest of our number?"

Just when I thought this was going to be easy, she smiled and looked at us. "Well, I can't tell you that unless you are authorized to access to the box. You understand."

"Umm, yes we do. Up until now we weren't sure what

we had. As I mentioned on the phone, this number came from my uncle, Carlo Bocci. We found a paper tucked in with his belongings and weren't sure what it was. This is amazing that you discovered this. Thank you," Katie said.

She was doing great and I let her keep going. "Can you tell us if it belongs to Uncle Carlo?" She said it with such a melodramatic flair I thought she was going to pull a tissue from her purse and dab at her eyes.

"No, I can't, dear. Unless you are authorized as an owner of the safe deposit box."

"Well, any chance my name is on there? Katherine Pitts."

"Ms. Pitts, if you rented a safe deposit box here at First National, I don't think you would be happy with us if we gave out information about your safe deposit box. Would you?"

"Of course not."

I flashed a badge. *My turn to take a shot.* "Mrs. Finley, this is not police business but please understand, we have the best of intentions here. My fiancée here, Ms. Pitts, is struggling with the death of her uncle and we—she—is at a loss on how to proceed. This could be nothing. Who knows? But if you could just give us something to go on, only so we can formulate a plan to resolve this. Is there anything you can tell us? Was Mr. Bocci on the account by himself?"

She smiled. The nonstop talker of a minute ago was now silent.

Katie turned to me. "Must be my cousin, Claire. Got to

be." When Katie said the name Claire I watched as Mrs. Finley's eyes furtively glanced to the computer monitor and then back to us. "Can you tell us if it's Claire? Claire Dixon."

"I'm sorry. I wish I could help, but I can't. Your uncle leave any instructions on how to handle his estate? Does he have a will and an executor?"

"We're finding out that he doesn't," Katie said.

She shook her head. "Pays to be organized. When my Grandpa William passed, took us months to sort out his mess. I'm glad we solved the mystery of the number, but unless you are authorized, I can't help you."

"Mrs. Finley, you have been extremely helpful. We appreciate it and the family does, too," I said. Her smile filled the small office, wall to wall. "But let me ask, should Claire come down here? Would it be worth her while?"

She clicked off her monitor and folded her hands in front of her. "I didn't catch your name?"

"Delarosa, Ma'am."

"Officer Delarosa. You know better than that." I sat back and nodded, smiled at her. "When is the happy occasion?" she asked. Katie and I exchanged a glance. "The wedding?" She smiled at Katie. "You did say fiancée, right?"

"Oh. Yes, yes I did." Katie buried her left hand in her lap under her purse. "We're deciding. It's all a little new at this point."

"Claire, I hope she comes," said Margaret.

Katie hesitated. She went from being intuitive and quick

on her feet at the beginning of the meeting to being a little slow on the uptake.

Mrs. Finley smiled again. "Claire. I hope she comes. To the wedding."

I jumped in. "Oh, yes, we do too. Thank you so much. You've been quite helpful." I stood and grabbed Katie up by the arm. "Shall we, dear? We're back to square one."

We thanked her again, shook hands, and though the bursting bust line was begging for a glance, I looked her straight in the eye and smiled.

41

KATIE AND I SAT IN MY CAR, DISCUSSING WHAT TO do next. After ten minutes I sent her off on an errand and told her to meet me back at the bar. There was now no doubt that I had to bring all the players together to achieve any sort of resolution. I called Claire's phone again but I knew she would not answer. I was not sold that she's being held in exchange for the money, but I now had an idea on how to play this with minimal damage. I hoped. A chain is only as strong as its weakest link and the weak link here was a junkie/drunk who had a bull's-eye on his back and Tony Scarazzini taking aim. If I could persuade Brindisi to listen to me, I could save everyone's life.

I called the phone number Brindisi provided and he didn't answer. I left a message telling him it was critical he call me back. I told him the situation was life or death—his. I also said I would keep my promise and make sure he gets paid. He'd call back. He needed to feed his habit and the big meal tickets promised to him were through me and Rosso.

I went back to City Salvage and a CLOSED sign was on the door but it opened when I pushed. Tony was behind the counter, sitting in his spot but no cigar in his mouth and no sports page in front of him. His eyes were red, grief taking a vise-grip hold around his emotions. Tony would never be the same with Sammy gone.

"I'm going to sell the club," he said, without looking at me.

"Tony, you shouldn't make any decisions on anything right now."

"I'll give Millie a deal. She'll buy it." Millie, a sixty-five-year old, skinny, leather-skinned, functioning drunk, with a pile of thin, bleached-blonde hair on her head, who ran the club for Tony and Sammy. Tony always claimed she was honest and great at handling the girls and the drunks. Tony liked the club because it was an all-cash business, but he hated dealing with employees, strippers no less, and gave Millie free rein on running the place. He paid her well and as long as she had her three martinis every night, she stayed loyal to Tony. She protected the place as if it were her own.

"Give yourself time. Don't do anything for a while."

"What's the point? I always worried that I would go first

and leave Sammy by himself. I never thought he would go first. This is a bitch."

"Tony, you have to give it time."

A customer's tires crunched on the gravel lot outside. "Would you lock the door for me?"

"Sure." I locked the door. We heard the customer approach and then go back to the car and drive off. I also realized I made it harder for me run out in case Tony wanted to end it all and take me with him.

"What would you do?" he said.

I pulled a stool over to the counter and sat across from him. "Tony, I'd want revenge. I would kill anyone in sight who had anything to do with the murder of my brother."

"Good, we're in agreement."

"Tony, we're not killers." He understood what I was saying but looked away. "I want to draw them out and I want you to help me. You'll get justice, but it will be less bloody my way."

"You can't be serious. You put Rosso or the other jerkoff in front of me, I can't be sure what I'll do. Either kill them right away, or wait a few seconds to blow their heads off."

"Tony, listen. What will that get you? Respond to this, yes. But don't react. Besides, we're not sure who did this."

"This all started when you stirred up about the money. And Rosso is back? How did he find out about this?"

"He's part of it. He brought Claire in or she pulled him in."

"You're giving him too much credit. She reached-out to him." He reached under the counter and pulled up a bottle of bourbon and two glasses. "And he brought in Brindisi, who can't keep his mouth shut. You know it." He poured two drinks.

"Yeah, I do," I said. We both downed them and he poured two more.

"Brindisi was in the club the night after Sammy got killed. Is he that stupid? He's running his mouth about him landing a big score. He'll be easy to take apart. Just like he broke Sammy in half, I'll break him in half."

"Tony, there's no doubt in my mind, but you have to be smart about this. Let me take care of this. I'm going to end this real soon."

"We're drinking which means we're friends, but if you bring the cops around, I will come down on you, too."

"No cops until we have to. Work with me, trust me on this." He shook his head. Threw back another shot. "Please?"

"You have one day. Then I go after Rosso first, Brindisi second."

"I'm going to call you in a bit. Need your help tonight. Okay?"

He didn't say a word. Just sat there, staring at the wall as I left. I didn't know whether he would help me or not. If he snapped, there was nothing I could do about that—and I couldn't blame him either.

42

I CALLED BRINDISI'S NUMBER AGAIN WHILE I DROVE, and he answered. "You got yourself in deep, Brindisi," I said.

"How so?"

"You listen to me. Rosso will give you up in a second. If you think he'll cut you in, then you're a bigger moron than I thought."

"Go to hell."

"What was the point of cracking me on the head last night?"

"What are you talking about?" he said, hacking a cigarette cough in the background.

"Where's Rosso holding Claire?"

"Like I said, what are you talking about?"

"Where are you?" He was silent. "Brindisi? Is Rosso there with you?"

"No."

"Where are you?" Again, silence. "You do realize the police are triangulating your position with the cell phones. I'm the only one who can help you now. Where are you?"

I heard voices and music in the background. He didn't say anything for a minute. I guess making an attempt at thinking. "Lucky's."

"Don't move. I'll be there in five minutes. You better be out front." I closed my phone. It didn't matter whether he would be there or not; I only needed to scare the hell out of him. And also remind him he hit the wrong guy on the head last night.

What this case needed from the beginning was luck and I was lucky that I was only a few minutes from Lucky's. A dive bar on the edge of town, it catered to redneck bikers and lowlifes like Brindisi. Harley Davidson fat boys and Ford pickups filled the small, gravel parking lot. I drove in and watched him for a minute as he paced around in a circle, talking on his cell phone. I pulled next to him and he ended his call. I reached across and opened the door. "Get in."

"I don't think."

"You're an accomplice to a kidnapping. Get in. I'm your only way out."

"Son of a bitch, Delarosa."

He got in and I pulled out of the lot. "Who were you talking to?"

"My mother."

"Not the time for you to be cute." I went two blocks and

turned in to an alley that ran along the back of an old, closed-down factory. I stopped the car, threw it into park, got out and went around to his side. I flung open the door, yanked him out by his shirt collar and slammed him against the building. "You try to take my head off last night?"

"No."

I took a step back and smashed a right hook into his jaw. His head snapped around and he crumpled to the ground. I stood him back up and pinned him against the wall. "This is nothing compared to what Tony Scarazzini will do to you."

"Who's he?"

I smacked him against the building again and the little weasel went into one of his repulsive coughing fits. "Jesus, why are you not dead yet?" He was doubled over with his hands on his knees, hacking and gasping for air. I decided to provide him some motivation and brought my right foot up hard into his solar plexus, which landed him on his back. He rolled over and I couldn't tell whether he was choking, screaming, or dying.

His convulsions and spasms subsided after a minute but he was still on his side, curled into a ball. I knelt beside him, gripped his neck and pushed his head into the dirt.

"Let's try this again. Sammy Scarazzini. What happened?"

"An accident," he said, in a raspy, halted voice. "Just supposed to scare him and the idiot stepped out in front of me." I ground his head down harder. "True. I swear. I didn't want to hurt nobody."

I got up and he rolled over on his back. "Get up."

He crawled on all fours for a few feet, leaving a trail of blood and saliva that dripped from his mouth. He made his way to my car, pulled himself up using the open passenger door and plopped down on the seat with his feet hanging out of the car.

"Don't get blood on my car. Where's Rosso?"

"No idea." He wiped his mouth and face with his sleeve. "Fuck, man, you didn't have to do that."

"Yeah, I did. Just be happy it's me and not Tony. Now, where's Rosso?"

"He don't tell me nothing."

I slammed the car door against his knees and he yelped in pain. "Try again."

"I swear. I always met him at this shit-hole motel where he works. Harbor something…"

"And he just called you after all these years?"

"He was in a bar one night. A couple of weeks ago. I kind of recognized him but wasn't sure. He looks different. Then I realize it is him and he remembers me. He starts talking about some big score he has going down. All secret. A few days go by and he calls me and asks if I want some work. Like the old days." He winced, grabbed his side. "I think you broke my rib."

"Consider that as getting off easy." He bent over, putting his head in his lap, and hugged his ribs. "Hey." He lifted his head and his face was pale, more pale than usual. I must have hurt him but I didn't care. "I want a meeting with Rosso. Tonight. Do you have a phone number?"

"He would call from the motel."

"Here's the deal. You set up a meeting with Rosso. Tell him I have what he wants in exchange for Claire. You do that and I'll keep Tony Scarazzini from breaking you in two. And after tonight, my advice for you is to be on the first bus out of town."

"What if I can't?"

"You'll be begging for a broken rib."

I yanked him out of my car and threw him to the ground.

He moaned, rolled around, and then struggled to his feet. "I won't forget this, Delarosa."

"I want to hear from you in one hour."

"I can't call him. He always calls me."

"One hour. You'll find a way."

He staggered down the alley; every few yards he would turn around and look at me. I stood beside my car and waited until he got to the end and turned on the street toward Lucky's.

He'd call.

43

I PULLED INTO THE HARBOR COURT MOTEL PARKING lot twenty minutes after leaving Brindisi staggering his way down an alley. I hustled to the office and went in with my old police badge held out in front of me. Leaning on the front counter was an overweight young woman in her twenties, with stringy, mousey-brown hair, wearing gray sweatpants and a white tank-top that barely covered her black bra and beer gut. She looked up from her phone and I didn't give her a chance.

"Detective Delarosa. I'm looking for Karl Boyd. Is he here?"

"Umm, no." She put her phone on the counter.

"Where is he?"

"I—I'm not sure. I'm actually filling in for him."

"Do you know where he lives?"

"Yeah. Here."

"He lives here?"

"In the back apartment." She jerked her thumb over her shoulder. "He's the manager."

"What's your name?"

"Candy."

"Well, Candy. Which way is the apartment?"

"Right there." She pointed to the office. Off the front desk area was a small office, and on the back wall of the office was another door. "He's not in there."

"Mind if I knock myself?"

"Well, I don't think—"

"Thanks." I went around the counter, through the office and pounded on the apartment door. "Boyd? PCPD." I waited a few moments and knocked again. Nothing happened.

"I told you." Candy had come back to the apartment. "Don't you need a warrant or something? I don't think you can just come in here."

"Is that what you think?" I said. "What if I said you are impeding a criminal investigation?"

"Umm…"

"If I bring a warrant, it allows me to search your purse, too. Is there anything in there you don't want me to find?" Her dull, brown eyes went wide and a dumbfounded expression took over her face. "So were okay, then?"

"Uh huh."

"Boyd, PCPD." I pounded on the door. I never expected to find him. Boyd/Rosso living at the Harbor Court explained why Katie couldn't find an address for him. I did hope the Mensa candidate behind the counter would tell him the cops were after him. It might work.

I followed Candy out to the front desk and the word PINK was written across her wide ass in large, purple block letters. Designer wear for the ghetto set?

"Do you have a cell phone number for him?"

"No, only the number here. I only call him here. I just started a week ago. He told me he needed part-time help 'cause he has some other job."

"Okay, tell him Delarosa was looking for him."

She picked up a pad and a pen. "How do you spell that?"

"You'll figure it out." I had already broken all kinds of "impersonating an officer" laws, so I split. I turned back as I got into my car and she was still writing.

I called Brindisi while driving back to McNally's and he answered on the first ring. "Your hour is up."

"I told you, he calls me."

"Not good enough."

"Delarosa, c'mon. All I do is to go around the motel where he works, and I can't do that."

"Why?"

"He has my car."

"The Lincoln is yours?"

"Yeah, and I need it. Man, this is not going how I expected. I'm steppin' out of this. If you find him, tell him

I need my car back."

"Not happening, Little Al. You're in this whether you like it or not. It's only a matter of time before the cops make the Lincoln as the car that ran down Sammy. Be smart, Brindisi. I told you I can help you, but only if you help me." The noise and clatter of a bar played in the background. He was probably still at Lucky's. "You hear me?"

"Yeah."

"Put me in touch with Rosso. You have thirty minutes." I ended the call.

I pulled into the alley behind McNally's, parked the car in the garage and went in through the back. I no sooner sat in the booth beside Katie and my phone rang. It was Brindisi and exactly twenty-nine minutes since I gave him a thirty-minute deadline to call me.

"Just telling you I can't locate him. Like I said, he calls me."

"Meet me in the alley behind Club Cuba tonight at eleven. Make sure Rosso is with you."

"Why, to get beat up again? I don't think."

"If you can't find Rosso, at least save yourself. And I'm your savior." I hung up.

"Was that Brindisi?" asked Katie.

"Yep. The poor sap is scared and doesn't know who or what to believe. How did you do on Boyd?"

"Nothing on one Karl Boyd. No criminal records, no traffic tickets, nothing. No real estate."

"Because he doesn't exist. He's Rosso. You won't find anything. What about Brindisi?"

She pulled a file out of her pile and opened it.

"We could paper a room with his rap sheet. Every little crime you can think of. Nothing big, though. He's never done any time."

"Address?"

"Says no known address."

"Not surprised. How did you do on your errand? Did you find anything?"

"You'll be pleased."

"Perfect. Now, I need to think through how much I want you involved."

"No thinking. I'm ready."

"I'll decide. I'm going up to the condo for a bit. Wrap it up here and come up and we'll talk."

I got upstairs and realized I hadn't eaten anything all day. In the fridge were three beers, a few slices of Genoa salami, and a half pound of provolone cheese that was two days past its sell-by date. I ate the salami and cheese and drank a beer. I craved a bourbon, but I needed to keep a clear head.

Katie came up and after we went through the plan for the night, I sent her home for the rest of the day and told her to meet back at my place at ten. I made two more calls and reassured myself that the plan would at least motivate Brindisi—or scare the hell out of him. I didn't worry about him turning tail and running, either. He had no money and no place to go. His circle of influence didn't have a big circumference.

I stretched out on the sofa with my hands behind my head. Rosso made a mistake pulling in the gutter-dweller Brindisi. Rosso (or Claire?) needed someone to handle the grunt work in exchange for enough cash to fuel his habits, but he forgot that Brindisi's loyalty was like a dog's. The dog was loyal to whoever fed him. All I had to do was offer Brindisi a better doggy-treat.

44

AT NINE O'CLOCK, I WALKED THE ALLEY BEHIND Club Cuba to do a quick reconnaissance. I did not want to leave anything to chance. Rosso and his boys got the jump on me at Pier 21 and I would not allow that again.

The alley ran north/south, divided the block in half, and was only wide enough for a trash truck to get through. Each store and restaurant on the block had a trash bin next to their back door with a light above it. The lights cast angular shadows from the trash bins that set an eerie film-noir mood that any Hollywood director would think perfect for the business at hand. The stores would be closed by our meeting time; only Club Cuba and one other restaurant on the north end of the block would be open. I did not want any unnecessary traffic to interfere with my intervention of Little Al.

Feeling comfortable on how I wanted to position myself and my surprise guest, I walked around the block and went into the front entrance of Club Cuba. It was crowded as usual, with Leah greeting patrons as if they were the only ones that night. She greeted each client—she called them clients—not able to shake the individual attention of her old profession—and led them to a table and took their initial drink order. She treated the clients as if they were guests in her house and the clients responded. Club Cuba was busier than ever, and Leah loved it. She was in her element. The club fulfilled her with a career and a passion. There was not enough room in her life for the club and me, and that suited me fine—for now.

She spotted me as I entered and I pointed to the bar. I sat near the end but ordered a ginger ale. No booze to cloud the night. A few minutes later, Leah came over and I followed her to the office. She closed the door and we embraced.

"Twice in a week," she said. "What have I done to deserve this?"

"You've been your gorgeous self."

"I don't believe that." She pushed me down into an office chair, hiked up her royal-blue dress and straddled me. She put her arms around my neck and her face next to mine. "I loved seeing you the other night. Please tell me you're here because you missed me," she whispered, as she kissed my neck.

"What if someone comes in?"

"I asked you a question."

She kept up the kissing and my hands traveled up and down her back. "Of course I miss you. And I loved seeing you. But…"

"You can't stand to be apart from me…" She kissed me lightly on the lips, and then back on my neck.

"Of course that's true…but…"

"You want me more than anything in the world…"

"Yes but…"

"What?" Her hand went to my lap. "There is only one reason you would be here tonight, right?"

"Of course. You're the love of my life, but…" And she *was* the love of my life and I loved it when she got into this teasing, playful mood.

"But, what? Are these questions—hard?" She gave me a squeeze.

"Very." My eyes rolled back in my head.

"What do we do about that?" She kissed the other side of my neck and nibbled on my ear. The strategy I worked out to draw out Rosso and save Brindisi at the same time was fleeing my head.

"Don't you have customers out there?"

"I'd say I have my hands full at the moment."

"Okay—I have business here tonight." I pushed her up and off me. I stood up and she laughed.

She pointed at the front of my pants. "What, are you going to stab somebody with that?" She threw her head back in a laugh, the beautiful eyes and smile filling my soul.

"Are you happy now?" I said, in all my bulging glory.

"Seems like *you're* the one who's happy."

"Funny. As much as I would like to continue, I need to fill you in on tonight's business." Club Cuba had an upscale clientele so there was never much rough stuff. An occasional drunk to toss out was the most trouble they had, but Leah kept her "strong arms"—that's what she called them—around to keep the peace. The strong arms, all former military guys, had a ninja-like knack for staying invisible. If some idiot got out of line or got loud, these guys magically appeared and quelled the situation. She paid them well and they stayed loyal. Tonight, I needed the strong arms ready, and invisible, in case my plan went the wrong way. I gave her the run-down and she was happy to supply some back-up. *Just keep it out of the club.*

She stepped up to me and planted a long, passionate kiss full on my mouth. "Come back when you can stay awhile."

"I'm thinking you and I go away on a long vacation as soon as this job is over."

"You know where to find me." She left me alone in the office.

I made another call and then went to the alley to wait.

I had a position next to a trash bin at the mid-point of the alley. Both entrances to the alley were covered by Leah's "strong arms." We would have eyes on Brindisi no matter which way he came in. At 10:50, we coordinated our watches. We agreed to abort if he did not show by

11:30. The throbbing pulse from the band in the club vibrated into the alley. Voices from couples or groups of folks leaving the restaurants would echo off the buildings, and at two minutes before eleven, a teenage couple walked into the alley, only to be intercepted by one of the strong arms. I could not hear what he told them, but they scurried out like scared cats.

At 11:05, Brindisi's slight silhouette appeared at the end of the alley. He shuffled a few steps—*was he drunk or high?*— and then stopped and leaned against a building. Damn, I wanted him sober for this party. I stepped out from my spot to let him see me. After a minute, he regained his shuffle and headed my way. A worker from the restaurant on the north end came out with two bags of trash and startled Brindisi. The worker sized him up for a second, and then threw away the trash and went back inside.

Brindisi straightened himself. I waved him on. He stopped ten feet from me and I took a few steps toward him.

"No. Stay right there," he said, his voice slurred. He was half-juiced and that worried me.

"Fair enough," I said. "Glad you came."

"They'll kill me if they know I'm here."

"Where are they? Where does he have Claire?"

"I told you. He calls me when he needs something."

"You're being played. He used you."

"He'll pay me."

"You better think long and hard. If he's holding Claire

against her will, you're an accomplice to kidnapping. Those boys in federal prison will love you. They'll pass you around like a dessert."

"What he has going with the girl is his business. As soon as he pays me, I'm outta here."

"Is that what you think?" I sent a quick text on my phone. "Pay attention, my friend." Fifteen seconds later, a car pulled into the south end of the alley and stopped. The driver's door opened and Mike got out. Brindisi shielded his eyes from the bright headlights. "See that guy?"

"I'm trying."

"He's my partner. He picked up Claire an hour ago. But no Rosso. Game's over, Brindisi."

"Bluffing."

"You sure? Where's Rosso?"

"Already told you. I would meet him at the motel when he calls me." He couldn't stand still. He shuffled around, would stuff his hands in his pockets, pull them out, and stick them in again. "I came here like you asked. Are we done?"

"Not quite." I waved to Mike. He reached into the car and cut the lights. The passenger side door opened and she stepped out. The light in the alley picked up the long auburn hair. She stood beside the car for a minute and then got back in.

"Are you shittin' me?"

"We have Claire. Now, where's Rosso?"

"Fuck, man. He told me this would be a score. He said she had big money coming." He was going in circles. "I need that money. Oh, man…" He fell to his knees. "I can't believe this."

"Where do I find him?"

"I—I think I may…wait…"

I pulled him back up to his feet and propped him against a trash bin.

"C'mon, Brindisi."

"Wait—if you have the girl, why do you want him? This is over."

"Not quite. If Tony gets to him first, it's just more dead bodies. Including yours."

"You cannot let him know I told you."

"I won't. And I'll help you get out of this."

His breathing was heavy and he was sweating through his clothes. He needed a drink or a fix or both. I stuck five twenties into his hand and I thought he was going to kiss me.

"Supposed to meet at Eighth Street Café at eight tomorrow morning."

"Stay clear. Go hide somewhere and come around my place in a few days." The hundred bucks in his pocket put some steam in his step and I watched as he got to the end of the alley and turned the corner.

I waved to Mike and he pulled the car forward. I yelled a "*Thanks, guys*" to Leah's men and slid into the back seat of the car. "You look good as a redhead."

Katie turned to me from the front seat. "Damn right."

45

THE EIGHTH STREET CAFÉ WAS IN THE LOBBY OF an old five-story office building with a small parking lot to the left of the front entrance. I parked on the opposite side of the street a block from the café and gave myself a vantage point from where I could observe.

Eight o'clock came and went. No sign of Rosso or Brindisi or the big Lincoln. It was approaching 8:20. Decision time. Giving Brindisi the money last night could have blown the entire plan. He might be on a bus to nowhere by now but I discounted that idea. Money in his pocket meant a drink or a fix, not a bus ticket. Or, he realized what he did and had second thoughts and told Rosso to try to save himself. Or they were just late, which was the case.

The Lincoln pulled into the lot. Rosso got out with another man, the goon who held Claire by the hair at our last meeting on the pier. No sign of Brindisi. I watched as they walked into the café. Brindisi not showing up was a bad sign. Did he give up Rosso and split town, or was he curled up in a gutter somewhere, or in a corner of a squalid room in a downtown flop house? Or did Rosso get wise to Brindisi and decide to plug the leak by taking him on an early morning fishing trip in the harbor?

I clicked the 300mm lens on my Nikon and focused on the café window. The glare from the early morning sun reflecting off office building windows made it difficult to see through the café glass, but I was positive it was them at a table. Rosso's long gray ponytail was a dead giveaway.

It was show time. Surprise was the credo to live by so I put on a ball cap and sunglasses and got out of the car. I stayed on the opposite side of the street and walked a block past the café, crossed, and then came back to the café, keeping an eye on the door. I went in and both men were at the table as I saw them, engaged in conversation. The place was more of a deli combined with a gas station-convenience store. You could order a sandwich from a deli counter that was so dirty you could trace your figure through the grime, play the lottery, and buy a pack of smokes, the newspaper, or a six-pack. It was only open through lunch and was really a hangout for the old-timers to kill a morning because they had nothing else to do while waiting to die. The place had eight tables and all were full. I wanted it crowded; less chance for them to make a scene.

I stopped at the coffee counter, drew off a cup and had to wait for three ahead of me to pay the clerk. Which was fine; it gave me time to survey the interior and I noted a side door in case I needed to make a quick exit. If they spotted me, they didn't react.

I walked to their table, pulled out a chair and sat down, taking off my sunglasses and looking Rosso in the eye. "Surprise." The goon was to my left and instinctively slid back; I slipped a hand inside my jacket. "Don't even." Both guys were tall: Rosso skinny but fit; the goon had some beef on him. The last thing I wanted was to tangle.

"Well, isn't this interesting." Rosso stayed calm but his eyes darted around the room. He must have wondered whether I was alone or whether Brindisi was with me.

"Beautiful morning, isn't it?"

"What do you want?" Rosso lowered his hands to his lap.

"No, no. Hands on the table, both of you. We don't want to make a scene in this fine establishment now, do we?" He brought his hands back up. So did the goon. "I thought I'd hear from you by now?"

"Got the money?"

"Maybe. Where's Claire?"

"Safe and sound. Waiting on you to deliver."

"You know that's a tough order, right?"

"You'll come through. Or the pretty redhead gets dead. Very simple."

"Not easy finding a half-million dollars that went missing thirty years ago. That money is long gone."

The goon piped in. "Half-million—"

"Shut up," Rosso snapped. "Nice try. More like two

million."

"That what she told you when she found you?"

"She didn't find me. I found her. And I was there when it happened."

"You know you have a Scarazzini problem."

"Don't know what you're talking about."

"Tell that to Tony the Scar. And this business with Claire, no matter who found who, just exposed you—Boyd."

"Don't matter. With my share, I'll be long gone."

An older couple sitting at the next table turned and looked at us and we both noticed. "Why don't we continue this outside?" I threw a twenty on the table. "See that side door? Go out that way and to your car. Or should I say Brindisi's car?"

Rosso nodded to the goon and they got up. I followed them out to the Lincoln.

"Let's wrap this up, Rosso."

"You have what I want?"

"Need proof she's okay."

"You got my word."

"I don't think. Prove Claire's okay and we get on with things. No proof, then I make a call and you go down for Sammy Scarazzini." He scanned around the lot. Picked at something in his teeth, folded his arms across his chest. "Proof."

He took out his cell and dialed. He spoke into the phone. "Put her on." A moment went by. "Tell Delarosa you're okay." He handed me the phone.

"Claire?"

"Johnny, oh my God."

"Are you okay?"

"I'm okay but you got to get—"

Rosso grabbed the phone from me and ended the call. "Happy?"

"No. I need to talk to her. In person. She hired me, not you," I said.

"We're way past that now. The money?"

"I might. But I want Claire. How about the three of us meet? Sort this out before it all goes real bad. Don't be stupid. Tony Scarazzini has all the motivation he needs to end this now. That includes me."

He pulled out a pack of smokes and lit one up. Threw the match on the ground and then opened the car door.

"Tonight. Midnight. Back at Pier 21. Bring the money."

"You bring the girl."

They both got into the car and drove off. I walked across the street to my car and my mind flashed to Brindisi. Poor guy. I promised I would protect him if he connected me with Rosso and he came through on his end of the deal. I called his phone but no answer. My sixth sense was tapping on my brain, like a Morse code operator sending an SOS. I hoped Brindisi was still a member of the human race.

46

I CALLED MARCO TO ASK FOR A FAVOR, AND HE CAME through like a champ. He wanted to be part of tonight's rendezvous and I agreed on one condition: he had to put the badge away until I saw what we were facing with the Rosso and Claire show. Was it possible that Rosso flipped on Claire and was holding her? My instincts said no but anything was possible on this gig.

I met Marco and Mike on Pier 3 at midnight. Marco arranged through a friend to have a twelve-foot sailboat waiting to take me to Pier 21. I wanted to arrive at Pier 21 via the water, avoid the access road, and secure a position before Rosso and his merry men showed. They got the drop on me two nights ago; I refused to be put into a defensive posture a second time.

An ex-cop named Tolliver owned the boat. Marco made quick introductions but I didn't catch his first name and it didn't matter. Tolliver had the sail down and had mounted an 8-horse power electric trolling motor on the back of the boat. A thick cloud cover hung low and obscured any moonlight. Lights from the piers reflected off the water and provided the only sight-navigation points other than yellow buoys, topped with a single flashing red light, anchored in the middle of the harbor. Tolliver and I cast off from the dock and into rough water, the result of the overcast sky and approaching weather. The chop in the water muffled the hum from the almost silent motor—which was the idea: to go in without a sound.

Marco and Mike stayed back at Pier 3, ready to move in, if and when I called. Once I had a visual on Claire, I signal Marco, and he closes in with some uniforms. Rosso collared on kidnapping and abduction, leaving me to figure out my red-headed client and what is left of this case.

The trip to Pier 21 took fifteen minutes. We stayed three hundred yards out from the piers and without a bigger engine to power through the choppy waves, it took everything Tolliver had—muscle and concentration—to keep us on a steady course. He did not say a word. He understood his job and it didn't include talking. He was to take me out to the pier and get himself back as quickly as possible without being seen or heard. Pier 21 was the last pier on the north end of the Harbor and designed for use by the PCPD Harbor Division and the Coast Guard. It was the only pier with a dock customized for smaller water craft.

Tolliver circled wide in the harbor before angling back

to the pier. He guided the small boat to a dock and when we nestled in, he pointed to a ladder. I grabbed the first rung I could reach, hoisted myself out of the boat and climbed up. I turned around and he was in reverse clearing the dock. I gave him a wave, he nodded back and then disappeared into the black.

The small dock led up to the larger pier deck but there was still a chain link fence between me and the harbor access road. A gate in the fence was marked for police and Coast Guard access only, but Marco came through for me again with the security code. I punched the code into a key pad and the gate clicked open.

I came up on the access road thirty yards from the meeting location. The wind picked up and a light rain began to spit down. I checked my watch: 10:45. An hour and fifteen minutes early. I stopped and stood motionless for ten minutes, listening for anything that would alert me to someone else waiting in the dark. The crunch of a footstep on the roadside gravel, the beep of a cell phone, a muffled cough or sneeze, or the click of a lighter: it's hard to stay silent. The wind picked up and the rain came down hard and steady. I found a small alcove near the door of a garage used for several forklifts and huddled there. I turned up the collar of my jacket and sent Mike and Marco a text telling them I was in place.

At eleven-fifteen, Harbor security rolled by on their rounds, not bothering to slow or even glance at the pier. The wind and rain made this a night to go through the motions. At eleven-thirty, just as I drifted to thoughts of a smooth bourbon warming my stomach, headlights appeared on the access road. The headlights went from two to four as they drew closer. Two cars. I sent another text: *company*.

Brindisi's Lincoln came to a stop on the side of the access road across from the Pier 21 entrance. The second car, a dark-colored Mercedes, stopped beside the Lincoln. The driver of the Lincoln got out and hopped into the passenger side of the Mercedes. I thought it might be the goon from the café this morning but I could not be sure in the rain. The Mercedes hooked a U-turn and sped off down the access road. The Lincoln sat on the shoulder of the road, illuminated by a street arc-light, like an actor at center stage under the spotlight. Rain blew through the light like shiny crystals as I stared at the car. *Did I approach or was the car a prop waiting for the show to begin?* I sent a text to Marco and Mike explaining what happened.

They responded: *Do not approach*. They were right. It was not midnight, so I decided to wait.

The sirens were first and then red and blue flashes lit up the pier. Two cars at first followed by two more. Two PCPD officers from each car jumped out and surrounded the Lincoln, weapons drawn. They shined flashlights into the car while one officer ran back to his cruiser and grabbed a crowbar from his car. He came back to the Lincoln and used the tool to pop open the trunk. They all took a step back; then, cautiously, they all came closer to the car and peered into the trunk. Something told me it was not an expensive set of luggage they were examining.

One officer quipped, "Dead all right. Call it in." My heart sank as the hairs on the back of my neck stood up. The officers huddled together and I knew what they were saying because I was the officer doing the talking in my previous life. *Decision time.* Their next order of business would be to notify the coroner's office, cordon off the area, and then begin a search. I can't move from here without them seeing me. If they discover me hiding, then I'm rung up as suspect number one. If I come forward, I might have a chance to get out in front of this and save myself. I sent a text to Mike and Marco. *Cops on scene. Need help.*

I stepped out from my alcove with my hands in the air. "Officer. Name's Delarosa. I'm retired from the job." The officers all instinctively reacted with guns drawn. I had eight 9mm Glocks pointed at me.

"Down on the ground—now."

I did not hesitate and went to my knees as they surrounded me. They pushed me flat on the pavement; they pulled my arms around my back and slipped a zip-tie around my wrists and pulled it tight.

"I'm on a job. I can explain." They yanked me to my feet, patted me down and took my Beretta. "Name's Delarosa..."

Two officers were holding me when a third got in my face.

"You're on a job? What kind of job?" the officer yelled. He had sergeant stripes on his sleeve.

"I'm ex-PCPD. Now a private investigator. Supposed to

meet a guy here."

"What's this guy's name?"

"Brindisi." *Can't give up Rosso just yet.* "I have a bad feeling it might be him in the trunk."

"How do you know what's in the trunk?"

"I don't but—"

"What *do* you know?"

"The car. It's Brindisi's."

The sergeant glanced around at the other officers. "You have any ID?"

"Of course. Jacket pocket." One officer reached in and fished out my wallet. He went through it, found my private investigator's license and my PCPD retired card and handed them to the sergeant.

"You want to explain what you're doing here?"

My mind raced—I didn't want to explain Claire and the money and the entire case but, I needed to come up with something legit. "This guy Brindisi was flipping evidence in a case I'm working on."

"What case?"

"Why don't we take these cuffs off and I'm happy to help?"

"Why don't I decide what we do?" offered the sergeant.

Another car pulled up to the scene and thank God, it was Marco and Mike. Marco got out and had his badge in front of him. "Who's in charge?" he asked.

A uniform guy pointed to a sergeant. The sergeant met him halfway. They talked for a minute and both came over to me.

"Is it Brindisi?" asked Marco.

"I haven't looked in," I said. The sergeant had two uniforms cops walk me over to the Lincoln. It was Brindisi all right. A beat-to-a-pulp version of Brindisi anyhow. His skull had a fatal four-inch gash and blood covered most of his head and face. "It's him."

The sergeant faced me. "Detective here says you're legit, but I still got to take you in."

Marco nodded at me and I knew the sergeant had no choice. "Tell Mike to call Jim Rosswell."

"Will do, buddy."

The uniformed officer grabbed my elbow to move me but I was fixated on Brindisi. He was a foul, repulsive example of a human being. A junkie, gutter-dweller, lived in the margins, and now dead in the trunk of his own car. The same car he used to kill Sammy. Maybe karma does have a place in the world.

47

I DROVE IN A POLICE CRUISER THOUSANDS OF TIMES over my twenty-year career but last night was the first time I was in the back seat. I have been in the city's main lock-up thousands of times but today was the first time I'd seen the view from the inside of a cell looking out. No fun.

I went through processing at two o'clock in the morning. Mug shot and finger prints. I wasn't charged with anything yet but they had plenty to hold me. I understood the sergeant on the scene last night had no choice. He had a dead body in the trunk of a car and me hiding in the shadows. A rookie cop would have locked me up, too.

My home away from home was ten-by-ten holding cell with benches along the three walls and a toilet in a corner. I sat upright with my back against a wall the entire night. I tried to sleep but the other customer in my cell, an old wino who was passed out on the opposite bench, snored so loud sleep was out of the question. He also wet himself in the middle of the night while trying to find the toilet so the cell reeked of urine. It was one of those odors that gets in your nose and doesn't leave.

I played the entire case back through my mind. Rosso got wise to Claire's quest from his step-mother Elena Garver, and, what? Suggested Claire use the Harbor Court as home base for the operation? Why would she do that? She had me on the search, why involve anyone else? I'm thinking Rosso injected himself into her plan and was holding her to make sure he got his slice of the pie. He sends me warnings to let me know he's a tough guy, involves Brindisi to do dirty work, and then kills him to tie up the loose end?

The old wino fell off the bench and landed on the floor with a thud. I called to the duty officer. "You got a man down in here."

Thirty feet away the officer grunted as he got up and moved his chocolate-frosted fueled body down the hall. He got to the cell and observed the scene. "Is he breathing?"

"Appears to be."

"Call me when something serious happens." He waddled back to his desk.

The jail got busier as the morning progressed. It's usually the case after the bars close down and people lose their minds. Two guys were brought in on DUI charges and thrown into the cell across from me, and a woman argued to the duty officer that she was not a hooker and it was all a misunderstanding. *Life's a misunderstanding, dear. Good luck.*

The fat duty officer slid in a tray of breakfast around seven: a cold piece of toast, oatmeal that tasted like concrete, and a cup of lukewarm coffee. *Talk about police brutality.* Mike and Katie came in at eight. Mike knew the duty officer, a Sergeant Peterson, and he allowed them back to visit me.

"It stinks in here." Katie had a frown on her face that said she couldn't wait to get out of the place.

Me too.

"Tell me about it."

"You look like shit," Mike said. "Get any sleep?"

I pointed to the drunk, who was still sawing logs.

"Jim?"

"He's on his way. Marco said he's coming, too. Try to spring you out without too much hassle. Raised a lot of questions last night."

"I'm sure."

"Rosso? Any idea where he is?"

"No. Any luck with Claire's phone?" Katie had her hand cupped over her nose and mouth.

"I called but it goes straight to voice mail. Must be turned off," she said, through her hand. "Anything else I can do?"

I shook my head. "I was thinking of getting a tracker on Brindisi's car but too late for that. If I can keep the cops away for another night or two, we'll hear from Rosso. He can't drag this out any longer. Brindisi's death will point to

Rosso."

The wino let go of a long, loud fart.

"I'm done." Katie flew out of the cell area. It was too disgusting to even laugh.

"All right, keep the faith. Peterson said he'd call me when something happens," said Mike. "I'm headed back."

"What about Claire's credit cards?"

"Ask Marco. He'll have to keep it quiet, though."

"Okay. At least it's an idea."

Mike left and I leaned back against the wall and slept for twenty minutes. I woke to the sound of Marco's voice. He was at the duty desk but I couldn't make out what he was saying. After a minute, he came back to the cell.

"You're leaving a trail of dead bodies, old friend."

"Marco." I got up and talked to him through the bars. "Find anything?"

"Only that everywhere you go we find a dead body."

"Did they process the car?"

"Yep. Didn't find one fingerprint."

"No way."

"Smelled like bleach. They sanitized it. Good for you, though. No physical evidence to tie you to Brindisi."

"They find a cell phone on him?"

"Nope. Nothing. Only one beat-to-a-pulp little junkie. You want to tell me what's going on?"

"Who tipped the cops last night?"

"Harbor police got an anonymous call about a body in a trunk."

"Unreal."

I had no way around this now. Rosso kills Brindisi—calls in the anonymous tip—and leaves him for me so I'm jammed. Didn't he realize that will shine the light on him? No telling what this dog would do. He stayed one step ahead of me now for a week, but I had to clue in Marco at this point—and beg him for one more day.

"Rosso. Remember, from thirty years ago? He's back."

"He's back in Port City? I told you the money would uncover the worst of the worst?"

"He's been in Port City. Goes by Karl Boyd. Manages a motel on Harbor Boulevard owned by his step-mother, Elena Garver. Which means he and my client, Claire, are cousins. Sort of. He's holding her till the money comes through."

"Damn. Holding her?"

"I think. He wants the money—says he's entitled. Says he'll release her when I come up with the missing two mill."

"That's kidnapping for ransom."

"But something tells me they're a team. I need to force his—or her—hand. Somehow."

"Did you actually find the money?"

"Maybe."

"Johnny…?"

"We have a lead, not confirmed."

"I'll be damned."

"Claire's credit cards. Can you run them?"

"Man—I don't know…"

"We have dead bodies. Probable cause."

"All right. I'll see."

Jim Rosswell walked in—my attorney, friend, golfing buddy. "Well, isn't this a mess— Jesus, it stinks in here." He turned to Marco. "Is that you?"

"It stinks like that when lawyers walk in."

"Could we cut the playful repartee? Jim, give me some good news, please."

"You're out of here within the hour. Officially a person of interest. The DA wants to interview you later this afternoon."

"Can you get me out of that?"

"I'm your attorney. Not a magician."

"You guys can take it from here. I'll check with you later." Marco left. Jim came closer to the bars, out of any earshot of the duty officer.

"Are you clean on this?"

"Yes. Brindisi was a CI on a case. He got caught up."

"Okay. I'll take your word. I'll meet you at three at the DA's office."

Jim left and thirty minutes later, I got sprung. I signed some documents and they handed me my wallet and phone. I got outside to find Katie waiting for me in her car in front of the building. I got in the passenger seat.

She put the car in gear but paused and lowered all four windows. "I can still smell it. I hope the stink doesn't stay in my car."

"Please drive." I laid my head back, closed my eyes and prayed for sleep.

48

WE GOT BACK TO MCNALLY'S, I WENT UP TO MY condo and poured a bourbon and allowed it to burn in my stomach as the hot shower burned my skin. I had the water as hot as I could stand it and feared it was not hot enough to ever get the stink off my skin and out of my nose. I toweled off, got dressed and went down to the bar. The warm aroma of fresh brewed coffee felt like a blanket wrapped around me and Mike, bless his soul, had scrambled eggs and toast ready. Katie stared at me while I ate. "What?"

"Since I started working for you, I've been on a stakeout, learned about GPS tracking, posed as a hooker to get information, pretended my uncle died to get access to his safe deposit box, stripped to my underwear to break into a hotel room, walked in on you having sex, and seen the inside of a jail."

"Told you it was boring."

"And it's only been one week. Just wanted to say thank-you."

"This is not a typical—"

"I know. Not a typical job. You keep saying that."

"So now that you gained all this experience, what do we do next?"

"We review. Claire is kidnapped by Rosso so he can get his share of the loot. But, we don't have any leads on the money except for Mrs. Finley at First National."

"Right. And don't forget, we're not sure that Rosso is holding Claire. They could be working together," I added.

We were sitting at the booth. She nodded and went back to her files which she now had in a fancy file box from an office supply store. An upgrade from my cardboard box.

"She hires you to find the money. Then all these other goom—what'd you call them…?"

"Goombahs. An Italian mob…"

"I know, I watched *The Sopranos.* Goombahs come around looking for their share."

"Only Rosso. Remember, Tony warned me to not dig around for money. What he said is exactly what happened and now Sammy is dead."

"And now Brindisi."

"Yep, Brindisi. Too bad, but he was on the fast-track to his two-by-six apartment anyhow."

"Two-by-six?"

"Coffin."

She smirked and crinkled her nose. "I guess I need to

learn these street terms."

"You will. Pull out everything we—you—have on Boyd/Rosso. He's gotta be somewhere and I want to find him before he contacts me again. He's not going to let this go past another night, though."

"How do you know that?"

"Cops are involved now. Matter of time before they find him. He's been one step ahead of me; he knows he's now on the clock. Time is now on our side."

"What about the money? He's going to want something. He won't give her up without the money."

"You're right." I finished the breakfast and gathered up my plate and went to the bar, fixed two drinks—my usual and a small vodka tonic—and brought them back to the table. "Short one for you."

"Good idea."

"What are we missing?"

She sipped the drink while she thought. "We don't know where they are. Brindisi is gone. So is his car. Rosso must have other guys working for him, right?"

"Right." My intuition about her was correct and it was good to have two brains on this. Rosso had been one step ahead of me for two nights now. My turn to be in front.

"The only thing we discovered was who his step-mother is and—hey, could they be staying there?"

"No. I checked on that. Too obvious. People would spot them. They're holed up somewhere."

"Well, we need to find something, so…we go back to the motel?"

"Not bad."

We got to the Harbor Court and burst through the front door with my badge held high, like I did with Candy-girl. This time the big black guy was working. I wore a jacket and jeans and Katie had on slacks and a blouse. At least we looked the part. "Detective Delarosa and this is Detective Smith. Looking for Karl Boyd."

"He's not here."

"Where is he?"

"He's on vacation. Been gone about a week." He talked to me but kept glancing at Katie.

"What's your name?"

"Maurice. Maurice Myers. I'm the assistant manager."

The TV blared out some mindless drivel from one of the afternoon shows where a bunch of pseudo-celebrity women sit around and talk about the issues of the day, as if they were some kind of experts. "Could you turn that off?" asked Katie.

"Sure, sure." He looked back at Katie while he picked up the remote and clicked off the TV. "Don't I know you?"

"No," she said.

He stared at her; his eyes went to the counter and he fidgeted with some papers. He knew.

"Who's he hang around with? Any scumbags come around here?"

"Look, I don't want to be mixed up in anything—"

"Maurice." Katie's voice went up, stern and strong. "We're investigating Mr. Boyd—and you know that's not his real name, right?—on some serious charges. I suggest you tell us anything you know or you'll never get that promotion to manager."

Damn, I was impressed.

"Boyd's not his real name?"

"Can you say witness protection?"

Maurice's eyes got wide. "Really?"

"So if the cops don't find him, you-know-who will. And if you-know-who gets here first, do you think they will care about you?" I said.

He shook his head. "Umm, lately this little slimy guy would come around. Drove a big Lincoln."

"Yeah, he made an untimely exit last night."

"You don't say?" His eyebrows shot up.

"Who else?"

"Umm, the only other guy I ever saw was this big white dude. Called him Mouse, I think. Yeah, Mouse."

"Mouse?" Katie took out a pad and wrote it down.

"Yeah, but I think his name was like Moskowski. Something like that. I heard Boyd say that once. He would pick Boyd up when his shift was over."

"What kind of car did he drive?"

"Mouse? Mercedes. Like twenty years old. One of those big boxy ones."

"Color?"

"Dark blue. I think. I always thought it was funny. The

little guy who came around should be called Mouse and the big dude ..."

"Enough, Maurice." I pointed at him. "But you did good. Thanks. You see anything odd, give us a call. Any guys hanging around, things like that. Give me a paper." He handed me a small note pad and a pen. I wrote my cell number on it. "I'm out of cards. If Boyd comes back, don't tell him we were here. Just call me. Got it?"

"Yeah, I got it."

We headed for the door. Katie stopped and winked at Maurice. "You did good."

We got outside and I said, "And now we have a lead." I winked at her. "And you did good."

No sooner than we got into the car, my cell rang and it was Mike telling me Marco was on his way to the bar. Said he had info for us.

49

MARCO WAS BEHIND THE BAR, HELPING HIMSELF. We met at my booth and I introduced him to Katie. He gave her the once-over and tried to say something to me, but whatever was going to come out of his mouth would be inappropriate, and he knew it. He gulped down his beer and threw a matchbook on the table.

It was from the Highway 6 Hideaway Motel. I knew it, fifteen miles south of town on Route 6. One of those motels that time passed by when the interstates came though. Route 6 led into Crescent Beach but now that Interstate 24 carried the weekend sun worshippers, only the truckers and couples sneaking away for a little afternoon delight had any use for a place like the Highway 6 Hideaway.

"Found it in Brindisi's personal effects. That, a lighter, and seven dollars. Thought it could be a start."

"You thought right, my friend. Thanks."

"Johnny, wrap up this case. You're too close to the edge. Hate to see you jammed up."

"We're trying."

"Pleasure to meet you," he said to Katie. He threw a look back at her, and then to me and shook his head as he walked off.

"You too," she said.

"Ready to go again?"

"Of course."

"Have some jeans with you? You need to dress down for this place."

It took forty-five minutes to get out to the appropriately named Highway 6 Hideaway because of traffic. We drove in Katie's red Honda Accord. Which, she volunteered, her Daddy bought her for a graduation present. I'm sure Rosso knows my BMW and we need to be as stealth as possible. If they were ensconced in this flea bag, I could put an end to Rosso's reign of terror and ring him up for Sammy's—and Brindisi's—demise. Again, I needed surprise on my side. My phone rang while driving out—Jim Rosswell. I let it go to voice mail, and then listened to his message. He not so gently reminded me the DA's office expected me at three which was ten minutes ago. *Please, Jim. Cover for me.*

I drove, with Katie looking for anything that could clue us in, and the only clue we had was Mouse's dark-blue Mercedes. We made two passes by the motel and didn't see anything. We parked across Highway 6 in a small dirt lot for a farmer's roadside vegetable stand. A teenage girl sat in the stand with her legs propped up on the counter and her nose in a paperback.

The Hideaway was built in a *L* shape with an office at one end and a small patch of grass in front. An old riding lawn mower was rusted in place on the grass, a beat-up pickup sat next to the office, and two other cars were in the lot. We waited for thirty minutes and nothing happened. We cooked up a quick plan and drove across the street. I called her phone and we kept the call open for me to listen. I stayed in the car while Katie went into the office.

I could only see a large lady with a white T-shirt and piled-up blonde hair behind the front counter; their conversation came through on the phone.

"Excuse me, ma'am," Katie said. "I'm hoping you can help me."

"I'll try and if I can't, we'll find somebody who can," said the lady with a down-home country accent.

"I'm looking for my cousin. Tall woman, about thirty with red hair. Real long red hair."

"We was wondering what you two were doing. We was watching you sit across the road. That's my daughter, Becky, working in the vegetable stand, and she and I was talking while youses all sat there. My name is Charlene."

"Oh, hi. Well, we weren't sure if this is the right place."

"It's the right place if you want it to be." I watched as she leaned closer to Katie and her voice went lower. "You two look like our typical customers. Older guy, younger gal come out here for an hour or so. We thought you two couldn't decide what to do."

"Oh, no. Nothing like that. Supposed to meet my cousin. Tall with red hair?"

"Actually, you all just missed them. They pulled out a few minutes before you two pulled in across the road."

"Oh yeah—what were they driving?"

"Big old Mercedes. Blue one."

"She with an older guy with gray hair and a ponytail?"

"She's with two guys. The pony tail man and another big guy. We wondered about the arrangement. All kinds of characters come through here but they didn't appear to be her type. She looked high-class to me. The only way she would be with those two was if they was paying big dollars…oh, sorry, excuse me and my mouth. This is your cousin we're talking about."

"No problem, she's a piece of work anyhow. Thank you for the information." She turned toward the door. "Which way were they going?"

"They headed back toward the city." *Thank you, lady.* "Real hurry, too. They all came busting out of the room, jumped into the car and off they went."

"Okay, thanks. You've been quite helpful."

"You're welcome, sweetie. Hey, if they come back, should I mention you stopped by?"

"No. I'm sure we'll catch up with them." *Get a phone*

number, Katie. "By the way, did they leave a phone number when they registered? I lost her number." *Good girl.*

"We don't ask for a lot of personal information when people pay cash. Know what I mean?"

"Yeah, sure do. Thanks again."

"You and your friend come back."

Katie came out and got into the car. "Did you hear all that?"

"I sure did. They are headed back toward the city and once again, he's one step ahead of us."

While I was listening to Katie and Charlene, two more calls came in from Jim. I listened to his voice messages and he was not happy. "I can't cover for you, Johnny. You better be dead someplace, that's all I can say." I'd face that music tomorrow, but for now, it was back to the office and to confirm a suspicion.

Traffic wasn't as bad this trip; it only took twenty minutes for us to make it back to town. I pulled into the alley and stopped in front of my garage. I opened the garage door and the trunk on my BMW. From my box in the trunk, I grabbed the GPS detector and switched it on. "Start your car," I said to Katie. She did and sure enough, the device beeped and the green LED lit up. My suspicion confirmed. "Son of a bitch." Katie got out of the car and came around to me. I showed her the device.

"So they tracked us and got out before we got there," she said. "Wow, they got my car, too."

"It also means they know you work for me. And I'm not happy."

I found the tracker under the left front fender. I handed it to her. "Souvenir from your first case." I put the detector back in the trunk of the BMW and closed the garage door. "Meet me inside. I want to figure out when my skills abandoned me."

50

MIKE, KATIE, AND I CAME TO THE CONCLUSION that we had to wait. Rosso would dictate the next move and that bothered me to no end—if Rosso was the mastermind. I'm sure nothing got past Charlene at the Hideaway Motel. If Claire was in distress, Charlene would know. Cops packed the bar and Mike kept going back and forth between the bar and our booth. He would add a new pearl of wisdom every time he came back.

"We somehow set a trap. Tell him you have the money."

"We tried that," I said. "That's when Brindisi showed up driving his car from the trunk. We wait until he contacts us."

"Just trying to think of every angle." He went back to the bar and we continued.

"Anything on Bocci that we didn't cover?" I picked up the Bocci file.

"Nope. His background came back clean," she said.

"Either very boring or very smart. Why would he kill himself?"

"Maybe he was sick. Cancer or something?"

"Say that's true. Why wait until I show up? He could have just sent the money to Claire. If there is any money," I said.

"More romantic this way."

"Huh?"

"Yes, his last dying wish. That sort of thing."

"Why make her work for it and start all this? I don't buy it. If the safe deposit box is real, why not tell her? Or, if he was dying, why not draw up a will and leave it to her?"

"Because it's money he stole?"

"True. But after all these years? He'd look like some old, senile geezer who stashed away every penny he made."

Mike came back and sat beside me. "The guy in the jeans and black T-shirt at the end. Recognize him?"

I scanned down the bar. "No. I don't. The guys at the far end are cops. I don't know this guy. Is he acting weird?"

"No. Just sitting with his beer and watching the game."

"Well, could he be just a guy in a bar?"

"You're right. Just saying."

He went back behind the bar, and Katie and I kept brainstorming. We went through every file, talked through every character. Claire's background was clean, too clean. She had nothing except for one credit card with a small balance on the credit report. The address she gave us matched her records. She had no employment history, which was unusual, but she did say she spent the last few years taking care of her mother. "Did we miss something with Jackie?"

Katie pulled her file on Jackie and flipped it open. "I don't remember anything standing out. No criminal past, nothing on her credit report that would indicate a problem. Had some medical bills, but that is what Claire said, right?"

My eye kept going to the bar and the guy in the black T-shirt. He got up, threw some bills on the counter and left. Just a guy in a bar. False alarm. "Right, Claire took care of her until she died. That's the story anyhow."

Katie swiveled around in the booth, put her back against the wall and stretched out her legs. "So we wait?"

"Yep."

Mike came back and threw a piece of paper on the table. "The guy in the black T-shirt left you a tip." Written on the paper: TELL DELAROSA. TONIGHT AT 1:00 A.M. CITY SALVAGE. BRING THE MONEY.

"You see him leave?"

"I noticed him getting up but a minute or so went by before I picked up his money and there was the paper."

"Damn. Here we go again. Tony. I gotta get to him before they do."

Katie grabbed the paper and read it. I called Tony's phone. No answer.

That was not good. I prayed he was drunk in his club or somewhere, anywhere. Just not at the salvage yard. I felt a showdown coming on and Tony was out of control as it was. If Rosso confronted Tony at the salvage yard, the irony would be as thick as the cigar smoke in the City Salvage office—it would be the end of the line for one of them.

51

I PASSED CITY SALVAGE THE FIRST TIME AT ELEVEN. No cars in the lot, no lights on inside; buttoned up for the night. I went a half-mile, turned around and came back toward the junkyard. I pulled off Lincoln Road and parked in the driveway of an old factory across the road and about forty yards away. I had a view of oncoming traffic and the salvage yard lot, plus I was tucked back far enough to be somewhat hidden.

Tony never answered his phone so Mike went to Stiletto's. Katie set up a communication center in my condo where she could monitor my GPS and my phone. Sounded more sophisticated than it was, but she said it was cool, like on TV. I reminded her that people died because of this case. It's not cool; not like TV.

Brindisi getting whacked left a mark on me. I felt responsible. Not responsible for his years as a junkie, but responsible for putting him in a situation that caused his death. It was inevitable, but without me forcing his hand, he would still be walking and talking. No, I'm wrong. Rosso would have whacked him and nobody would give a second thought. Brindisi didn't deserve it and neither did Sammy. These guys were vulnerable; Rosso took advantage and that bothered me to the point where I didn't want Rosso breathing.

My phone buzzed and broke me from my contemplation of the unfairness of life. I answered: Mike. "I'm still at Stiletto's and nobody had seen Tony all day. Listen to this—he signed over his truck to one of the dancers. Told her he wouldn't need it anymore."

"What is that? Death-wish thinking? He feels the end is near and got rid of his truck?"

"Hell if I know. Are you at the junkyard?"

"Yes. All quiet."

"Okay, I'll head that way and lag back until I hear from you."

"Copy that."

I closed the phone and waited. Two cars passed and then the road was empty. The lights went off in the gas station next to the salvage yard. The clerk locked up the store, threw away a bag of trash, then got in his car and pulled off. Now midnight. The windows were down in my car for me to listen for approaching vehicles, but the cool air coming in soothed out the adrenaline that rushed through me.

The night was quiet, except for my breathing, an

occasional cricket, and a light rustling of tree branches. I had to stay put to see the parking lot but I noticed I could pull my car closer to the factory and out of view from the road if I needed. The element of surprise evaded me this entire case and I couldn't allow it to happen again. The only way into the field of junked cars was through the office. Rosso would have to come through the front parking lot to access the property. An eight-foot fence surrounded the six acres of the salvage yard and the back line of the property went down to a small stream and a wooded area beyond. Tony's battle against city planners to keep them from re-zoning the junk yard to eliminate the eyesore of a junkyard had played out in the newspaper for years. The point was, I couldn't imagine Rosso's crew coming through the woods and the stream, over or through the fence, and across six acres of rusted-out cars and trucks. They would use the front door.

At twelve forty, a car passed me and swerved into the salvage yard parking lot, stopped, cut off its lights, and sat idling. The blue Mercedes. A moment later, two men ran out of the office and jumped into the car. It sped off spraying a shower of gravel and dust. *Had they been in there the entire time? So much for my element of surprise.* I backed my car into the spot to block it from the road. I hopped out, pulled my Beretta from the shoulder holster and ran to City Salvage.

The front door was ajar with a makeshift CLOSED sign tacked to it. I pushed it and stepped into the office. The permanent stench of cigar smoke hit me, and Sammy flashed through my mind. It was odd being in this office without Tony and Sammy behind the counter. Narrow shafts of light filtered in through the window and door from outside street lights. Newspapers were spread on the counter and a pile of new daily papers, still wrapped in plastic sleeves, were on the floor by the door. I scanned around with the Beretta in front of me. A twinkle of light caught my eye and drew it to the wall behind the counter. The glass case for Tony's Samurai sword—his prized possession—was smashed and the sword was gone.

Tony. The office had a back door that led to the junkyard. I turned the knob and it opened to a set of rickety wooden steps. A small spot light was mounted on the outside of the office above the back door. I went down the three steps to the ground and moved away from the light into the shadows a few yards to my right. I stopped and waited for the quiet of the night to tell me something. And it did.

Breathing. Heavy, raspy, and slow came from my left. Between me and the breathing was the cast of light. I didn't want to illuminate myself in case someone was ensconced in the maze of junked cars, waiting to take a shot. I walked out and around the light, putting the field of cars to my right and the office building to my left. I aimed toward the breathing, my heart pounding, my adrenaline spiked, more than afraid of what lay ahead.

I moved forward no more than five paces when the glint of a reflection caught my eye. Two more steps closer and I noticed the slow rise and fall of an oblong object, gold in color, reflecting light every time it would rise. Another step and the horror came into view. "Tony?"

His back was against the office building, which was no more than a shanty, and the gold handle of his Samurai sword stuck out of his belly. Blood from the wound had soaked his shirt and pants. "Tony, Jesus." I used the flashlight on my cell phone. The sword went through his belly and out his back, impaling him to the wooden wall of the building.

His breathing was the bubbling gurgle of the death rattle every time his body gasped for air. He stood erect against the wall, his eyes wide, his mouth gaped open. The only movement was his chest and stomach, rising and falling with every strained breath. Every time he sucked in air and his chest rose, blood would trickle out of the wound.

"Tony, I'm calling for help."

"No." He struggled to talk. It came out as a whisper. "Johnny."

"I'm here. I'm calling 911." I opened my phone to dial.

"No. Listen." The words came slow and heavy. Tears rolled down his cheeks. "They are coming back."

"Who? Rosso?"

He nodded. "Will you help me?"

"Tony, of course. I'm calling..."

"No...my gun."

"Tony..."

"Under the counter. You have to. Look at me."

Tears rolled down his cheeks as he struggled through

another breath. His skin was pale gray; he had to be in shock. "Tony. I don't…"

"Get my gun. Don't get prints on it."

"Tony, bad idea. Let me help you."

"Too late." Every word difficult. "I'm doomed."

"I'm getting help..."

His eyes went wide, or as wide as they could. "Get the fucking gun."

He was right; he was doomed. The sword was clear through him. If it was pulled out, the blood would flow like water from a burst dam and take his life with it.

"Okay." Everything in my being told me this was wrong, but I did it anyway. I went back into the office and searched behind the counter for the gun. Broken glass from the frame crunched under my feet. I used the flashlight from my phone and found a compact Colt .45 in a box below the cash register. It was wrapped in an oily rag that I used to hold the gun. I hurried back to Tony. His breaths were shallow; the gurgling in his breathing was gone. Must not be enough air going in to make a gurgle. Last call for Tony—he'd die at the hand of his own sword. Literally and figuratively. His right arm came up and he opened his palm. I put the gun in his hand and threw the rag aside.

He nodded, struggled a whisper. "They're coming back."

"Okay, okay. Stay strong, friend."

His eyes went past me toward the yard of cars. A small smile crept onto his face. "Sammy?"

The hair stood up on my neck and my skin crawled. I looked behind me but only saw the dark field of rusted metal. I turned back to Tony and his eyes were open, gazing toward the yard. He had this peaceful presence about him. I'd heard stories about people near death who sometimes see people who have gone before them. His teary eyes came back to me. He didn't say anything, or even try. He didn't have to.

At one fifteen, tires crunched on the gravel of the City Salvage parking lot. I had a view of the back door and Tony, still breathing, ten feet to the right of the door, from the backseat of a junked Plymouth SUV. The doors and the windshield had been removed, but it gave me a vantage point and an angle on Rosso. A few moments later, Claire came through the door, followed by Rosso and Mouse the goon. The trio walked out of the light and toward Tony when a gasp came from Claire. Her hands covered her mouth and she turned away. *Genuine?*

"What did you do?" she said to Rosso as she backed away.

"What had to be done."

Tony's right hand was behind his back. He needed Rosso in front of him and I decided to help. Not my moral best, but forgiveness could come later. I had to pay for Sammy and Brindisi, and karma stood beside me with an invoice in hand.

I got out of the SUV but kept it between me and the

trio. “Rosso.” I shouted, with my gun leveled at them across the hood of the car. He pulled a handgun from his waistband as he pulled Claire in front of him as a shield. Mouse moved away from them and into the car yard. He had a shotgun and I had to be cautious he didn’t circle around behind me.

“You have the money?”

“I’m not happy about Tony.” The cars were organized in a grid of rows and aisles with each aisle marked with a sign on a pole. Mouse ran up one aisle to get a position on me. I moved to my right, parallel to the building, crouched low.

“C’mon, Delarosa. We can end this as businessmen and go on our way.”

The spot light at the door only cast twenty feet or so. Enough for me to see them, but I was in the dark, a good thirty yards away. “Tell your monkey to come where I can see him.”

Rosso swiveled around, following my voice.

“He’s just making sure we have no surprises.”

“Tony didn’t deserve that.”

“He had a lot of enemies. Too bad. Have the money?”

“Let her go. Then we can talk.” I scurried more to my right, crouched below the tops of cars, staying concealed. A clink of metal came from my left. Mouse the goon was not too skilled in the art of silent surveillance and tracking. Rosso waved his gun back and forth, scanning the dark junkyard, keeping an arm around Claire. “C’mon, Delarosa. Just wasting time.”

“Let her go.”

"I need to see the money."

I made my way through the maze of cars to a point where Tony was now between me and Rosso. I walked out of the yard with my hands raised, my gun in my right hand and a white envelope in my left.

"There you go." I waved the envelope.

"That supposed to be the money?"

"A map to the money. Two million in cash would be kind of bulky."

"The money, Delarosa."

"It's all right here. How about you put the gun down?" I took a step closer to him, but his goon came out from the yard and came up behind Rosso and Claire. "Tell him to stay right where he is. I'm here alone. We can handle this."

Rosso took a quick glance behind him. "Hang back, Mouse."

Mouse kept the shotgun pointed at me but he stopped ten feet behind Rosso. I took another step forward with the envelope held high. "It's all right here, but we'll need to work together. The money belongs to Claire. Not you."

"That's between me and Claire."

"Fair enough." I laid the envelope on the dirt, five feet in front of Tony. "There you go. I'll back off. Look for yourself." I stepped back a few paces. "Put your guns down and I'll do the same." I set my gun on the ground; he nodded back to Mouse, who did the same. "No, have him move away."

"Do it," Rosso said. Mouse slid away from the shotgun. Rosso put his pistol down.

"Perfect. Nobody gets hurt. Money's all yours."

A bead of sweat trickled down my spine. He held Claire's arm and they came forward. Exactly what I didn't want. As they got closer to the envelope and to Tony, Claire swiped Rosso's hand from her arm and backed away from the horror scene. Perfect.

Rosso bent over and picked up the envelope. "Rosso," Tony said, in a raspy whisper. Rosso flinched, turned to Tony, and stepped back just as Tony's arm came up. He squeezed the trigger with what had to be the final bit of strength left in his body.

Rosso went down and Claire froze in place. Mouse, stunned to see a dead man shoot his boss, hesitated long enough for me to dive for my gun and fire a shot past Claire and into the dirt beside his shotgun. That backed him off. As I scrambled to my feet, he bolted through the door. The car squealed out of the lot. *Turned tail and ran. So much for loyalty.* PCPD will snatch him up within an hour. I picked up Mouse's shotgun and then checked Rosso. Dead.

I called Mike and told him it was over and to go back to the bar. No sense in having both of us answering questions. I dialed Marco. "Two dead. Plus, one took off. An old Mercedes." I closed the phone and went to Claire, who hadn't moved. "The envelope," I said. She hesitated, and then slowly walked over to Rosso and pulled the envelope from his fingers.

She came to me and a noise—a thud—made us react. We turned to Tony; the gun had fallen from his hand.

"I didn't think this would ..." She couldn't finish her thought. She seemed as stunned as Mouse the goon.

"Open it," I said.

Her hands trembled as she slid a finger under the flap and opened the envelope. She pulled out a card on which I had Mrs. Finley's name, the bank, and the number broken down into the safe deposit box number and the pass code.

"You found the money?"

"Bocci set up the box and there's a good chance you're authorized. I have no idea what's in it. You're on your own from here."

Claire read the card again. "I can't believe you even got this far."

"We did but we also racked up five dead bodies. Not my style. Did you enlist Rosso or did he find you?"

The cool self-assurance came back. The corners of her mouth turned up in a devilish way. She didn't say a word. She folded the envelope and stuck it in a back pocket of her jeans and sat down on the steps below the door.

Lives were lost because of what she started. Directly or indirectly, I'm not sure. But her not talking to me was not the way to stay on my good side.

"They're going to take you in."

She shrugged and leaned back against the door and folded her arms across her chest. "All I did was hire you to do a job. I never dreamed all this would happen. Did I now?" Calm, cool, and cocky and I couldn't take my eyes off her. She returned my gaze and I stood there while she read my mind.

"Not what you think," she said.

Sirens approached and within a few minutes, the place swarmed with blue uniforms. Marco arrived and took charge, thank God. Claire didn't say much, only that she hired me and was abducted by Rosso. Two young male ambulance techs were on the scene and fell over each other making sure she had no injuries.

After securing the area and calling for a coroner, Marco came to me with his palms turned up. "What the hell?"

"I got a call to meet them here. He wanted the money in exchange for Claire. I found Tony pinned to the building; they showed up and Tony got the last word."

"You're telling me they ran the sword through Tony but he held onto his gun?"

"That's what it looks like to me. Just when you thought you saw it all, huh?"

His face was red and his neck bulged against his collar. I thought his head was about to explode. "How many bodies you collect on this case? Four?"

"Five."

"Damn, Johnny. Hope you can explain all this."

I jerked a thumb toward Claire. "I'm hoping she explains it."

He watched the EMTs fawn over her as she played the victim. She wasn't a victim any more than I was the Pope. "She doesn't look too bothered at leaving a trail of bodies. Ever find out if her long lost money was real?"

"Nope."

"You're telling me all this was for nothing?"

I shrugged. "The thought of all that money..."

He scanned around. "Jesus. Sammy and Tony both gone. The city will get its way now. This place will be shitty affordable housing within a year. You got to come down and make a statement."

"I know."

"I'm taking your girl's statement personally. I can't wait to hear this."

He took Claire out by the arm. Two more ambulance techs arrived, along with the coroner. After declaring him positively, absolutely dead, the four techs went to work removing Tony's sword. I couldn't watch but I heard the jokes that came from the callous insensitivity that builds up from years on the job. "*Guess he got the point.*" "*Wonder if he squealed.*"

"Delarosa." It was an older, veteran officer who I worked with years ago. "Gotta go."

He was waiting to take me to the station. "Okay."

I turned around to take in the scene one more time. They had the sword out and Tony on a stretcher. My heart was heavy.

52

"OMERTÀ?"

"Code of silence."

"Oh, cool. Message job?"

"When you shoot someone in a specific part of the body to send a message. If I shoot you in the eye, that tells your crew we are watching."

She wrote on her notepad. "Damn. Harsh. How about goombah?"

"Crony or pal."

"Then what's a goomah?"

"Mistress."

"Does every mobster have a mistress?"

"Katie…"

"Well, do they?"

"Yes, every one. Mandatory."

"Do you have a mistress?"

"Too many to count."

"Mandy would be your mistress."

"When do I get to meet Mandy?"

"Never. I'm protecting you."

"Oh yeah?"

Three days had passed since the showdown at City Salvage. The police and the DA questioned me for three hours, and questioned Claire for a day and a half. She hadn't called me and would not answer her phone. The DA flirted with charging her with accessory to murder but she played the innocent victim and blamed everything on Rosso.

"Okay, a couple more," she said.

"Why are we doing this again?"

"I want to be familiar with mob-speak before our next job comes along."

"All our jobs don't involve old wiseguys."

"Well, just in case. One more…jamook." We were in the back booth of McNally's and both on our second pre-lunch drink. Katie noticed her as she came through the door. "Damn. Show time, boss."

I turned around. Claire was headed our way. She wore a low-cut, black dress that accented her slim waist and stopped a few inches above her knees; black heels; and a black beaded necklace with matching earrings. The long, auburn hair flowed behind her.

"Wow, she knows how to make an entrance."

Well, I'll be damned. "Yep, she sure does." Claire came to the booth and Katie stood; the two eyed each other for a second. "Claire, this is Katie. Does research for me."

"Nice to meet you," Katie said.

Claire nodded at her dismissively. Katie brushed past her and Claire sat. She pulled an envelope from her purse and slid it across the table.

"Thank you," she said. I opened it. This is the way Claire and I started—me opening an envelope full of cash. "One hundred and eighty thousand. The balance I owe you."

"Well. What do ya know. Bocci came through?"

"Safe deposit box. Had four hundred thousand in cash and an account number and passwords for a bank in the Cayman Islands. One point five in there. Not quite two million but close enough. You did a good job."

"You have Katie to thank for that. She must have called fifty banks and brokers within three states."

"I will."

I sipped my bourbon to pave the way for what should be an interesting visit. "I have a lot of questions."

"I'm sure you do," she said, with a cool confidence. She was not the same woman I met two weeks ago. Her eyes were now a dull, hard emerald, no sparkle of personality.

"Did you know Bocci had the money?"

"Suspected."

"I don't understand. Why not go to Bocci yourself?"

Her mouth turned up in the devilish smile again. "You *don't* get it, do you? After everything that happened?"

Too many lives lost to sit here and guess her motivations. "Claire, listen to me. No guessing games. Tell me the truth."

"Can I get a glass of wine, please?"

"No. Start talking."

She bristled as she leaned back in the booth and folded her hands in her lap. "Mother and I knew Mr. Bocci had the money. Never thought he would kill himself, though. That surprised me. Also made a lot more work for you. Or her." She nodded at Katie, who now sat at the end of the bar.

"Why did he do it?"

"He knew that when somebody came around asking about the money, it meant my mother was dead. She forbade me to go myself."

"Why?"

"Bocci was in love with her. Since they were teenagers. My mother hated him because he's the one who had my father killed. He wanted Donny out of the way, wanted my mother for himself. Nothing but a troubled, weak, selfish, cold-hearted bastard who obsessed over my mother. When my mother rejected him, he decided to hold the money and give it to me when he died. But my mother did not want to give him the satisfaction of meeting me in person. He committed the ultimate selfish act—suicide."

"He said to me, tell her I kept my promise."

"He always told my mother he would take care of me. Damn, he actually kept the promise."

"So he skimmed the money?"

"Sure. He was in the perfect position. All the cash that came in off the street went through him. He betrayed my grandfather but made sure to cast blame on others. My mother held him—and the other goons—responsible for the attack on her.

"Tony and Rosso."

"Yep. They thought Donny had the money and hid it with her. Since Donny was dead, they didn't care what they did to her."

"Why involve Rosso at all? Or Tony? We found the money, that's all you needed."

"Still don't get it?" she said. My mind raced to link all this together but it didn't make sense for her to involve the goons to complicate things. Her hard, green eyes focused on me as if she was controlling my mind.

Then it hit me. "Revenge."

"Of course. My mother was loaded. I don't need the money. She made me promise to exact vengeance on the scumbags who broke her legs. And I was happy to do it. I witnessed what they did to her."

"So you got Rosso to scare up Tony?"

"I prayed they'd kill each other and they came through like champs." She completed my thought. "I'm a cold-hearted bitch, Johnny Delarosa."

My drink needed a refresh after that. I got up and poured another for me and a glass of Chardonnay for her and came back to the booth.

"Rosso went along? The lure of the money?" I asked.

"Rosso was a pathetic waste of human cells. I gave him a little treat one night. He would've followed me to hell."

"Why Sammy?"

"Collateral damage. Sorry."

You are a cold-hearted bitch. "The argument with Elena Garver at the Marquis? What was that about?"

"You saw that? I'm impressed." She held the wine glass up to me in a salute and then took a sip. "Old Aunt Elena wanted me to forget the entire thing and not get her stepson involved. She knew Little Jimmy was out of his league and was afraid he'd get himself killed. God bless her, the old bag was right."

"So now what? You got what you wanted—your plan worked."

"Not entirely what I wanted. I wanted to sleep with you. You're the first real man I've come across in quite a while. I'm tired of the effeminate metro-sexual wimps who want to *make love* then talk about our feelings." She gulped down the rest of her wine. "Not too late, you know. I'm in town one more night."

Now that would literally be sleeping with the devil. I raised my glass to her. "Our business is finished."

She reached across and grabbed my hand. "Too bad. It would be unforgettable." She winked at me, got up from the booth and went to Katie, thanked her, and walked out.

Katie came back and sat down. "Tell me, tell me. What did she say?"

"Moron or idiot."

"What?"

"Your last question. A jamook? It's a moron or an idiot."

"Oh, okay." She jotted it down on her pad.

She played us all right from the beginning and I refused

to believe it. My instinct, my sixth sense, my gut screamed at me and I didn't listen.

I'm a jamook.

53

ST. ANTHONY'S CATHOLIC CHURCH WAS ON 24TH Street two blocks from my boyhood home. It was a large parish that served the Italian neighborhood. It had an elementary school, an adjacent hall for bingo, socials, and every other type of event imaginable, a separate basketball gym, offices, and a rectory for the pastor and his two associate priests. Growing up in an Italian family meant our entire life centered around the church. From elementary school, to being an altar boy, to playing basketball in the Catholic Youth League, to helping with food drives, drinking beer—and trying to kiss girls—behind the gym, fund-raising dinners, and even the annual spring dance. The church was our life.

I parked in the church lot and found Fr. Franco Azzolino on his knees, tending to a flower garden in back of the rectory. "You missed a weed over here," I said.

Frankie, as I called him—we'd known each other from first grade—shaded his eyes as he looked up at me.

"Confessions are Saturday at four."

"Well, you better block out a couple of hours for me."

He got up and put his hands on his hips. "How long has it been?"

"Well, I'm here every Sunday—I guess I miss your Mass."

"Like I said, confessions on Saturday." He came over and we hugged.

"You look good, Frankie," I said. We were the same height but he packed on a few pounds around the middle and lost more than a few hairs on his head. He was destined for the priesthood from high school. He loved being an altar boy, he loved the history of the church and he loved the Mass. We went to Central Catholic together and after graduation, he went directly to the seminary, was ordained eight years later, spent six years doing missionary work in Haiti and Honduras, came back to the States and somehow finagled his way back to St. Anthony's as an associate pastor, and then was appointed pastor four years ago. He was a good priest, respected by both the diocese and his congregation.

"How are things around here?"

"They're good, Johnny. School's at capacity. A lot of young families in the parish."

"No kidding? That's wonderful."

"Yeah, evidently, the Little Italy is the place to live. We're now hip, cool, and fashionable. Gentrification of the neighborhood. New restaurants, shops."

"I heard as much but I haven't been over here in a while. How are you?"

"Not bad. They keep me busy here nonstop."

"And you love it, right?"

"Of course. There are a few folks here I'd like to ship off to the Lutherans but other than that, everything is good."

I took an envelope out of my pocket that contained twenty thousand in cash and handed it to him.

"What's this?"

"Donation. In the name of Tony and Sammy Scarazzini."

He peeked into the envelope. "I thought I heard your name on the news."

"Unfortunately."

"Too bad. I did Sammy's funeral. Now we'll have Tony. I guess you can't live a lifestyle like theirs forever." He opened the envelope again. "This is generous. You sure?"

"I'm sure."

"It wouldn't do me any good to ask what happened, would it?"

"Nope. Like you said, you can't live that lifestyle forever. Can you use that for the kids' sports programs?"

"Absolutely."

"Tony and Sammy would like that."

"We're not laundering dirty money, are we?" He winked.

"You never know, Padre. But I'll let you get back to the garden."

"You need to come by more often. I'll even take you out to dinner. One of those new trendy restaurants we have over here."

"You got a deal."

We shook hands and he walked me around to the parking lot with his hand on my shoulder. "Don't be a stranger," he said.

I got into my car and put the window down.

"I'm going to take you up on that dinner."

"You're a good man, Johnny Delarosa."

"I only wish." I pulled out of the lot and glanced back in the mirror to see Fr. Frankie standing there, waving to me as I drove away. He's the good man.

I called Cara's phone on my way back to McNally's. She didn't answer so I left a message. "I owe you dinner and an apology." I thought I did apologize, but another wouldn't hurt. "I like our times together. I miss you, my friend. Call when you can."

Next, I called Jim Rosswell's office. It took two tries before I got through to Jim. On the first call, the receptionist cut me off when trying to transfer the call. On the second call, it took two transfers before Jim's assistant put me through.

"You're not in jail, are you? I just got you out."

"My life is your job security."

“Ha! You’re right. How can I help?”

“Wanted to thank you again plus I have some work for you.”

“No need to thank me. What’s the job?”

“Kelly and I still own a house on Crescent Beach.”

“Really?”

“Yeah, long story, but I’m buying out her half.”

“A beach pad all your own.”

“Yep. Can you draw up the papers?”

“Sure thing. Send me an email with the details.”

“Thanks, buddy.”

“Stay out of trouble.”

He hung up and my phone beeped. It was a text message from Cara: a smiley face.

My heart was warm.

54

THE EVENING SKY WENT FROM A LIGHT PINK TO A burnt orange to a deep purple as the sunset gave way to a canopy of twinkling summer stars. I gazed in amazement from my balcony and wondered whether Sammy was now one of those stars. *Are the innocent the only souls rewarded with star status after they arrive at the final destination?* Rosso wouldn't deserve to be a star; neither would Brindisi.

I had a bottle of a California cabernet beside me and I did a good job of getting halfway through the bottle. The Claire Dixon case had taken a toll. I'd had plenty of jobs where the client was less then forthcoming: The suffering spouse who wants her cheating husband followed but conveniently leaves out that she's also having an affair. Or the bank manager who wants me to expose an employee embezzlement scheme to cover up his own swindle. Claire played us all; she got the revenge she was after by pitting Rosso and Tony against each other. I wondered what her plan was if Tony was dead when they got to City Salvage. Figure a way for me to kill Rosso? Or maybe she also gave Mouse a little treat and he was primed to finish out her scheme?

I needed some Coltrane on this night of contemplation and the soothing sound of John's alto-sax filled the condo. I left my screen door open to hear the music and my neighbors in the apartment below, two sixty-eight-year-old hippies from Greenwich Village, always thank me the next morning after an evening of Coltrane. They say his music enhances their sexual experience and I must admit, his *Blue Train* album and a good bottle of wine would amp up the romance. But, tonight I needed to sort through the last two weeks.

My condo door opened and closed. Katie came out to the balcony.

"Hi. Mike said you wanted to see me."

"Yep, sure do. Sit down." She sat on my spare lounge. I pulled my chaise up to a sitting position and swiveled around to face her. "You did a good job and I want to thank you."

"Hey, no problem boss. I told you I'd be good for you."

"I never thought we would find the money and we did because of your persistence and hard work. I found myself a good partner."

"Partner?"

"I mean, employee. I shouldn't have serious discussions

when drinking wine." I poured another glass. "Want one?"

"Can't. I'm on duty downstairs. Are you drunk?"

"Not yet." I had an envelope on the small table and gave it to her. "Your bonus."

"A bonus? Oh my God." She opened the envelope and pulled out the cash. "Are you serious?"

"This was a good payday and you earned it. But listen to me." She was counting it and I slapped my hand on the pile of bills. "Five thousand."

"What? No way." She came off her chair and threw her arms around me.

"Okay, sit back." She sat down and doled out piles of bills on the table. "Put that back in the envelope. This is between you and me. I should give you a check but I'm not. So you can't be flashing cash around. Stick it in the bank. Don't tell your father, neither. I don't think he would understand. And don't ever count your money in front of anyone. Ever."

"Yes, boss. I understand. I knew this would be the greatest job ever. I wanted to work with you from the minute you rescued me." She stuffed the money back in the envelope.

"This job was not typical. They never pay this well."

"Yeah, yeah, you keep saying that. But somehow…"

I grabbed her hand to make sure she was listening. "It paid well, but we don't like it when people get killed while we're working a case. You understand?"

She nodded, her blue eyes magnetic. A moment passed and I realized I was still holding her hand. I pulled it away and felt my face flush. If she noticed my embarrassment, she was considerate enough to not say anything. The problem was the moment was too easy and natural.

"You understand, right?"

"Of course I understand."

"Good. Remember what I said about always playing it cool."

"Got it."

"If you want to grab a late dinner after your shift, I know a Chinese place. Your treat."

"I would love to, but I promised to meet Mandy and some friends."

"Any guys?"

"No, no guys. Besides, I decided I want to be a goomah."

"Is that right?"

"Yep, so if you run into a sexy Italian man who wants a mistress, keep me in mind."

"Will do."

She waved the envelope as she went into the condo. "Thank you."

"You earned it." I admired the view as she left.

She's too young, jamook; she's too young.

I stretched out on the chaise and poured another glass of the cabernet. The measure of success on a case: did we complete the job we were hired to do? Yes, we were hired to find the money and we found it. That's a success. But losing three old wise guys, one street junkie, and one old, crooked mob accountant in the process negates any positive. I don't care how bad or corrupt they were. I'm in the investigative business and not used to getting into the middle of a mob war, no matter how manufactured or orchestrated.

Claire controlled the puppet strings and Rosso danced when she tugged. My instincts told me to wise up, but I ignored them. Not my shiniest moment and I was a contradiction in the flesh. Five deaths on the case disturbed me, but not enough to prevent me from accepting the two-hundred-thousand-dollar fee. Sammy and Tony would approve—would tell me to not be an idiot and take the money. I offered a prayer and hoped that Tony and Sammy were together again, right where they belong.

Claire played us all and she was damn good. She cut a slice through this town and left an auburn wake of death and revenge and managed to leave without a scratch.

I raised my glass to the blanket of stars.

One hell of a ride, Claire. One hell of a ride.

ACKNOWLEDGEMENTS

Writing a novel is a solitary experience, but it takes a team of people to clean it up, comb its hair, straighten its tie, and push it out to the world.

Faith Williams (www.theatwatergroup.com) did a masterful job editing this book and making my words make sense. Thank you, Faith! Thank you to the talented Brandi McCann (www.ebook-coverdesigns.com) for creating the incredible cover!

A special thanks to the talented novelist, P. J. O'Dwyer, for sharing her experiences on writing and publishing. Also, a grateful nod to the Writing Prose critique group of Columbia, Maryland who set me on the right track!

I am forever indebted to my parents, George and Evelyn Stever, for instilling in me a life-long love of reading. They are two very special people and the best parents a man could have. All my love and thanks to both of you.

A special thank you to my late, great father-in-law, Chester Hildreth, for a career's worth of cop stories that will serve me for years.

I am proud to call Mark Stever and Matthew Stever my brothers. Two finer men I do not know. Thank you guys for your friendship, love, and support.

My children give me an enormous amount of pride. Thank you to Brian, Kevin, and Cassidy, and daughter-in-law Jessie for your love, humor, encouragement, and friendship. And to granddaughter, Lucy, who is the light of our lives and keeps us all young and energized.

This book is dedicated to my wife, Helene Hildreth Stever, for her constant support, encouragement, friendship, and unconditional love. Thank you! I couldn't have done it without you!

Johnny Delarosa returns in:

Toxic Blonde

2017

Please visit:
www.davidstever.com
to join David's mailing list for news, reviews, and updates!

CPSIA information can be obtained
at www.ICGtesting.com
Printed in the USA
LVHW090817040720
659722LV00001B/88